CW01475980

THE
MARTINMAS
PLOT

Robert Broomall

BLUE STONE
MEDIA

A Bluestone Media Publication

ISBN: 9798854675680

Cover design by bespokebookcovers.com

For James, Heather, Diane,

Claire and David

CHAPTER 1

Trentshire, England – 1117 A.D.
September 13 – Feast of St. John Chrysostom
59 Days Until Martinmas

$\mathfrak{I}$T WAS STILL warm, but the days were growing shorter. The harvest was in, and it had been a good year, thanks be to God. Miles and Blanche watched their children at the archery butts, which had been set up in the open field west of the manor house. The old poacher Sewale was the children's instructor. Sewale still limped from the hip wound he'd suffered in the taking of Brightwood Castle, eleven years before. Because of the limp and the constant pain from the wound, he left the heavy work in the fields to his sons these days and spent his time repairing equipment and in general labor around his house and the manor.

Sewale leaned on a cane. "Draw it all the way back," he told Miles's oldest boy, Richard. "Aim, but don't hold it too long, and release. Trust your instincts."

Richard was lean and ascetic, with his mother's dark good looks. He let fly, hitting the target just left of center. "Good," Sewale said, patting the boy's shoulder.

Blonde Alice, age seven, raised her small bow and shot effortlessly, hitting the target dead center.

"That's it!" Sewale cried, pounding his cane on the ground. "Well done, Lady Alice! We'll make a poacher of you yet." He realized what he'd said and turned to Miles and

Blanche. "Your pardon, Miles. My lady. Just joking, of course."

Blanche arched a brow. "Of course," she said. She turned to her husband with feigned exasperation. "It seems our daughter is to be a poacher."

"She'd be a good one, too, I'll wager," Miles said. Miles was 51 now, still heavily muscled but grey of hair and beard. Blanche's linen headdress covered a grey streak on the left side of her dark hair, a streak which looked even more dramatic when her hair was braided, as it was now.

John, the middle child, burly and strong like his father, missed with his arrow and stamped his foot in exasperation. Richard cuffed him playfully. "Don't worry about it, you're bound for the Church, anyway."

"No, I'm not," John argued. "I'm going to be a knight, a soldier like Father."

"They're getting so big," Blanche said. "It seems hard to believe that Richard will be off to squire at the new year."

"Aye," Miles said. "I'll miss him, even if he's not going far." Richard would squire for Guillame of Edsworth, who was married to Blanche's former maid, Millicent. Guillame was the only lord who would take the boy. No one else wanted him because he was half English.

Miles had been a common ploughman, though he was descended from English nobility. He had become Blanche's steward, and her lover. He had been given permission to marry her by King Henry, for services rendered against Baron Aimerie, who had plotted against the throne. Because of that marriage, he was now a knight and lord of three manors.

Miles went on. "I don't hold with sending boys off to be squires and pages. They can learn all they need to learn at home. That's the way it was done in England before."

"It's the custom," Blanche said.

"Your custom, not ours," Miles said out. Blanche was a Norman, widow of the earl of Trent.

"Like it or not, you're one of us now," she reminded him.

"Aye, and well hated for it."

"That's why we have to be like everyone else," Blanche said. "The other nobles are just looking for a way to attack you. You know that."

Miles grumbled, but she was right. He had wanted to name his first-born son Edwulf, after his own father, but Blanche had insisted on a French name. "He's going to have a hard enough time as it is, being part English. Give him an English name and you'll make it worse."

Now she said, "John will have to find a sponsor for the Church soon."

"Don't tell him that," Miles joked. "He's dead set against the idea."

"He's a second son," Blanche said, "and second sons go to the Church. It's a shame their ages aren't reversed. I've an idea that Richard would do well in the Church."

"Aye, he's even learning to read, for some reason," Miles said. Miles had long ago learned to write his name, but that was all. "God knows, he's more pious than John."

"Should John be a monk or a priest, do you think?"

"A priest," Miles said without hesitation. "Can you imagine John locked away in an abbey all day, praying and copying books?"

Blanche laughed. "No. Either way, we need to find him a good sponsor if he's to go far. And that's going to be difficult because you're English."

She went on. "We'll have to start looking for a husband for Alice soon, as well. We'll need someone with land and prestige. There's no sense looking in England, so we'll have to think about Normandy or France. Even Flanders."

Miles crinkled his brow. "She'd be far from home. Be a long while till we'd see her again. If ever."

"It's the best we can do," Blanche said. "I don't like the system, either, but it's the system we have, and we have to deal with it."

They became aware of horsemen approaching from the direction of the manor house. Sunlight glinted off arms and armor. "What's this about?" Blanche said.

There were a dozen of them, cantering up the path in the autumn sun. Two wore mail hauberks, but they all wore helmets with nose guards and had long shields slung across their backs. All but the leader had spears, as well. Activity at the archery butts stopped as everyone watched the newcomers.

The party grew closer. They were led by Blaise, a knight who had been in service with Aimerie but after Aimerie's death had switched his allegiance to the sheriff of Trentshire.

The horsemen drew up and formed a half-circle around Miles and Blanche.

"Blaise," Miles acknowledged.

"Lord Miles," Blaise said formally. His polished mail gleamed in the sun. He was a good-looking blond with a dimpled chin, in his late thirties. Of all the men who had attended Aimerie, Blaise was the most decent.

Blanche frowned. "What's going on?"

Blaise ignored her. "Miles of Redhill, by order of the sheriff, I am placing you under arrest."

Miles and Blanche looked at one another.

"Arrest?" Miles said. "What for?"

"For treason," Blaise said.

CHAPTER 2

"WHAT!" MILES SAID. "I've committed no treason. You know that."

Blaise wasn't here to argue. He spoke in a formal voice. "I must ask you to surrender your sword and dagger."

Blaise's men edged their horses closer, some of them no doubt eager for an excuse to strike down this upstart Englishman.

Miles pulled his short sword from his belt and handed it, hilt first, to Blaise, followed by his dagger.

"I protest!" Blanche said. "I'll go to the king if I have to. Miles is no—"

"I understand your concerns, Lady Blanche," Blaise said, "I do. But it's out of my hands. I have my duty."

Sewale stared at the Frenchmen with undisguised contempt; Miles hoped he didn't lose his head and try to use his bow on them. That would get everybody killed. The children ran over to Miles. "Father, what's happening?" "Are you in trouble?" "You didn't do anything wrong."

Miles hugged them and patted their heads. "It's just a misunderstanding. We'll have it cleared up in no time."

He acted unconcerned, but there was a sinking feeling in his stomach, because he knew the other nobles of the district, save for Guillame of Edsworth, would like to be rid of him. Had one or more of them given false evidence against him?

Blanche continued to glare at Blaise. Miles turned her toward him and kissed her. "Don't worry. I'll be home soon."

Miles's son Richard came up. "Father . . ."

"It's all right," Miles reassured him. "Take care of your mother while I'm gone. Take care of John and Alice, too."

Richard straightened and squared his shoulders manfully. "I will, Father."

The sheriff's men had brought a spare horse for Miles. He mounted and the party rode away.

* * *

As Miles and the sheriff's men started off, Blanche turned to her children. "I'm going back to the house. You help your Uncle Sewale with the bows."

Richard took charge of his siblings while Sewale supervised the gathering of bows and arrows. Blanche started off, walking as fast as she could. People crowded the bridge to the manor house, watching Miles being led away, talking about it amongst themselves.

Wada, the steward, left the bridge and hurried to Blanche across the grass. Wada was big and strong, his nose skewed from a long-ago beating. "What's happened, my lady?"

"Miles has been arrested," Blanche said. "For treason."

"Treason?" Wada said. "That don't make—"

"I know," Blanche told him. She was on the verge of tears, but she held them back. She had to be strong at a time like this. She was the lady of the manor, and she had to act like it.

"Did they say anything more than that?" Wada asked her.

"No, just that it's treason."

Wada considered. "Think Lord Guibert's behind it?" Guibert of Haverham was the leader of the shire nobles who were opposed to Miles.

"Possibly," Blanche said. "Or it could be the sheriff. He hates Miles, too. Have Father Albinus come to me, I must send a letter to the king. Wait here, first."

"Yes, my lady," Wada said.

6

Blanche's youngest handmaid approached. Ediva had entered Blanche's service four years earlier. She was followed by Blanche's other maid, Estrild, who came huffing up from the village, where she'd been taking religious instruction from Tostig, the vicar. Estrild was about Blanche's age but seemed older. She'd been with Blanche since Millicent left.

Blanche said, "Ediva, I want you to go to the manor of Ravenswell. Find Miles's son Garth and tell him what's happened. See what he can learn."

"Yes, my lady," said Ediva. Ediva was twenty-one now, a beautiful young woman. "Only . . . I don't know where Ravenswell is, exactly."

"Mody does," Wada said. Mody was a groom who had accompanied Miles and Blanche on visits to Miles's family in Ravenswell. "She'll need protection for the road, anyway."

"Very well," Blanche said. "Give her Mody and one of the beadles. Now, get going."

"Yes, my lady," said Ediva, bowing.

"Yes, my lady," said Wada, bowing as well and leading Ediva off.

"What about you, my lady?" said Estrild, still a bit out of breath. "What are you going to do?"

"You and I are going to Brightwood Castle," Blanche said.

7

CHAPTER 3

"YOU KNOW I'M no traitor," Miles told Blaise as they put Redhill behind them.

"I do," Blaise admitted. Miles and Blaise had been on opposite sides when Miles captured Brightwood Castle, eleven years earlier, but Blaise had behaved honorably then, and if the two men were not exactly friends, they respected each other.

"So what's this about?" Miles said.

Blaise made a face. "The sheriff issued a warrant for you, that's all I know. I've no idea what's behind it." Onfroi of Buchy was sheriff of Trentshire, replacing old Lord Tutbury, whose heart had seized up one evening while he was enjoying the favors of a young woman, a very young woman.

The party rode on in silence. They turned onto the river road, and eventually Brightwood Castle loomed in the distance, its whitewashed stone keep gleaming in the September sun, its window and door arches painted bright red and blue. King Henry's flag—a gold lion on a red field—hung from the battlements, signifying that this was a royal castle. Onfroi's banner, a red boar on a white field, flew from the staff, indicating that Onfroi was in residence. The flag of Brightwood's castellan, Theobald of Jumièges, which normally adorned the staff, now hung from the battlements, but lower than the king's.

Memories came back to Miles, as they always did when he saw this castle—memories of storming it, of taking it from Aimerie and killing him. Memories of his friend Blackie, of Ivor the smith, of Ediva's father Ailwyn and young Will, of so

8

many others who didn't make it back. Sometimes he could see their faces clearly, and sometimes they ran together in a blur. It seemed like a long time ago.

They passed through the fields and village of Brightwood. Cattle grazed in the stubble of the harvested fields. Men prepared equipment for the autumn ploughing, which would begin soon. Women and children picked apples and pears in the orchards. Brightwood was one of Miles's and Blanche's manors, and the people called greetings to him, though the greetings were hesitant because Miles seemed to be under guard, and they wondered why.

The castle's bailey was ringed by a turreted stone wall. They crossed the bridge over the ditch, entered the bailey and halted near the old wooden hall, now used as a barn. "Dismount," Blaise said.

Followed by two of his men, Blaise led Miles up the stairs to the hill, then through a crenellated forebuilding and into the keep itself. They mounted more stairs and entered the arched hall, halting near the head table, where Miles had killed Aimerie's son Ernoul years ago. Like the castle's exterior, the hall was whitewashed to make it seem brighter inside, the window arches painted. The window shutters were open, letting in fresh air and sunlight.

Onfroi rose from the table, where he had been waiting. Onfroi was a big man with a shaved head. He had small, mean eyes and heavy jowls. It occurred to Miles that it must be expensive to keep his head shaved like that. Cold, too, in the winter. Theobald of Jumièges, the castellan, stood to his left.

"Here is the prisoner, my lord," Blaise said.

"Very well," Onfroi told Blaise. Blaise gave Miles a sympathetic glance and murmured, "*Bonne chance.*" Then he left with his men.

Onfroi stepped from behind the table and looked Miles over. "You can't imagine how much I've looked forward to this day, Miles. I knew you'd do something stupid and get yourself arrested."

9

Miles tried to act casual. "What am I supposed to have done, my lord?"

"Don't pretend you don't know," Onfroi said.

"I don't."

Onfroi scoffed. "Then I expect you'll find out soon enough. Actually, I wasn't the one who preferred the charges."

That surprised Miles. "Who was?"

"You'll learn that soon enough, as well," growled Theobald of Jumièges. Theobald was dark and lean, with a scarred face, like most knights. A corner of his left ear was missing. Theobald and Miles were familiar with each other, since Brightwood furnished most of the castle's food. Miles could count on one hand the number of Frenchmen he liked, and it wouldn't take the full hand. Theobald wasn't one of them.

To Onfroi, Theobald he said, "I'll enjoy watching this one being questioned, my lord."

" 'Questioned?' " Miles said blandly. "That's the term you French use for 'torture,' isn't it?"

Theobald smiled, revealing front teeth broken as a result of a long-ago blow from a sword hilt. "You're funny now, Miles. You won't be so funny later."

"Enough," Onfroi said. "We've no time for banter. Treason is serious business, Miles. There's only one way this ends for you."

"You're right," Miles said, "because I'm not guilty."

Onfroi snorted. "Of course you're not." To Theobald, he said, "Take him away."

Theobald shoved Miles back across the hall to the stairs, accompanied by a guard. Theobald gave Miles a harder shove designed to make him fall down the curved stairwell, but Miles was expecting it and was able to maintain his balance.

They went down two floors, past the guard room and storeroom, to the cellar. It was damp and chill down here, and it reeked of feces and urine and body odor. The only light came from two horn lanterns at the bottom of the steps. A large metal cage occupied the dirt floor. There were no other prisoners.

"In," said Theobald.

Miles obeyed. The guard squealed the door shut and locked it.

"What happens now?" Miles asked Theobald.

"You'll find out when somebody tells you," Theobald said. Beckoning the guard, Theobald turned and left.

The cell was empty save for a bucket to be used as a latrine. There was no bed. Rat droppings littered the floor.

Miles sat with his back against the metal bars. He wished he had his cloak for the chill. He couldn't imagine how cold it must get here in winter, and winter was not far off.

He waited. And waited.

He had no idea of the passage of time; the light down here never changed. It could still be day; it could be night. It could be tomorrow, for all he knew. He heard the skittering of feet as the rats appeared, and he resigned himself to eventually being bitten by them. A guard with a scarred left eyebrow came down the stairs and passed a pail of water through the bars, along with a crust of bread. Miles threw a small piece of the bread across the floor to occupy the rats, while he devoured the rest. The bread was moldy, but he had expected that. The rats didn't care.

He started to wonder if he would be in here forever. He wondered about Blanche and the children. How were they doing? Would he ever see them again?

He dozed off . . .

Footsteps on the stairs. Two people.

Theobald rounded the stairs and stood before the cage. He was followed by another man. Miles started with surprise when he realized that this second man was Galon of Monteaux, earl of Trent.

CHAPTER 4

ℑNVOLUNTARILY, MILES ROSE to his feet, cursing himself as he did because it showed deference to Galon.

Galon stepped into the cell with a big smile. "As I live and breathe, it's Miles the Englishman. The 'free man.' Been a long time, Miles."

"Not long enough," Miles said.

Galon wagged a finger playfully. "Impudent as ever—that's what I like about you. And I notice that you still don't call me 'my lord.' "

Galon was greyer and thicker in the waist, but otherwise little changed from when Miles had last seen him. He still wore the Norman bowl haircut shaved up the back and a drooping moustache—he was about the only one who did, these days. He still dressed simply, as well, his clothes as out of date as his hair. He looked around the cell, eyeing the rats dispassionately.

"You've come a long way, Miles," he said. He smiled and indicated the cell. "Well, until this, of course. The first time I saw you, you were at the end of a rope, which is where I should have left you. Now you're a knight, married to a prosperous widow, and lord of three manors. Clever of you, using Blanche to get ahead like that."

Miles felt his face redden. "I married Blanche for love. Do you honestly think I want anything to do with your French nobility?"

Galon waved a hand. "Spare me the hypocrisy. And how is my father's lovely widow?"

"She's well," Miles said. "Now that we've gotten the pleasantries out of the way, I presume I've been arrested because of you?"

"You presume correctly," Galon told him.

"Why? You must know I'm no traitor. And why are you in England? You never come here."

"Nor does anyone with half a brain," Galon said. He regarded Miles evenly. "I'm here because I need your help."

"You want to kill yourself?" Miles asked hopefully.

Galon said nothing.

Miles went on. "What help could I possibly be to you? And why in God's name would I want to do it?"

"As you may or may not know, I am now chief councillor to King Henry," Galon said.

"That doesn't say much for the king," Miles said.

"I am also the king's chief gatherer of intelligence."

"You mean his spy?"

"That's the common term for it, yes. Stigand does most of the work, of course, he enjoys that sort of thing." Stigand was an Englishman and Galon's seneschal. Before that, he'd done Galon's dirty work. "And lo and behold, he seems to have uncovered a plot."

"A plot?" Miles said. "What kind of plot?"

"That's just it—we don't know."

Galon began pacing the cell. He almost stumbled into the latrine bucket, which was nearly full, and wrinkled his nose. "Don't they ever empty this thing?"

"Apparently not," Miles said.

"Interesting," Galon said. He continued. "At any rate, one of Stigand's agents was in the Saracen's Head, in Badford, and he overheard a drunk say something to the effect of: 'His Martinmas has come, as it does for every king.'"

Miles's eyes narrowed. "Martinmas? That's when we—"

"Slaughter the animals. Yes, I'm aware of how a farm works."

"So it's a plot to kill the king?"

13

Galon shrugged. "We presume so. Stigand's agents detained the man—he was a Scot, of all things. Stigand and I crossed over to England as soon as we were told. Stigand questioned the fellow, but he died before he could tell us anything useful. All we know is that it apparently has something to do with Martinmas."

"You said this man was in Badford. So the plot originates here in Trentshire?"

"Possibly," Galon said. "It could come from Scotland. It could come from Normandy, for all I know. There's no end of disaffected barons there."

Suddenly Miles understood what was happening, and it was all he could do to keep his jaw from dropping open. "Wait. You want me to find out what this plot is about?"

"I do indeed," Galon said.

"Why me?"

Galon sighed. "Because, believe it or not, you're the only man I can trust."

Miles had to laugh. "*You* trust *me*?"

"I know, it sounds ridiculous, doesn't it? The fact is, unlike anyone else I know, Miles, you're honest. Disgustingly so. You don't lie, you don't cheat, and you don't give up when you set your mind to something. You proved that when you found my father's killer. Plus, you're not one of us, so it's unlikely you're part of the plot." He paused. "You aren't part of the plot, are you?"

"Of course not," Miles said. He added, "You do realize that it's hard to investigate anything while I'm in this cell."

"That's why you're going to escape," Galon told him. "It's been arranged. A ladder will be waiting for you by the southeast wall tomorrow night."

"Brilliant idea," Miles said. "Then I'll be a criminal, wanted by the king. The sheriff will come after me with all his men. I'll have to hide in the forest, and it's precious little investigating I'll be able to do from there."

Galon was unfazed. "It's my belief—and Stigand agrees—that, as an outlawed noble, and a man of repute among the English, the plot's leaders will eventually get in touch with you and try to get you to join them."

Miles paused. "That's the best idea you can come up with?"

"Do you have a better one?"

"It's not my job to have one," Miles said.

Galon said nothing, so Miles went on. "For laughs, let's say that everything goes the way you want it, and I foil this plot. What then? I'll be welcomed back with open arms and my name cleared?"

"Precisely," said Galon.

"There must be something else in it for me if I succeed."

"Well, you'll still be alive, so there's that. Look, I'm not completely evil, Miles. If you're successful, I'll see that the king rewards you."

"And if I fail?"

"Then you'll be dead. I'll have to find another way to stop the plot, but at least I'll have gotten rid of you."

"And if I simply refuse to help you?"

Galon spread his hands. "In that case, you know the penalty for treason." He smiled. "So, English, what say you?"

Miles swore. "I say I have no choice."

Galon's smile broadened. "What a clever fellow you are."

CHAPTER 5

Accompanied by her maid Estrild and two armed guards, Blanche approached Brightwood Castle. Blanche's white palfrey had been put down some years back, and she now had a chestnut mare, which she rode sidesaddle, as this was a formal visit. It was late afternoon, so she and her party would spend the night at Brightwood's manor house.

Next to Blanche, Estrild fussed. "Aren't you worried, my lady?"

"Why should I be worried?" Blanche said.

"They might lock you up, too. And me."

"If they were going to arrest me, they would have done it already. I need to make sure that Miles is being well treated, and I need to find out what they've arrested him for. This is Onfroi's doing, mark you."

Estrild said no more, but she didn't seem happy.

The day had turned cloudy and cool. Even though she was in a hurry, Blanche was mindful to be a good lord, so she stopped to greet her tenants as she rode through the fields and village of Brightwood Manor, chatting about the weather, crops, births and deaths. At last she entered the castle bailey, where, to her surprise, she was met not by the castellan, but by her late husband's son.

With his worn clothes, clipped back hair, and drooping moustache, Galon looked like an aging relic from another era. The brooch that held his cloak was not made of gold or silver or laden with jewels, as it would have been for most of his class; rather, it was a battered clasp of cheap brass that

Blanche had thought old when she had been married to Galon's father, years before.

A groom took Blanche's horse and she hopped from her sidesaddle to the ground, while Estrild shooed the two guards out of earshot.

As he always had, Galon bowed low to Blanche in a manner that skirted outright mockery, though not by much. "Greetings, Lady Blanche. I guess I can't call you 'Mother' anymore. To what do we owe the honor of your visit?"

"You're the last person I expected to see here," Blanche said. "What are you doing in England?"

"I'm here on affairs of state," Galon said.

She nodded toward the keep's whitewashed battlements. "Why isn't your flag displayed?"

"I'm staying at St. Mary's Lodge."

"Is Lady Rosamunde with you?" If Galon's wife, Rosamunde, was here, custom demanded that Blanche pay her a visit, and Blanche detested Rosamunde.

Galon's dark eyes narrowed. "You haven't heard?"

"Heard what?"

"I sent Rosamunde away."

"What? What for?"

Galon tried to make light of it. "She was having an affair. With a groom—with a groom, can you imagine it? What was she thinking? I was going to kill her, but like a fool, I let myself get sentimental and remembered she was the mother of my children. Don't know why, my children hate me. Now I know how my father must have felt."

He cleared his throat. "Anyway, I forced Rosamunde to join the Church and packed her off to the Holy Land as a nun. With any luck, the bitch will be captured by the Turks, and they can have their way with her."

"And the groom?" Blanche said. "What happened to him?"

"I had him cut into pieces and thrown on the trash heap."

"How magnanimous," Blanche said. "So you'll be looking for a new wife?"

"Yes."

"She has my sympathy, whoever she is. Now, I've come to see my husband, who is being held in the prison here."

"I'm afraid that's impossible," Galon said. "He's being held on a charge of treason."

"You know as well as I do that's a false accusation."

"I know nothing of the kind. That's what you get for marrying an Englishman, Blanche. I thought you had better sense." He paused. "Miles says it was a marriage of love. Is such a thing possible?"

"It is. So you've talked with Miles?"

"Naturally. 'Twas I who had him imprisoned."

A jolt of fear ran through Blanche, but she tried not to show it. "Why does that not come as a surprise to me?"

"All these damned English are traitors at heart," Galon said, "you know that. All save Stigand, of course. That's why I never come to this country. These people live in the vilest squalor, yet they constantly brag about how free they are."

"What treason is Miles suspected of?" Blanche said.

"Name one, we'll build a case for it."

Blanche drew a deep breath. "You . . ."

"Now, now, spare me your famous temper. My father is no longer your husband, you do not enjoy his protection. I can have you thrown in prison, as well—and not alongside Miles."

She controlled herself, because what Galon said was true, and he would do it. "What is going to happen?"

"As luck would have it, Miles has been given an opportunity to redeem himself," Galon said.

"What kind of opportunity?"

"I'm not at liberty to say."

"Is it dangerous?"

"Of course it's dangerous. That's why he's doing it and not me."

"And if he fails?"

"If he fails, you'll be a widow again. And, as I'm in need of a wife . . ."

Blanche's stomach went cold. "You wouldn't."

"Oh, but I would."

"The king—"

"I am the king's chief councillor, he'll grant me what I wish." Galon smiled. "So, you see, I win either way. Now if you'll excuse me, I have matters that need attending to."

He gave her that mocking bow again and started away, back to the keep.

CHAPTER 6

September 14 – Feast of the Exaltation of the Holy Cross
58 Days Until Martinmas

THE GUARD WITH the scarred left eyebrow brought Miles water and a bowl of slop that was supposed to be pottage. The guard closed the cell door but did not lock it. Miles heard his feet scraping back up the stairs.

Miles gulped down the brackish water. The rats beat him to the pottage, but they could have it. Miles waited a bit, then eased the unlocked cell door open. The squeal of its rusted hinges could probably be heard in the next village. Better to do it all at once, he thought. He gave the door a hard push and opened it all the way with another tortured squeal.

From above—no response. Silence.

Miles stepped from the cell. One of the rats preceded him, scampering up the stairs like a loyal pet scouting the way. Galon had told Miles that his escape was arranged, but was Galon lying? Maybe this was a plan to kill him. "Killed while trying to escape." There could be no questioning the finality of that verdict. No appeal from it, either.

Miles started up the circular stone stairs, moving as quietly as possible. He hoped it was night and that he was not walking into a daytime hall filled with people. That would be interesting. He passed the storeroom on the floor above the cell, then the guard room on the ground floor. The guard room was lit by a single candle and, inside, men were snoring. So it was night.

He kept going up, reached the first floor and the hall. Peeked around the staircase into the arched hall. The hall and the gallery surrounding it were dark save for a few candles. No one was about, though Miles heard snores and grunts from the servants who slept there.

He made for the keep's door. With luck, there wouldn't be a guard. In peacetime, the castle lacked a large garrison— a couple of knights and a score of soldiers. The king couldn't afford to pay for more, and the surrounding manors couldn't provide food for more. The door was reinforced with iron and barred from the inside, so no one was getting in without a battering ram. There was no need for a guard—or so Miles hoped.

Miles went down the steps to the door. He eased up the heavy bar and set it on the floor. Opened the door and made a left turn into the forebuilding. The forebuilding replaced the ramp that had once led to the keep's door. It was a mini-castle in itself, constructed of stone, with its own battlements and steps that led to another door on the ground floor. It smelled strongly of urine.

Miles reached the ground floor and the forebuilding's door. This door was barred, as well. Miles removed the bar, cracked the door open.

It was raining. Not a heavy rain, but enough to hide the moon and keep anyone who didn't need to be outside indoors. No guards were visible.

Miles stepped into the rain and pulled the door shut behind him. It felt strange to be in the fresh air again after his time in the fetid cell. He breathed deeply. No sense pushing his luck by going down the steps that led to the castle hill, in full view of anyone who might be watching. So he slid down the steep hill instead, sometimes on his butt, sometimes using his hands and feet, almost like crawling in reverse. He got to the muddy bottom and started up the other side.

He reached the top and peeked over. Still no one in sight. In the stables, horses whinnied. Galon had told Miles a ladder would be waiting by the southeast wall. Miles hoped Galon hadn't been lying. Otherwise, it was a good drop from the battlements, and it would be hard to get out of here with a broken leg.

He left the ditch and crossed the bailey, walking normally, as though he had every right to be there. It was open space; he had no choice. But there was no one about. No one challenged him from the walls.

He reached the bailey's stone wall. He let out his breath with relief and kept to the shadows, creeping behind the chapel and the old hall. Despite the rain, his nose told him people frequented this area as a latrine.

He expected to find the ladder, if there was one, halfway between the two guard towers, in an area just behind the guards' barracks. He moved slowly, feeling his way with his feet in the near total darkness.

His right foot hit something. He bent and touched it. It was the ladder. With difficulty he picked up the unwieldy ladder and raised it against the catwalk above him, hoping the rain drowned out the noise he was making. He tested the ladder, made sure it held, then put a foot on the first rung.

"Qui êtes-vous!" someone shouted from his right.

Miles turned. One of the guards had come out.

The guard recognized Miles. "You!"

Before Miles could reply, the guard lunged at him, catching him with one foot awkwardly on the ladder. As they fell, the ladder fell, too, and it knocked Miles on the head, stunning him. The guard took advantage of Miles's momentary weakness and threw him onto his back, placing his hands around Miles's neck and squeezing hard.

The guard was big and strong. Miles fought, but he couldn't get leverage against the man. The guard squeezed and squeezed—catching the escaped traitor would bring him a large reward. He was choking the life out of Miles, making him gasp for air.

Miles's efforts weakened. Desperately he flailed around with his hands, looking for some kind of weapon. One hand landed on the guard's waist, felt a dagger at his belt. Drew it from its sheath.

The guard realized what was happening, but before he could react, Miles plunged the dagger into his side. The guard grunted and relaxed his grip, giving Miles more leverage, and this time he plunged the dagger into the man's chest all the way to the hilt.

The guard groaned deeply this time. There was something wet on Miles's hand, something that wasn't rain. The guard's grip relaxed almost to nothing. Miles pushed him away and stood. He put the bloody dagger in his own belt, retrieved the ladder and leaned it against the wall.

Sound of hands clapping.

"Well done!" said a voice, and Galon stepped from the deeper shadows.

"You bastard." Miles was breathing hard. "You did this."

Galon's mouth turned down in mock disappointment. "Miles, Miles. You didn't think I was going to make it easy for you, did you?"

"I've killed a man. Now they're going to want me all the more."

"Gives your escape more credence. Gives you more incentive to do your job."

"What if that guard had killed me?"

"I told you—I have faith in you."

Miles's temper rose. "You—"

"If I were you, I'd stop nattering and get going. Before the alarm is raised."

Miles swore and started up the ladder. His head was woozy from being choked and from being hit when the ladder fell on him. He made it to the catwalk. He hoped the men in the covered towers were asleep, which they might well be in this weather. Otherwise, they couldn't help but see him. He dragged the ladder noisily up behind him, lugged it across the catwalk, and lowered it through the merlons to the ground below. He squeezed through the merlons, found the ladder's rungs, and started down.

"Alarme!" cried a voice from below. Was that Galon? *"Alarme!"*

"Quoi?" shouted a sleepy voice from one of the towers. Then: *"Arretez!"*

"Arretez!" cried a voice from the other tower.

"Alarme! Alarme!" shouted the voice from below.

Miles climbed down faster, though the ladder was not all that steady.

"Gardes!"

An arrowed whizzed by Miles's head. Too close.

He dropped from the ladder, fell hard to the ground below, stumbled awkwardly, and toppled backwards into the bailey ditch. The ditch was half-filled with muck and water, with garbage and refuse from the latrines. Spitting God knew what from his mouth, Miles scrambled across the ditch, cries coming from above and behind him, an occasional arrow aimed at him in the dark and missing wildly. He climbed the ditch's other side, reached level ground, and started for what he hoped was the safety of the forest.

CHAPTER 7

September 15 – Feast of St. Mirin of Bangor

57 Days Until Martinmas

AT SOME POINT during the night, Miles lost the pursuit. They'd set dogs after him, and he'd tried to throw them off his track by walking a ways in the middle of a stream. He couldn't hear barking anymore, so maybe his trick had worked.

But that didn't mean they'd give up the chase. They'd regroup and come after him again. He was an accused traitor and he had killed, or seriously wounded, one of the castle guards. The sheriff and Theobald would want him badly.

They would want him dead.

He stopped to say his morning prayers and continued on his way. He was covered head to foot with muck from the castle ditch. He could probably be smelled a mile away. He'd tried to wash the taste of the ditch from his mouth in the stream, but only partly succeeded. He was still finding little bits of things he didn't want to think about stuck between his teeth, or lodged in his gums, or under his tongue, and he spat them out whenever they appeared. Plus he was freezing cold in his wet clothes.

Damn Galon. Damn the French.

The rain had stopped—unfortunately, because it had cleaned him off a bit. The rising sun shimmered between the trees. Weariness dragged at him like the proverbial millstone tied to his waist. He wanted to lie down and sleep.

Later.

He needed to get further from the castle before he rested. What was he going to do now? His life had been upended. What would happen to Blanche and his children? Would he ever be able to go back to his old life, or would he have to start over? All the while on the run from the king's justice.

But that was for the future. Right now he needed shelter, food, clothing, and fire. He had no money, nothing but the guard's dagger he had taken. How the Devil was he supposed to foil a plot this way? He didn't know what use he was going to be to Galon, or even how he was going to survive out here. Only yesterday he had been worried about finding his children spouses and sponsors. Now he was worried about staying alive.

The truth was, he'd gotten soft. He'd gotten used to having clean linen more or less every day, gotten used to having a hot bath and a shave every week or so, to sleeping in a warm bed. He wasn't a young man, like he'd been in Wales, able to face discomfort. He was getting older, and a life in the woods was going to be difficult. He'd have to toughen up. But did he still have that kind of toughness in him?

He traveled west; he was deep in Alton Forest now. He drank from another stream, washed the filth from his face and beard and hair as best his could. At last he could go no farther. He found a hollow that offered a bit of concealment, dropped to the ground, buried himself under new-fallen leaves, and slept.

It was late afternoon when he woke. He was so thirsty that it hurt to swallow. He listened, but heard no horses, no men. He seemed to be alone. He picked himself up and kept going, his leg muscles wobbly. After a while, he saw a clearing ahead, with what appeared to be wooden structures inside it.

A village? Here in the forest? It couldn't be. Surely he'd have heard of it.

He approached the clearing cautiously, scouting it from behind a low rise. There was no one about. There might have been a village here once, but now it was deserted, the structures falling down. And if it had been a village, where were the fields and pastures? The trees around here were not new growth.

Then he realized what it was. The old camp of the Viking—Fromont, his name had been—and his Brotherhood of outlaws.

Miles entered the camp. There wasn't much left after eleven years. Anything of value remaining after the outlaws had pulled out had been looted long since. Fallen down structures, a few scraps of rag. No metal, of course—that was far too valuable. Some of the wooden poles were still serviceable, and he would have used them to start a shelter, but he couldn't stay here. This was the first place the sheriff's men would look for him. They had visited this camp a number of times in the months after Fromont left, searching for any outlaws who had defied old Tutbury's edict and remained. A few had, of course; they always did. The sheriff's men hung them.

Miles refreshed himself from the stream that had once provisioned the camp, then slept again about two miles away. The next day he went deeper into the forest, angling northwest, in the direction of the river. Following a game trail, he at last came upon a glade. On one side of the glade a rugged outcropping of rock afforded protection from the northerly winds. There was water nearby. This would make a good spot to camp while he figured out what to do next. He could shelter in the rock's overhang, at least for a bit. Right now, he had to get food.

In the distance, he heard horses.

Someone was coming.

CHAPTER 8

September 16 – Feast of St. Edith of Wilton
56 Days Until Martinmas

MILES WORKED HIS way through the trees toward the noise. It sounded like two horses, and men accompanying them. As Miles eased behind a large oak, the party came into view, framed by the dense forest's yellowing leaves. Three men, English by their dress, leading two pack-laden sumpter horses.

"Should've turned at that track back there," said the party's leader, a wrinkle-faced man wearing an old-style blue cap. "I told you."

"Track?" A young fellow with a coarse linen coif scoffed good naturedly. "That weren't no track. 'Tweren't nothin'."

"Well, this ain't nothin', neither," retorted the oldster. His cap had a pointed top that folded forward. "Where's it taking us, I ask you? We could wander around these woods for—" He stopped. "Say, you boys smell somethin'?"

The party halted. "Smells God awful," said the third fellow, a husky young man with blond, curly hair.

The one with the linen coif sniffed tentatively. "Dead animal?"

The old one scrunched his nose. "Nah, smells worse'n that. Smells like the inside of a . . ."

This wasn't the entrance that Miles had intended to make. Still, he stepped into their path, the dagger by his side.

The dagger's blade was crusted with the blood of the guard Miles had taken it from, and the three men took note of that.

"Gentlemen!" Miles cried jovially. "What brings you to our fair forest?"

The men stared at him, wide-eyed, as though he had been conjured out of thin air—or out of a latrine, given his appearance and odor.

The blond recovered first. He spoke in an awed voice. "You're him, ain't you?"

"Can't be nobody else," said the one with the coif. "Not way out here."

"You're Brock the Badger," the old man said. He was careful not to get too close to Miles, lest he pass out from the smell.

Brock the Badger was the legendary outlaw of Alton and Dunham Woods—of all Trentshire, really, and parts of the surrounding shires, as well. There had been a Brock the Badger in these woods for as long as long as Miles could remember. There had probably been one since the time of the Old Ones. When one Brock died or departed, another took his place. Originally, Miles supposed, these "Brocks" were men cast out by society for their misdeeds, forced into the forest to live as best they could, usually as thieves. With the coming of the French, however, the Brocks had been English nobles, exiled from their lands, fighting a lost war against the invaders. The last Brock had been captured some years before by the sheriff's men. He had been brought to Badford Town and chopped into quarters, the pieces being sent to the far corners of the shire as a warning to those who violated the French king's law. A new Brock had not yet risen to replace him.

At least . . . not until now.

These three men might have overpowered Miles had they put their minds to it, yet Brock's reputation had them awed. If they wanted to think Miles was Brock's latest incarnation, let them. He flourished the blood-stained dagger. "Who are you?" he demanded in a gruff voice.

"Pedlars, yer honor," said the old one, removing his cap. "I'm Grugan by name. This here's my grandson, Brand, and his friend Hugh. Good, honest men we are."

"You two are strong young fellows," Miles remarked, indicating Brand and Hugh. "Shouldn't you be working the fields?"

Grugan was old, and he looked old. The furrows on his face were as regular and evenly spaced as if they had been made by a plough. "Bless yer honor, but I brung them with me for protection. Also maybe to get them into the trade. My eldest, you see, he took up farming in Lower Wynchecombe. My other boys, one's a tanner, one's a fuller. There's no one to follow me."

Brand, the one with the coif, spoke up. "You goin' to rob us?" he asked Miles.

"No," Miles replied. On a whim, he added, "I only rob the French--and those among the English who collaborate with them." He scowled and leaned in close. "Do you collaborate with the French?"

"Oh, no," Grugan said.

"Not at all," said Brand.

"Never," added Hugh.

"I rob the French, and I give to the English," Miles said on the spur of the moment. *Rob the French and give to the English*. He liked the sound of that. "What are you doing out here?" he asked the men. "This is hardly country for pedlars."

"We was lookin' for the river road," said Brand, "but we got lost somehow."

Miles returned the dagger to his belt. "Unfortunately, you'll not reach the road tonight. Tell you what, camp here with me, and by all that's holy, if you've a bit of food to share, I'd be glad of it. I'll take you to the road in the morning."

" 'Twould be an honor to share our food with you," Grugan said.

"Aye," said Brand.

"Aye," echoed Hugh.

Grugan said, "Beggin' your pardon, but what kind of adventure was you on to look—and smell—the way you do?" He squinted at Miles. "Say, ain't you Miles? Lord Miles of Redhill? I remember you from around Badford, back in the old days, when you was hundred pledge."

Miles saw no need to lie. "That's right."

That seemed to give them even more respect for him. " 'The last English lord,' " Brand said. That was what some people called Miles. "And now you're Brock the Badger."

"What're you doing out here?" asked Hugh.

Miles lifted his brow, as if amused by his situation. "I'm on the run. I was falsely arrested by the sheriff, and I escaped from Brightwood Castle."

Grugan slapped his thigh. "Escaped from Brightwood! Wait'll people hear that one."

"What'll you do now?" Grugan asked Miles.

"Try to clear my name," Miles said. "Until then, I'll enjoy being Brock."

"Miles of Redhill as Brock the Badger. They'll make a song out of that one, so they will," Grugan said.

"A song about how he escaped Brightwood Castle, too," Hugh added.

"He robs the French and gives to the English," Brand said.

Miles grinned. He was starting to enjoy this. Being an outlaw might not be so bad. "See here, I don't like to beg, but do you fellows have any clothes to spare? I can't stand the smell of these, and I can only imagine how bad it must be for you to be around me."

Brand scratched his head. "Let's see, I got some hose in one o' my packs . . ."

"I got a shirt might fit," Hugh added.

"Sorry I can't pay you," Miles said. "I escaped with naught but what I was wearing."

Grugan waved a hand. " 'Tis no matter, my lord. Bless me, but we're proud to help. The stories we'll be able to tell are more'n worth the price of some food and clothes."

"Aye," said Hugh, "we'll be the toast of the Saracen's Head, we will. Should help us no end with the ladies." He poked Brand in the side.

"Much obliged," Miles told him. "And I hate to keep imposing, but I wonder if there's one more favor you might do for me."

CHAPTER 9

September 16

"**T**HERE IT IS," said Mody, pointing. "You can just make out the church tower."

It had been a hard, two-day ride for Ediva, along with the young groom Mody and the glowering beadle Simon, who formed her escort. One of the benefits of being Lady Blanche's maid was that Ediva had learned to ride. That was a lot better than having to run here, like she would have done in the old days. She wasn't sure she was up to running like that anymore, and that made her feel sad, like she was getting old.

They had spent the previous night at the manor of a baron named Hugo. Most lords welcomed travelers, eager to see new faces and hear news of the outside world, and Hugo had been no exception. Ediva had half expected the old man to try to force himself on her during the night—some lords regarded that as their right—but he hadn't. Ediva had long ago learned to keep a dagger in her belt for such emergencies.

They approached the village. Ediva had heard Miles speak of Ravenswell so many times, it seemed like a legend—a myth, almost. But the reality was that it was just another village, not so very different from Redhill.

Ediva and her party rode down the narrow, tree-lined street to the stares of men, women, and children. They weren't used to seeing strangers here.

"Who are you?" a boy called.

"Where you from?" shouted another.

Ediva didn't answer.

As they drew opposite the stone church, Mody pointed again. "That's Garth's house over there."

Ediva pulled up opposite the gate to Garth's cottage—where Miles had once lived. Chickens and a goose roamed the well-tended yard, along with an orange cat. There was a good-sized orchard in the croft. The roof thatch on the house was new; there were no holes in the walls, and the lime wash wasn't worn away; the shutters were sturdy and fit tightly in the windows. There was a separate building for the animals, as was becoming the custom for better-off ploughmen.

On this sunny day, two men were drinking ale at a trestle table set under the broad roof eave. The one with bunched shoulders and the shock of wheaten hair must be Miles's son—they looked too much alike for it not to be. The other was older, with a dark, humorless mien, like a traveling preacher. Garth appeared to be in his early to mid-thirties. He wore a knee-length shirt, belted at the waist, and dark hose. The other man was dressed much the same, save that his hose were green. A large brown dog lay by the table, one eye focused on Ediva and her party.

Ediva waited expectantly, but the two men ignored her presence outside the gate and kept talking. Irritated, Ediva dismounted and handed Mody her reins. She shoved open the fence gate and went in.

The dog sprang up and ran at her, but instead of attacking her, it put its paws on her shoulder and licked her face. She laughed and scratched behind its ears.

Still, the men paid her no attention. She pushed the dog down and stepped forward.

"I'd also like a milk cow," Garth said to the older man.

The older man straightened. "A cow isn't part of her dowry."

"I'd like it added in," Garth said.

The older man thought. "I could do a pig, maybe. Maybe two pigs."

"I'd prefer the—"

Ediva cleared her throat loudly.

The two men ignored her.

The older man said. "A horse, a colt, but that's as far as I'll—"

"I'm looking for Garth," Ediva interrupted.

"Good for you," said the older man, visibly annoyed by the intrusion. "Go away."

Garth looked up. "We're busy."

"I am Ediva of Redhill."

That got Garth's attention. He stood, frowning. "Ediva? *That* Ediva?"

Now it was her turn to say nothing. She faced him, looking smug.

"My father's often spoken about you," Garth said. "You're one of Blanche's maids now, aren't you?"

Ediva was about to snap, "That's 'Lady Blanche' to you," but at the last moment decided not to. As Miles's son, Garth must know Blanche. Maybe he was permitted to address her that way.

The older man said, "Let's finish our business, Garth. I haven't got all day, and it's a long walk back to Risby."

Garth held up a hand for him to wait.

"See here—" the man started.

"What do you want?" Garth asked Ediva.

Ediva brushed muddy paw prints from the shoulders of her dress. The dog wanted to jump on her again, but she pushed him down. "I bring urgent news."

"What news?"

She hesitated.

"Spit it out," Garth said.

"I don't like speaking in front of strangers," she told him.

"Just say it."

"Your father has been arrested."

"What!" said Garth.

"What?" said the older man, rising.

"What for?" Garth said.

Ediva hesitated once more, looking at the older man.

"What for?" Garth demanded. "Tell me."

"Treason," said Ediva.

Garth stared.

The older man cleared his throat. "I must go. We'll speak again."

"Wait, Oli," Garth said. "I was hoping to make our terms final today."

"Another time, perhaps," Oli said stiffly. "Good day to you." He nodded to Ediva as he brushed past her, heading for the gate. "Miss."

Garth stepped closer to Ediva, cheeks red. "I hope you haven't ruined my marriage contract. I've been working on Oli for months, and now it may all be for naught."

Ediva knew that Garth's wife had died last year. Of course he would need a new one. "I told you I didn't want to talk in front of a stranger," she shot back. "But, no, you had to insist."

Garth bit back a retort. "So now what?"

"Lady Blanche wants to know what you can do to help."

"Damned little, if Father's been arrested for treason," Garth said. After a second he added, "Sounds suspicious, though. Father's never said anything treasonous around me." He stopped, "Well, not recently. In the old days he . . ."

"He what?" said Ediva.

"He always said he wanted to lead a revolt against the French, to drive them out, and make Mercia an independent kingdom again."

Ediva was surprised by that. "He's never expressed those sentiments in my presence, nor in Lady Blanche's, as far as I know."

"I think he realized it was impossible," Garth said. "So there's no truth to the charge?"

"Of course not. Miles owes everything to the king. He'd be a fool to throw it away, and Miles is no fool."

"Then why-?"

"That's what Lady Blanche wants you to find out."

Garth let out his breath with resignation. "All right, you've delivered your message, now be on your way. You need to find shelter before it gets dark." He started for the gate. "Tell Blanche I'll let her—"

"Where are you going?" Ediva said.

"There's someone I need to see."

"About Miles?"

"Yes."

"Then I'm coming, too," Ediva said.

"No, you're not."

"If Miles has spoken to you about me, he must have told you I don't take 'no' for an answer. Now where are we going?"

CHAPTER 10

EDIVA FOLLOWED GARTH down the village street. "Where are we going?" she repeated.

"*We're* not going anywhere," Garth said. "I told you, there's no need for you to stay here. You've delivered your message, now leave."

She continued following him. He sped up, but she effortlessly matched his pace. At last he stopped and sighed in frustration. "If you must know, I'm going to the mill. To see my brother."

"See, that wasn't so difficult," Ediva said. She added, "Look, I'm sorry I interrupted your marriage negotiations. I thought your father's life might be important to you."

"It is," Garth said as he started walking again. "It's just that these negotiations have been going on for months. Oli's daughter, Millette, brings a handsome dowry. The marriage will cement relations between my family and his—Oli is the wealthiest man in Risby." He paused. " 'Would have brought,' I should say, because Oli may not want to do business with the son of a traitor."

"I heard about your wife," Ediva said in a conciliatory tone. "You have my condolences."

"Thank you," Garth said.

"Did she die of disease? Plague?"

"It's none of your business what she died of," Garth snapped. Then he slowed his pace and let out his breath. "Every year, on Midsummer's Day, there's a race to the bottom of Lookout Hill. The winner gets a silver penny. Mary—my wife—and her childhood girlfriends decided to run it one last time before they got too old. It had been raining, and the grass was slick. Mary tripped and fell. She broke her leg. Broke it so bad the bone was sticking out. The vicar and the midwife treated it, but it didn't set right. It festered. She developed a fever . . ." His voice tailed off, and he had a faraway look in his eye.

"I'm sorry," Ediva said. "I shouldn't have asked."

"What's done is done," Garth said. "It was God's will, though till my dying day I'll wonder why. Mary was everything to me. I'd known her since we were children. Known I'd marry her since then, too. I don't really want to marry again, but I have no choice. It's expected of me."

"Because of who you are? The most important man in the village, like your father was?"

"And hundred pledge, like he was, too. Everyone says it's time I remarry." He turned on her. "Just as you should be married."

"I'll marry when I chose," Ediva said, "not when someone tells me to do it."

"Aren't you worried that you'll end up like Estrild? I've met her, you know."

"Estrild has a good life," Ediva said. "She's happy." She thought of something. "What about your children by Millette? What will happen to them?"

"Oli has no living sons," Garth said. "Millette will inherit from him. Which means my children by Millette will inherit from her." He smiled proudly. "Which means I'll have united the two largest holdings in Risby and Ravenswell."

They turned off the street and followed a well-worn path to the stream and the mill, its wheel grinding monotonously in the shade of yellow-and-orange leafed oak and ash trees. The stream undercut the wheel's blades, rotating the wheel on a shaft that turned the millstone located inside the building. A small dam had been built upstream, diverting water into a millrace so that there was always enough water to make the mill wheel turn.

A line of women, most of them old, waited with sacks of grain to be processed, gossiping while they passed the time. Most of the sacks were on small carts. A good-looking man, the hem of his shirt drawn up partway through his belt on this warm day, weighed one of the sacks and hefted it onto a platform. "Ready, Wat!" he cried.

The platform was hoisted by means of a pulley to the mill's upper floor by a dark-haired youth who was either the miller's apprentice or his son, where the grain would be fed into a hopper and ground by the millstone. The man saw Garth approaching and waved.

"A fine day for hunting," Garth said as he and Ediva drew near.

"You've the right of it there," the man replied wistfully, "but I don't do that anymore, as you know. Seen the error of my ways." Where Garth was big and blocky, this fellow was slender, with merry blue eyes. He looked to be a few years younger than Garth. His hair was short and his beard trim. He flashed Ediva a grin, revealing even white teeth. "Who's your lady friend?" he asked Garth.

"She's not my friend," Garth replied testily. To Ediva, he said, "This is my brother, Aelred. Aelred, this is Ediva, Lady Blanche's maid."

Aelred's brow knit. "Ediva . . ." He brightened. "I remember you. A runner, aren't you? Good one, too. Near as good as me, as I recall. Seen you at the Shrove Tuesday races."

"That was a long time ago," Ediva said. "I don't run anymore."

"Ediva brings news from Redhill," Garth said in a lowered voice. "Father has been arrested. For treason."

The words jolted Aelred as though he'd been struck by an arrow. He gestured with his chin, and they walked out of earshot of the waiting women.

"Been expecting something like this," Aelred said. "Surprised it hasn't happened before time. Father threw in his lot with the French. He should've known they'd turn on him."

"He didn't 'throw in with the French,' " Ediva snapped. "He and Lady Blanche love each other, and they were married."

"Same thing," Aelred said dismissively. "And seein' as you're her maid, I reckon you've thrown in with 'em, as well."

Ediva started to say something when another boy on the mill's ground floor brought out a sack and called, "Flour!"

"Wait here," Aelred said.

He went back to the mill. He weighed the flour, then dipped a scoop into the sack and lifted it. He scraped off the excess flour with a rule and poured the scoop into a barrel. This scoop was the miller's fee, part of which went to the lord. There were barrels for wheat, barley, rye, and one of mixed-grain flour, whose bread was highly prized by some. Garth tied the sack of flour and returned it to the woman, who smiled and wished him good day. He weighed the next sack of grain and lifted it onto the platform to be hoisted to the top floor, then he headed back to Garth and Ediva.

When he returned, Ediva started in on him. "Instead of calling people names, you should be thinking about how you can get your father out of this. That's why Lady Blanche sent me here."

"Where's he being held?" Aelred asked her.

"Brightwood Castle."

Aelred shook his head. "Then there's naught we can do. No way to break him out of there."

"I know your father, and he's no traitor," Ediva pressed. "The charges against him are false. There must be something you can do. At least find out why he's been accused. They won't tell my mistress anything."

Aelred looked to Garth. "You could speak to Stigand."

"Who is Stigand?" Ediva said.

"Earl Galon's seneschal," Aelred said, "also lord of Ravenswell. He's at the manor right now for the first time in years. On account of his master's in England."

Garth scratched his bearded jaw—in much the same way his father did, Ediva noted. "Kind of a coincidence that Galon's in England and Father gets arrested, don't you think, Brother?"

"I do," Aelred said.

"Why?" said Ediva.

"Bad blood between 'em," Garth said. "Galon hung Father once, for insolence. He was saved at the last moment by our old lord, Geoffrey."

"Insolence?"

"Galon didn't like that Father was a free man," Aelred explained. "I imagine he likes him being a lord even less."

Ediva said, "I don't know much about Galon, but what I've heard about him isn't good. Don't they call him Galon the Cruel? Something like that?"

Aelred snorted. "They do, and what you heard doesn't begin to cover it. I was there when he beat your steward, Wada, near to death with his bare hands."

So that's where Wada got the scars, Ediva thought. "You think Galon made up these charges?"

Aelred shared a look with Garth. "That'd be my guess," Garth said.

"So what do we do?" Ediva said.

"*You* don't do anything," Garth told her. "It's none of your affair."

"And you?"

Garth shook his head. "I don't know."

"Your father would know what to do," Ediva said.

"Thank you for reminding me," Garth said. "I've been hearing that my whole life. 'Miles would have done this. Miles would have done that.' It gets wearisome." He sighed. "I wish old Lord Tutbury was still sheriff. He was a fair man, and he liked Father. This new fellow, Onfroi, hates Father."

"Why?" said Ediva.

Garth exploded. "My God, do you do nothing but ask questions?"

"That's how you learn," Ediva said.

"Then why don't you learn to do what you're told and go home?"

Chuckling at Garth's frustration, Aelred answered Ediva's question. "Onfroi hates Father for the same reason all the Frenchies hate him. Because he's English."

To Ediva, Garth said, "Your mistress must appeal to the king. It's her only recourse. The French will have to prove treason in court."

"Courts can be rigged," Ediva pointed out.

Garth nodded acknowledgement. "Still, Aelred and I aren't nobles. There's not much we can—"

There was a commotion in the village. "Now what?" Garth said.

"Do you do nothing but ask questions?" Ediva smirked.

Garth flared with anger, but he held it in. He went back up the lane to the village, Ediva and Aelred trailing him.

Armed horsemen filled the street in front of the church, led by an armored knight. The knight was lean, but his red-veined nose and cheeks betrayed a fondness for drink. Ediva recognized him. "That's Guibert of Haverham. He's no friend to your father, either."

"What Frenchy is?" Aelred said.

"Better see what they want," Garth said. He made his way closer to the gathering, Ediva behind him. "Stop following me," he told her.

Ediva ignored him. She turned to Aelred, but he was headed back to the mill. "What's wrong with him?" she asked Garth.

Garth sighed with irritation, but answered. "When the old earl of Trent was killed some years back, Aelred was the chief suspect, on account of his arrows were used in the crime. He was thrown in the castle gaol and fared badly there.

The French were ready to hang him when Father found the real killer. Since then, Aelred makes himself scarce when the French are around. He doesn't like drawing attention to himself." Pointedly, he added, "Any more questions?"

"Not at the moment," Ediva said primly.

Garth muttered something under his breath.

The manor's steward, Pierre Courtenay, had arrived, and Guibert addressed him. "We've been sent by the sheriff," he announced. "We're looking for the Englishman Miles, who calls himself lord of Redhill."

Pierre, a stout fellow with thinning grey hair, was puzzled. "Miles isn't here, my lord. He hasn't been here for years. He lives—"

"I know where he lives, you clod."

Pierre spread his arms. "Then why do you—?"

Ediva stepped forward. "Why are you looking here? Lord Miles has been arrested. He's at Brightwood Castle. You should know that."

Everyone turned and stared at her, including Guibert.

Guibert said, "Aren't you one of Blanche's maids?"

"I am, my lord," she said.

"What are you doing here?"

She gave Garth a look. "Asking questions."

In spite of himself, Garth almost laughed.

"Don't be impertinent," Guilbert told Ediva. "Other lords may allow it of you, but I won't." He turned back to Pierre. "The wench is wrong. Miles isn't at the castle. He's escaped."

"What?" said Ediva.

"How?" said Garth.

Guibert ignored them. He turned to his men. "Search the village."

The men dismounted, brandishing spears and swords. As they did, a deep voice said, "What's this about searching my village?"

The speaker was a tall man, clad in black.

Ediva was awed. "Who's that?"
"Stigand," Garth said.

CHAPTER 11

STIGAND APPROACHED GUIBERT and his men, walking purposefully. He had a high-cheeked, intelligent face and piercing blue eyes. His thick, greying hair was swept straight back, and his beard was trim. He made no ostentatious show of wealth; black cloth was expensive, and that was enough. His black shirt was offset by gold thread at its yoke. "If anyone orders this village searched, it will be me," he told Guibert. "Is that understood?" His French was perfect, though tinged with the trace of a broad, North Country accent.

Guibert hemmed. "Of course, Lord Stigand. We didn't know you were here, or we would have—"

"You know it now. You were sent by that idiot Onfroi, I presume?"

If Guibert was offended by Stigand calling the sheriff an idiot, he knew better than to show it. "We were, my lord."

"Miles isn't stupid enough to come here, but we'll double check, just to satisfy you and your master. Pierre, take the beadles. Search the village and the woods."

"*Oui*, my lord," said Pierre, hurrying away.

Guibert said, "Thank you, my lord." He was careful to show deference to Stigand. Stigand might be English, but he was also Earl Galon's seneschal, and thus an important man. He had married into a wealthy Norman family, and held rich lands across the Narrow Sea.

"Long time since I've been here," Stigand said to no one in particular, looking around the village. "Be longer before I come back, I expect. My life's in Normandy, now."

"You're fortunate, my lord," Guibert said. "I've never been to Normandy. Never been away from England."

Stigand grunted, as if that information reinforced Stigand's already low opinion of him.

Garth sensed Ediva readying herself for something. Before he could stop her, she stepped from the crowd and approached Stigand. "Lord Stigand."

Stigand looked her up and down. "And you are?"

She bowed her head. "Ediva, my lord. Lady's maid to Blanche of Redhill."

Stigand frowned. "Miles's wife? What are you doing here?"

"Seeking information, my lord. About why Lord Miles was arrested. About what he's supposed to have done."

"What is that to you?" Stigand said.

Ediva was undeterred by his tone. "It's for my lady. She's distraught. No one will tell her what's happening."

"Well, the reason for his arrest is a moot point now that he's escaped, isn't it? He proved his guilt by running away, so the main task now is bringing him to justice."

Ediva did not wilt under Stigand's baleful gaze. She had guts; Garth gave her that. "Lord Miles is innocent, my lord."

Stigand curled his lip. "You would say that, you're a member of his household. Plus, you're English."

"As are you, my lord."

Stigand stared at her for a long moment. "You'd do well to curb that insolence before it gets you in trouble. Were you one of my villeins, I'd have you whipped."

"Yes, my lord," Ediva said, but she didn't give in. "So what shall I tell my mistress?"

"Tell her she married the wrong man," Stigand said.

He turned away, heading back to the manor house, leaving Guibert and his men looking foolish.

Ediva returned to Garth. "He's almost as friendly as you are."

She saw the look on Garth's face. "What is it?"

"My father's escaped," Garth explained patiently, as though the answer were self explanatory. "That changes everything."

"Why? What are you going to do?"

"I'm going to find him, of course."

CHAPTER 12

September 17 – Feast of St. Stephen (Martyr)
55 Days Until Martinmas

EDIVA AND HER party stayed that night in the church of St. Wendreda, cold and uncomfortable. The following morning, she sent the groom Mody and the beadle Simon back to Redhill.

"Lady Blanche won't like this," Mody warned Ediva.

"Wada told us to stay by you no matter what," the glowering Simon added.

"I'll take the responsibility," Ediva told them. As a lady's maid, she outranked them. "Now, go."

Mody said, "But—"

"Go."

Mody and Simon left, and Garth and Ediva made their way from Ravenswell to Alton Forest. Ediva rode while Garth walked. They kept off the well-traveled paths. In the afternoon, they found themselves in a sunken lane, with the autumn trees arched overhead, their high branches almost touching, forming a tunnel of red and orange and yellow. Fallen leaves crackled underfoot.

"We could go faster if you'd brought a horse," Ediva pointed out.

"I don't have a horse," Garth said.

"You could have borrowed one."

"I don't ride. Look here, must you come along?"

"How well do you know Alton Forest?" Ediva asked him.

"I don't know it at all," Garth said.

"Then how do you expect to find Miles?"

"Well, I . . ."

"I know Alton Forest like the back of my hand. I've explored those woods since I was a child. Like as not, you'd wander around in there, get lost and die, and then what use would you be? Assuming you're any use now, of course. And that's if you don't get caught by the sheriff's patrols. Bet they'd be only too happy to lay their hands on Miles's son."

"Why?" said Garth. "I haven't done anything."

"Why?" she repeated. "Well, suppose the sheriff announces that he's caught you, and he says he'll hang you unless Miles turns himself in. What do you think Miles would do then?"

Garth had no answer. She was right. He changed the subject. "Why do you keep calling my father 'Miles?' It's disrespectful. He's your lord."

"It's what I've always called him," Ediva said. "I've known Miles since I was a girl and he was Lady Blanche's steward. All of us on the manor call him Miles. He's not big on all that 'my lord' nonsense." She paused. "I guess it's difficult for you, having Miles for a father."

"You could say that," Garth admitted glumly. "I've lived in his shadow all my life. I've yet to make my mark in this world. I've yet to prove myself, and I sometimes wonder if I'll ever get the chance. Father was a famous soldier. He defied the French to find the earl of Trent's killer. He became a lord. I just raise wheat and barley."

Ediva realized something. "That's what this big marriage is about, isn't it? You're trying to impress your father."

"No," he said a bit too quickly. "I told you, it's expected of me."

"Expected by who? If I did everything that was expected of me, I'd be . . ."

"You'd be a lot quieter, I'll wager."

They continued through the colorful tunnel of trees. Ediva said, "You know, your father has lived in the shadow of his father and grandfather—especially his grandfather, Wulfstan. That's been one of the things that's driven him all these years. It's eaten at him. Probably still does."

"How do you know about that?" Garth said, irritated.

"I've known Miles for eleven years. I hear things. My advice to you—"

"Just what I need, advice from a child."

"My advice is to be yourself." She couldn't help herself and added with a smile, "Garth the Gormless."

Garth saw no humor in her remark. "How old are you?"

"Why do you ask?"

"Just curious."

"I'm twenty-one."

"And you're not married?"

"I haven't found anyone who interests me. I've had offers, but I'm happy where I am."

"You're happy being a spinster?"

"I'm not a spinster!" Ediva said. After a bit, she continued. "There was a man I liked, Ulf—Blackie, we called him. He was an ex-soldier, a friend of your father's. He was fond of me—in a fatherly way, of course, and I looked up to him. I liked him a lot, but I was just a child. I kind of hold him up as an example, hoping to find someone like him."

"And you haven't found anyone who measures up?"

"Not even close," she said.

"What was he like, this Blackie?"

"Brave, clever, funny, kind. Good looking, too."

"What happened to him?"

"He was killed during the attack on Brightwood Castle. I've always pretended that Blackie would have waited for me to get older and married me, but the truth is, there was a woman who liked him, too, Hild. If he hadn't been killed, like as not they'd have got married. Hild is married now, with a family, but we're friends, and I know she misses Blackie."

"And you? Do you—?"

"Must you keep asking questions?"

"Now you know what it feels like," Garth told her. "Remember, you were the one who insisted on coming."

"I didn't insist on listening to you talk the whole time," she said.

They went on in silence.

* * *

They spent the night in some woods; Garth didn't know what manor the woods belonged to. He built a small fire in a hollow, where it would be unseen save by someone directly approaching it. Remains of other fires told him that he and Ediva were not the first to camp there. Ediva unsaddled and fed the horse—she'd brought grain with her for just such an occasion—then hobbled the animal.

The sky was clear and the stars were visible in their uncounted numbers. Ediva leaned against her saddle, eating bread in the light of the fire. "The souls of the dead," she said, looking at the stars, "or so they say. How far away do you reckon they are?"

Garth had never thought about it. He looked at the sky. "Five miles, I'd guess. Maybe ten."

"But, look, some are much smaller than others. Those must be fifteen miles away, easy."

Garth didn't want to talk about the stars. He said his prayers and curled up in his cloak near the fire. "Good night."

Ediva slept on the fire's other side, dagger ready, just in case Garth tried something. "Good night."

CHAPTER 13

September 18 – Feast of St. Hygbald
54 Days Until Martinmas

𝕿HEY WERE ON their way before dawn. The day was cloudy, a bite in the air signaling winter's inexorable approach. "How do you plan on finding my father?" Garth asked.

"We'll examine the likely places," Ediva said, "but it's my belief he'll find us."

"*He'll find us?*" Garth said in disbelief. He stopped in the path. "I didn't really need you to guide me, did I?"

The smirk on Ediva's face said everything.

"You tricked me," Garth said.

"You fell for it," she replied.

Garth said, "You're really here because you want to be part of whatever's going on."

"That's right," she said.

"Why didn't you just say so?"

"Because then you would have forbidden me to come. You wouldn't have succeeded, but you'd have tried, and I didn't feel like arguing."

Garth rolled his eyes.

They kept going, and Ediva thought of something. "That Stigand fellow, does he have to approve your marriage?"

"No," Garth said. "I'm a free man, I may marry whom I please. I'll give him a gift, of course, even though I don't have to. Best to stay on his good side."

"What about your partner in the contract, the sourpuss?"

"Oli's not free. He'll need to pay his lord so he can marry his daughter off the manor, but it's worth it to him to be connected to my family."

Ediva headed for the western part of the forest, reasoning that Miles would want to be far away from the Viking's old camp. She followed the streams, assuming Miles would camp near water. In the end, as she predicted, Miles found them. One moment he wasn't there; the next, he was. Standing in the path, hands on his hips, short sword at his belt, almost as though he'd been expecting them.

"You certainly made enough noise, Ediva," he said. "That's not like you."

"Wanted to make sure you heard us coming," Ediva replied.

"Lady Blanche is probably worried sick about you."

"Had to get Garth here, didn't I?" she said.

"Yes, and I'm glad you did." Miles clapped Garth's shoulder. "It's good to see you, son."

"Got yourself in a right mess this time, haven't you, Father?" Garth said.

"That I have, and it's going to be hard to get out. Where's Aelred?"

"He stayed in Ravensell," Garth said. "Too busy to come, he said."

Miles tisked in disappointment, then said, "Come, visit my camp. Rest and have something to eat."

It was late afternoon when they reached Miles's camp. Garth wished he'd brought provisions for his father; he should have thought of that. The camp was in a clearing, with an outcrop of rock providing protection from the north. There was a partly constructed hut with a fire pit inside, along with piles of cut saplings and pine branches to be used for walls and roofing. A hare hung in the smoke of a bunkered fire. And there was wine.

"Where did you get wine out here?" Garth asked.

Miles grinned. "I found some obliging pedlars. They gave me this cloak, too. It seems I'm Brock the Badger now."

"You're serious?" Garth said.

Ediva said, "You've become Brock the Badger?"

"Yes. Lord of the Greenwood." Miles put his hand over his heart. "I rob the French and give to the English."

Garth and Ediva laughed.

Miles cut them some of the hare and gave them bread left over from the pedlars' supply.

While they ate and drank, Miles saw to Ediva's horse, then told them about the plot. When he was finished, Garth said, "You don't actually believe that story, do you?"

Miles spread his hands. "I don't know what to believe. Galon seems to believe it, and that's the important thing. He's chief councillor to the king, and he wants to learn the truth."

"Which has somehow become your job," Garth said.

"Yes," Miles said.

Garth wiped his hand on the hem of his shirt. "So how do I help?"

"Ask around, see what you can learn. Be discreet. Get Aelred to assist you, if you can. The plot, if there is one, may have originated in Trentshire."

"Why do you say that?" Ediva asked.

"The original conspirator was apprehended at the Saracen's Head."

"Huh," said Garth.

"And what will you do?" Ediva asked Miles.

Miles wrinkled his forehead. "I'll try to stay alive, and I'll see what information I can glean from travelers. Now, you two can stay here for the night. We'll make beds from these pine branches and leaves. Then, Ediva, you must return to Redhill."

Ediva protested. "But I want to—"

"No," Miles said. "I won't see you hurt because of this. Nor will Lady Blanche. You've risked enough for us over the years. It's someone else's turn."

"How will I get in touch with you?" Garth asked.

"You know where my camp is," Miles told him. "Come here. That's safer than me trying to come to you."

With the sunrise, Miles saw Garth and Ediva on their way. "God speed," he cried, raising a hand in farewell.

The two of them traveled in silence. When they reached the path that led south, toward Redhill, Ediva ignored it and continued east, back toward Ravenswell.

"You missed the path," Garth told her.

"I know," she said.

"Father bade you return to the manor."

She made no reply.

"He's your lord," Garth said. "You can't disobey him."

"I've done it before," she said. "This will be more fun."

"Well, you're not going to Ravenswell," Garth told her. "Where would you stay? And don't say at my house. An unmarried woman? A scandal like that would ruin any chance I still have of marrying Millette. And there's nowhere else in the village for you save the church, and I doubt Father—"

"I wasn't planning to stay in Ravenswell," she informed him.

"Where, then?"

"I'm going to the Saracen's Head, in Badford."

CHAPTER 14

September 18

BLANCHE SMELLED THE vats of fermenting grapes in the back room. Others might hate that smell, but Blanche loved it. One of her fondest memories as a child was of crushing grapes with her feet, stomping around in them with her brothers and sisters, lower legs soaked with juice, grape skins squishing between her toes. She wished she could still join in, but he was a great lady now, and she had to maintain her dignity. There could be no tucking up her kirtle and chemise and exposing her legs to the manor workers. Ediva, of course, had no qualms about that and joined in readily, but Ediva had not returned from Ravenswell. Mody and Simon had brought word that she was going with Garth to find Miles, but she should have been back by now.

"My lady?" Father Albinus prodded.

Blanche looked up. "Oh, sorry. My mind must have wandered."

"Not surprising, with all that's going on," Albinus said in a kindly tone. "Are you sure you don't want to put this off until—"

"No. No. Let's get it over with. It helps me keep my mind off things."

They were in the winery. The winery's back room was a low, barn-like structure that housed the vats for fermenting and the oak barrels in which the wine was stored. The front room, which had been added onto the other building, was smaller and used as a sort of office, a storehouse for tools and records, for tally sticks that only Dragobert, the vintner, could understand.

Blanche and Albinus sat at a small trestle table, attending to the winery's finances ahead of the next quarter day, which was in eleven days' time, at Michaelmas. A pot of ink and two quill pens lay on the table. Albinus was there because he could write numbers and do sums. Estrild should have been in attendance on Blanche, but she was off again, getting religious instruction from Tostig.

Dragobert the vintner had once been part of Baron Aimerie's staff. Blanche had poached him after Aimerie's downfall, and was glad she had. The easy slope of Ghost Hill, and its chalky soil, had proven a fortuitous location for a vineyard. Redhill's wines were sold throughout Trentshire and in Badford Town. Profits from the winery kept Blanche's manors going during the lean years—and there had been a couple of very lean years. During those times, Blanche and Miles had distributed the winery's profits among the common folk, to help them buy what little food was available. Blanche had been born a peasant—no one knew that save for Miles—and she remembered facing starvation while those at the great house had full bellies. She wouldn't permit that on her lands if it could be avoided.

Right now she had other things one her mind, which made it hard to concentrate on the business at hand. In the village, sheep shearing was underway, and cries and laughter could be heard from that direction. She sighed. "I'm worried, Father. God knows where Miles is, or even if he's still alive. Ediva, too."

"Oh, they're all right," Albinus assured her, "you'll see. I have faith in them." Albinus hadn't changed much over the years, save that he moved more slowly, and his wooly hair and beard had gone grey.

"Miles is supposed to be doing something for Galon. Redeeming himself from the treason charge, Galon says, but . . ."

"Working for Galon is like working for Satan himself," Albinus said, crossing himself.

"And like to have the same result," Blanche added.

"I'm sure everything will turn out, my lady. Now let's get this finished, so I can bless the new-shaved wool." Albinus went back to his list, which was written on a scrap of parchment he'd scissored from the blank end of one of the old church rolls. "We've promised five barrels of best red to the castle for the winter, at two marks the barrel, and two barrels of second best at a mark and a half. That's ten marks plus . . . three, which is . . . thirteen." He wrote something on another sheet. "Will we have them?"

"We will. Do you mind if I put poison in them?"

Albinus cleared his throat. "I won't, but God might object. That Theobald . . ."

Someone approached the shed. It was the steward, Wada, tufts of wool clinging to his sweaty clothes and hair. "Sorry to interrupt, my lady, but there's someone to see you."

"Who?" Blanche said.

"Dunno, my lady. A pedlar. Calls himself Grogan, Grugan, something like that."

Blanche didn't know anyone named Grogan. "Why would I want to see a pedlar?"

"Says he has a message for you."

"Find out what it is. Then give him a half-penny and send him on his way."

"Tried that, my lady. Says he won't speak to nobody but you."

Now what? "Very well, bring him up," she said at last.

Wada departed and returned with an old man, twisting a faded blue cap in his hands. The man's face was furrowed, his clothes worn and travel stained. He bowed to Blanche, attempting panache and not succeeding. "Good day, my lady. My name is Grugan."

Blanche didn't have time for pleasantries. "I understand you have a message for me?"

The pedlar cast a wary glance at Father Albinus.

"Father Albinus is my confessor," Blanche told Grugan. "Anything you have to say, you may say in front of him."

"I was told to—"

"Have you a message or not?"

Grugan cast another look at Albinus and went on. "I do, my lady. It comes from Brock the Badger."

"*Who?*" Blanche said. She looked to Albinus. "Brock the . . .? Wait—isn't that your mythical forest outlaw?"

"It *was*, my lady," Albinus said, "but there hasn't been a—"

"Beggin' your pardon, my lady, but he didn't look too mythical when I seen him," Grugan said.

"And when was that?"

"Couple days back."

"Where?" said Albinus.

"Alton Forest."

"And the contents of this message?" Blanche said.

"Brock, he said, 'On the feast of St. Maurice and the Thebans. By the lone oak where he fought Aimerie.' "

A chill rippled up Blanche's back. Her dark, almond-shaped eyes narrowed. "What did he look like, this Brock?"

Grugan shrugged. "Dunno. Big fellow, maybe fifty. Wore a fancy black ring, I remember that. Took it from a Frenchy, I expect."

Blanche shared another look with Albinus. "And that was it?" she asked Grugan. "The message?"

"Aye, my lady."

"Did Brock rob you?" Albinus asked.

"No, Father, he didn't. Says he only robs the French— sorry, my lady. Robs the French and gives to the English, he says."

Blanche laughed at that. It was the first good laugh she'd had in a while. "The cheeky devil. Thank you for bringing the message, Grugan." She took a silver penny from her purse and handed it to him.

"Thank *you*, my lady. I must say, it's an honor to do a favor for Brock the Badger. Worth more'n money, that is."

That's a new one, she thought. "You'll take a glass of wine, for refreshment?"

Grugan cleared his throat and cast a sly eye. "I'd prefer a bumper of ale, if it's all the same to you, my lady. For me and my party—my nephew and his friend. And mayhap a bit o' bread, with jam mayhap."

Blanche smiled. "Very well. Wada, show our friend and his companions to the brewhouse. Take your bread and ale, Master Grugan. Tell the brewer I said it's all right."

"Thank you, my lady." Led by Wada, Grugan bowed again and departed, putting his pointed cap on his head.

Blanche turned, and Father Albinus was smiling as well. "So Miles has become Brock the Badger," Albinus said.

"So it would appear," Blanche said. " 'I only rob the French.' " She laughed again. "Do you know where this oak tree is?"

"I do, my lady," Albinus said, and his tone turned grim. "I could find it in my sleep."

CHAPTER 15

September 22 – Feast of St. Maurice (Martyr)
50 Days Until Martinmas

FATHER ALBINUS GUIDED Blanche to the oak.

Blanche assumed that the sheriff had men watching her at the manor, so she had ridden out with the huntsmen that morning, as she frequently did. Once in the forest, she broke off from the hunters and, by prearrangement, met up with Albinus, who was leading a sad-faced sumpter horse laden with goods.

The oak stood by itself in a glade beside a stream. Across the stream, trees and brush grew to the water's edge. Albinus held the horse's reins as Blanche dismounted. "This is where the battle was fought?" she said.

"More a massacre than a battle, my lady," Albinus said. "Those of us who got away that day were lucky."

Blanche nodded. She remembered standing in the rain that night, waiting for Miles to return, thinking he never would, until finally he appeared, the last man back. "It seems so peaceful now."

"Lost a lot of good friends that day," Albinus said. There was a hitch in his voice, and he said, "I'll wait in the woods, my lady, give you a bit of privacy."

Albinus left and Blanche walked around the glade. She tried to picture the grass piled with bodies, splashed with blood, but couldn't. She did find a few rusted arrow points, a pitted knife blade, and, by the water, what must have once been part of a helmet. It was all so quiet in the September sun. She sought the shade of the oak and leaned against the trunk, eyes half closed, listening to the birds and the hum of insects.

A familiar voice behind her said, "Good day, my lady."

She jumped. She had not heard him coming.

She turned and threw herself into his arms. "Oh, Miles."

They kissed passionately, their bodies pressed together. "God, I've missed you," she breathed. "Are you all right?"

"Right as I can be," Miles said. "Living in the woods isn't as much fun as the stories make it out to be. I could use a bath and a good meal." He kissed her again, growling, "Most of all, I could use you."

She returned his kiss hard, her teeth grinding against his. "Not as much as I'd like to be used," she said, breathing heavily. "Unfortunately, there's no time today."

They caught their breaths and held each other close. "Father Albinus has brought you some things that may help," Blanche told Miles. She looked into his blue eyes. "So what's the truth of your situation? Galon all but admitted that the charges against you were made up. He intimated that you're working for him."

Miles seemed surprised. "You've spoken to Galon?"

"Right after you were arrested. He informed me that I'm to be his wife should something happen to you."

"That bastard," Miles swore. "Still, it's no more than I'd expect of him." He paused. "I'm supposed to be uncovering a plot."

Blanche arched her brows. "A plot?"

"It's supposed to come to fruition on Martinmas, that's all Galon and Stigand know about it. Their informant died under questioning before he could say more."

"What kind of plot?" she said. "And why would Galon pick you, of all people, to uncover it?"

"It's an attempt against the king, presumably. Galon says he picked me because I'm the only honest man he knows, the only one he can trust."

"He's probably right about that," Blanche said.

Then she realized something, and she went cold. She moved out of Miles's arms and eyed him. "You know what this is, don't you?"

Miles waited.

"It's a plot, all right," Blanche said. "It's a plot to have you killed."

Miles let that sink in.

Blanche went on. "Galon hated you as a free man, he hates you more as a lord. He won't have an English lord in Trentshire, and he wants to be rid of you. Now that you've escaped the castle and killed a guard, you've validated his charge of treason. Onfroi is free to hunt you down and kill you without a trial."

Miles rubbed his chin. "You may be right."

"Of course I'm right."

"That doesn't sound like Galon, though. If he wanted me dead, he'd just get a sword and do it himself. At the worst, he'd send Stigand."

"He must have a reason for doing it this way," Blanche said. "It's probably because the king holds you in high regard, and Galon doesn't want to do anything to anger him."

Miles thought about that and sighed in agreement. He turned and stared across the stream. "I've been expecting Galon to come at me for eleven years. I'm just surprised he's waited so long."

Blanche stood beside him and put her arm through his. "He won't stop until you're dead."

Miles placed his hand over hers. "I know."

They were quiet for a moment, then Blanche faced him and wrapped her arms around him. "What will you do?"

"Well, I'm already pegged as Brock the Badger. I guess I'll try to live up to the name."

"That's not a strategy," she said. "It means you can never come home. What will happen to the children if I'm forced to marry Galon?"

Miles said nothing. He knew what would happen to the children. They both did.

She let go of him. "We'll come live with you in the forest."

"Not yet," Miles said. "Not with winter coming. I'm hoping there may yet be a way out of this."

"I've sent a letter to the king, but Galon is the king's chief advisor, and his word is bound to carry more weight than mine."

"It's still worth the effort," Miles said. "In the meantime, I guess I'll look into Galon's so-called plot."

"Why?" said Blanche. "You know it's not real."

Miles shrugged. "It'll give me something to do." He grinned. "Besides robbing the French and giving to the English, that is."

She made a face at him. "You love that phrase, don't you?"

"I do. I'll work on the off chance that Galon wasn't lying, and there actually is a plot. Galon reckoned the plotters would contact me."

"Why would they do that?"

"I'm well known, and now I'm wanted by the king. If the plot exists, and it is against the king, Galon thinks the plotters will want me on their side."

"As the last English lord?"

Miles nodded. "My job would be to win the common people's support."

"If there's a plot against the king, Galon is probably behind it," Blanche said. "I swear, if anything happens to you, I'll kill that man myself."

"There's a pleasant thought," Miles said.

"Now I must rejoin the huntsmen," she told him. "They're waiting for me, so we can be seen returning to the manor together. I sent Ediva to Ravenswell, to tell your sons what's happened. She's not back yet, so God knows what's happened to her."

"I've seen her," Miles said with a concerned frown. "She brought Garth to me. I sent her back to Redhill, but that was days ago."

"Well, she hasn't returned."

"I hope nothing's happened to her," Miles said.

"Could she have gone back to Ravenswell for some reason?"

"I can't see why."

"You've got me worried about her," Blanche said.

"Me, too. There's naught we can do, though. Not for the moment. Now, you must go."

They kissed again. Blanche took Miles's hand and placed it on her breast, kneading her breast with it, massaging his thumb and forefinger around the nipple. "I can't stand not having you with me," she gasped. "I'll come to you as soon as I may."

"No, don't," Miles told her. "I'll come to you."

"How? When? The manor will be watched."

He winked. "I'm Brock the Badger, remember? I do as I please. I'll leave a chalk mark on the inside of the vintner's door." He gave her another kiss, then helped her onto her horse.

Blanche rode off, with a last look behind her. Miles waved to her, then went into the woods, where Father Albinus waited. "Miles, my boy, it's good to see you."

Miles hugged the old priest warmly. "Good to see you, as well, Father."

Albinus indicated the sumpter horse. "I've brought you some things. If you're going to be Brock the Badger, best do it in style."

On the horse were a bow and two quivers of arrows, along with a spear, an axe, a sword, fishing line and hooks, and several coils of rope, as well as a heavy cloak and a cowl with a hood. There were also loaves of bread, a wheel of cheese in wax, sacks of oats, peas, and beans, and a small iron pot. "For making pottage," Albinus said with a knowing twinkle in his eye. There were also sacks of apples and pears and a pot of cider.

"Where did you get all this?" Miles asked him.

"They're donations," Albinus said. "From the parish. Sewale sent the bow. Says it's better than yours."

"He might be right," Miles said, admiring the bow. "Thank you, Father, this will be a great help. Now if you'll give me your blessing, it's best you get back before you're missed."

Miles knelt while Albinus made the sign of the cross over him. "*In nomine Patris, et Filii, et Spiritus Sanctus.*"

"Amen," said Miles, crossing himself.

Miles rose and Albinus said, "Stay safe, my boy."

"You mean stay alive?" Miles said.

"That, too."

"I'll do my best, Father."

Then Albinus was gone, as well, leaving Miles and the sumpter horse alone in the autumn wood.

CHAPTER 16

September 22

𝕸ILES WALKED THE heavily laden sumpter horse through the forest, back to his camp, following a path that was little more than an animal track. Trees crowded in all around. Miles patted the horse's muzzle. "What shall we call you, boy? Maurice, I think, in honor of the day."

The horse stared at him, unimpressed.

"Don't worry," Miles went on, "we'll soon get all that heavy gear off you and let you graze. We'll be able to set up a proper camp now."

Blanche had been right about the "plot," Miles realized. Galon was trying to get him killed. The job had been neatly done, too; Miles had to give the bastard credit. In nearly the blink of an eye, everything Miles had worked for was gone. Fifty-one years turned to naught.

Was there anything Miles could do? Could he get a pardon from the king? Unlikely. Not after he'd killed that guard, which, of course, was why Galon had him do it.

"He outwitted me, this time, Maurice," Miles said. The horse snorted, as if agreeing.

Miles would likely live out his days in the forest. "We'd better start exploring," he told Maurice. "We'll go southeast first. Easton Manor is over that way somewhere. Maybe we can buy you some grain there."

He sighed. He remembered his best friend, Leofric, long dead in Wales. He wished Leofric was with him now. The two of them could have fun. Well, as much fun as two old men could have living in the forest and robbing people. He'd have the rheumatiz ere long, he guessed. How had the Viking and his people stuck it out all those years . . .?

Stephen flicked his ears.

The forest had gone silent.

Miles was not alone.

Miles stopped. Ran his eyes slowly over his surroundings.

Someone was out there.

He waited, but saw and heard nothing. He couldn't stay here all day, he had to keep going. He drew the sword from its sheath on the horse's back. It was his own sword, from the manor. He thought about the bow, but the bow was useless for close-in work. Anyway, he'd only have one shot if there was trouble.

He started forward. Let them show themselves.

And they did.

There were three of them, ragged and dirty. One was huge, a brawler by his look. His nose had been broken so many times that it had bumps and ridges on top of each other. The second was a banty rooster of a man, bouncing on the balls of his feet. There were more patches on his clothes than there was original material. The third man was sturdy and intelligent looking, and he was missing his right hand.

"What have we here, boys?" said Patches.

"Easy pickin's," said the brawler. "Look at the load on that horse."

"Our friend carries a sword," Patches said, "a good one too, the kind that belongs to a noble. Who are you, friend?"

Miles tried to keep his tone light. "I'm Miles of Redhill, but you may call me Brock the Badger." He indicated the horse. "And this is my good friend Maurice."

"Brock the Badger?" Patches belted a laugh. "Sure, and I'm the Virgin Mary."

"That's funny," Miles said. "I thought the Virgin was better looking."

Patches' face clouded. "Go on, hand over that horse. The sword, too. And if you're quick about it, we'll let you go on your way."

"I'm afraid I can't do that," Miles said.

The man with one arm tried to be conciliatory. "Please, we don't want to hurt you."

"Maybe you don't," the brawler said, "but I'd like to put the bugger in his place."

"See, that's the difference between you and me, Wiggy," Patches told the brawler, rapping him smartly in the chest. "I'd have a go at him meself, but he's too old."

"And not like to get much older," said Wiggy.

Wiggy rushed forward. Miles didn't want to kill him. He stepped into his advance and hit him in the nose with the hilt of his sword. Wiggy cried out and bent over, holding his nose, which was gushing blood. "That wasn't fair."

Patches lunged at Miles. Miles dropped the sword and, using Patches' own momentum, caught Patches and threw him into a tree.

Something hit Miles in the back of the head. The world spun and he dropped to the ground.

CHAPTER 17

MILES'S HEAD SWAM. Then he remembered where he was and he reached for his fallen sword. A foot was on the sword, pinning it to the ground. The foot belonged to the one-handed man, who carried a thick branch, presumably what he'd hit Miles with. "Sorry," he told Miles, and there was genuine sympathy in his voice.

Nearby sat Wiggy, his lower face covered with blood from his broken nose. Patches climbed to his feet, moaning.

"Stay down," the one-handed man told Miles. "I don't want to hit you again."

Wiggy spit blood. "You might not want to hit him, but I do."

He got up and started forward, fists balled. Miles wobbled to his feet to meet him.

"Stop!" cried a voice.

They turned to see three more people in the path—two men and a woman. All wore packs on their backs. The man in the lead had burn scars over the right side of his face.

"Who the Hell are you?" Wiggy said to the newcomers. "By all that's holy, this woods is as crowded as St Hugobert's square on Market Day."

Patches was on his feet now, if a bit unsteady. "This one's ours," he told the newcomers. "Keep going, if you know what's good for you."

Miles took advantage of the distraction. Pushing the one-handed man aside, he grabbed the sword and placed his back to a sturdy tree. "Now, if you gentlemen wish to continue our discussion, I'll be more than happy to oblige, but I warn you, I'll not be so gentle this time."

He saw the second new man sliding toward Maurice. "Touch that horse, and you'll find out how sharp this sword is."

The man stopped, hands up.

"Who are you?" the disfigured man asked Miles. His burned skin was pinkish against the rest of his weather-beaten face. The ear on that side of his head had been turned to a nubbin.

Miles eyed them, sword ready, waiting for someone to try him. "I'm called Miles of Redhill."

" 'The last English lord?' " said the burned man. "Are you really him?"

"You told us you was Brock the Badger," Patches countered.

"I also told you I was Miles," Miles said.

"Can you prove it?" Wiggy said.

Miles held up his left hand, showed them the niello-inlaid ring. "Best I can do."

"If you're Brock, then it's you we've come to find," said the man with the burned face. "We heard you were active again."

"How?" Miles said.

"Word spreads. You robbed some pedlars and they haven't stopped talking about it. Bragging about it, really."

"That was you?" the man with one hand asked Miles.

"It was," Miles replied.

"Well, whyn't you say so in the first place?" Wiggy complained.

"I did, but you wouldn't listen."

Miles's three assailants were somewhat abashed. "You don't look like Brock," Wiggy said by way of an excuse.

"What did you expect me to look like?" Miles said.

"I dunno. Thought you'd be all clad in green, like."

"And be clean," Patches added.

Miles shrugged. "Like I said, this is the best I can do."

"I guess we should apologize," said the one-handed man. He tossed the heavy branch to the ground. "I'm Bondo." He indicated Patches. "This is Autti. And the handsome fellow with the broken nose is Wighelm."

Miles said, "Sorry about the nose, Wiggy."

"It's all right," Wighelm said. "Not like it's the first time."

"Or the last," Patches joked.

Wighelm growled.

The man with the burned face came over and took Miles's hand. "I'm Oswald. This is my brother, Oshere, and his wife, Diote."

"We was run off our land," Oshere said. "Our French lord decided to get rid of his people and raise sheep."

"We were actually hoping to find you and join up with you," Oswald said.

It had not occurred to Miles, though it should have, and doubtless would have in time, that the jolly outlaw of the greenwood needed a gang of jolly men.

Oswald caught Miles looking. "You're wondering about my face?"

Miles shook his head. "No, I—"

"If he ain't wonderin' about it, I am," Patches said.

"He got it savin' me," Oshere told them. "Pulled me out of our burnin' house when I was two."

"How old were you?" Miles asked Oswald.

"Seven."

"Damn," Patches muttered.

Wighelm shook his head in admiration. "Seven years old? That took some guts."

To Bondo, Miles said, "I assume you lost that hand for poaching?" Loss of a hand was a common penalty for poaching.

"Aye," Bondo said. "Guibert of Haverham done it."

Miles snorted at Guibert's name.

"For taking a rabbit," Bondo went on. "My hand for a fucking rabbit, do you believe that? And my first time, too. French bastard. Lost my future wife cause o' him. Couldn't work the fields no more, so her father wanted no more parts o' me. Nor did my own father, come to it. So I took to the woods." He shook his head. "I miss that life. Ever get enough money, I'd like to try and go back to farming."

"Ah, that's a chump's game," Patches said, waving a dismissive hand. "Spend your life breaking your back, and for what? So the lord can give you a meal at Easter and Christmas? Not me."

"Where are you from?" Miles asked Patches.

"Lower Wynchecombe," Patches said, rolling his shoulders. "Father's a day laborer, when he can get work, which ain't often. He had a lot of free time and spent most of it beating me. No future in that, so I run away."

"And you're outlaws now?" Miles asked the three men.

"Trying to be," Bondo said. Ruefully, he added, "Ain't been all that successful so far."

Patches said, "Tried to rob some pilgrims, but there was too many of 'em, and they run us off. I gave one of the guards a good sock on the jaw, though."

"And you?" Miles asked Wighelm. "Too many trips to hallmoot?"

"Aye," said the big man. "Some months, I think they only had hallmoot cause o' me. Seems me and ale don't mix. Time for a change of scenery, says I."

Oswald said, "So can we? Join you?"

Miles looked around. "You're all agreed on this?"

Wighelm made a face like "Why not?" The others nodded or muttered "Yes," though Patches looked like he'd have been happier were it him in charge instead of Miles.

"Very well," Miles said. "You can join me, but there are rules. First, we share all profits equally, with extra to the sick. We're brothers."

"And a sister," chirped Diote, a mousey woman who seemed out of place here.

There was laughter, and Miles went on. "Second, no unnecessary killing. Third, no raping. Fourth, and this is the big one, we may steal from others, but we never steal from each other. And we never take each other's women."

"And the penalty for breaking the rules?" asked Wighelm.

Miles was grim. "You know what it is."

They did. The men, and Diote, shared looks.

Miles went on. "If you don't like these rules, leave now. Going forward, each of you is free to leave at any time, and no hard feelings. Does that suit you?"

Mutters and nodding of heads.

"Very well." Miles held out his right hand and the others piled their hands on top of his. "Do you swear to be loyal to each other and to abide by our rules?"

"We do." "Yes." "Aye."

"Good." Miles fetched the pot of cider from the horse. He passed it around, and everyone drank to seal the bargain. "Everyone who joins us will swear the same oath. Now let's get Maurice back to camp and get something to eat."

CHAPTER 18

October 4 – Feast of St. Amon the Anchorite
38 Days Until Martinmas

*"Jolly Brock and his men sang and danced
And took their leisure in the greenwood . . ."*

MILES PLACED ANOTHER pine bough on the roof of his hut, arranging it so that it didn't obstruct the smoke hole. The boughs formed a thick layer; the hut should be fairly waterproof now. Next he'd use mud to chink in the spaces between the saplings and branches that formed the hut's walls, to keep out the winter chill. He was using a deer hide as a door. Maybe two hides, back to back, would ward off the cold better. Burlap backed with wool would work even better than that, but he didn't have either of those.

Around him, the camp bustled. Sweating profusely, Wighelm and Ioco chopped at a huge oak that obstructed the center of the expanding camp. Oswald and Diote worked on huts. Patches was clearing brush, and Oshere led a group of newcomers gathering firewood. Over the last eleven days, men had trickled in, until Miles now had about twenty. A few of the newcomers weren't outlaws. They were common ploughmen and laborers, who wanted to join Miles of Redhill, "the last English lord," unjustly accused of treason by the hated French. These men professed loyalty to Miles, a man they barely knew, when of course they were really professing loyalty to a cause, an idea, to a free England. Miles represented that cause, had represented it all his life, and these men were willing to surrender their livelihoods to follow him. It was a humbling experience, and Miles wondered if he could live up to their expectations.

The newcomers had to be assigned camping spots. Latrines had to be dug in a safe spot, the men had to be organized into groups. Hunting parties were sent out daily, as well as scouts looking for travelers to rob. One of the new men had already died from the flux and had been buried.

As Miles stopped for water, one-handed Bondo approached. "A word?" he said in a quiet voice.

Miles nodded.

Bondo said, "I keep my purse in the hut. It's inconvenient to carry it around. I had six coins in it, now there's only five."

"You're sure?" Miles said.

"Count 'em every night."

"What are you saying? We have a thief?"

"Don't like to think so, but how else could a coin go missing like that?"

"Any idea who it is?"

As if the answer was obvious, Bondo cast a sideways look at Wighelm's partner chopping at the oak.

"Ioco?" said Miles.

Bondo nodded.

Ioco was a dark-haired Cornishman, a refugee from the mines, or so he claimed. He had corded muscles, a nasty demeanor, and a face like a fist. He kept largely to himself, and most were glad of it.

"All right," Miles said, "I'll keep an eye on him. Thanks for letting me know."

Some of the men began singing a ballad another of the newcomers, Scarlet, had written. No one knew why he was called Scarlet. It was a name he had given himself. The song told how Galon the Cruel and his henchman, the traitor

Stigand, had hung Miles from a beech tree, but by a miracle Miles managed to escape death. The song made it sound like the incident happened when Miles was accused of treason, when in reality it had taken place over a decade before. The song also made it sound as though Miles had escaped by the use of his wits, not that he'd been rescued by a French lord named Geoffrey.

Miles didn't like people singing songs about him. "All right, all right," he called to the men. "Enough of that."

Grinning, the men complied. But Miles knew it would only last for a while. Soon they would start again—maybe with Scarlet's latest, "The Ballad of Brock and the Sheriff," whose verses mocked "Onfroi the Fat" and "Theobald Hack-Ear" in their futile attempts at bringing Miles to French justice.

"Miles!" cried a voice. It was one of the scouts, a man called Frithric, who had joined Miles's band one step ahead of the foresters. "Found this fellow wandering the woods," Frithric said. "Says he's looking for you. Got a horse with supplies, and all."

He ushered forward a burly man with wooly hair and beard. A rope cincture girdled the man's waist; a crucifix hung from his neck.

"Father Albinus!" Miles cried, hugging him. "What brings you here?"

"Looking for you, of course," Albinus said.

"It's all right," Miles told Frithric, "he's a friend."

As Frithric went back on scout, Albinus said, "I've come to be with you in your hour of need, Miles. Can't leave you and your lads without spiritual guidance."

"What about the parish?"

"Oh, Tostig can handle that, least till this mess gets cleared up."

"That may take a while," Miles pointed out.

Albinus didn't seem to care about that. "Come a long way, Tostig has. Not ordained, of course, but he can do everything else. Your wife's maid Estrild helps him when things get hectic." He looked round the camp. "You've gathered quite a flock."

"Good sinners, all," Miles said proudly. He turned and called, "Quiet! Men, meet our new priest, Father Albinus, as fine a man as ever donned the stole."

There were cries of greeting. Others waved as they worked. Meanwhile, Miles examined Albinus's pack horse, which held flour, bread, cheese, apples, and pears, as well as grain for Miles's sumpter horse, Maurice, and a cask of ale from the manor's brew house.

"Hersent wanted to come with me," Albinus told Miles. "In the worst way."

Hersent was Wada's wife. She had been an outlaw once herself, part of the Viking's band. She and Wada had fought alongside Miles during the assault on Brightwood Castle. "We could use her bow," Miles admitted. "There's no better shot in the shire."

"That's so," Albinus said. "In the end, she decided she couldn't leave her family."

"She made the right decision," Miles admitted. "How is Blanche?"

"Holding up as well as you'd expect, her and the children."

"I'll have to visit her soon."

"Be careful when you do. The manor is watched by Onfroi's spies. He counts on you trying to make contact with her." Albinus went on. "Don't underestimate Onfroi, Miles. He's not happy with these songs being sung about him."

Miles was surprised. "He's heard them?"

"Everybody's heard them. Why, you're famous, boy. The whole shire is behind you; they're already comparing you to Hereward. Making up tales about you and your men living free here in the greenwood."

"If only they knew," Miles said ruefully.

"One song even says you captured Brightwood Castle from Galon, not from Aimerie. Says you defeated Galon in single combat, but let him live on the condition that you be permitted to marry Blanche."

"God help us," Miles said. Galon wasn't going to like that. "Well, let's introduce you to the others and get you situated . . ."

"Miles! Miles!" It was Odda, another scout, a big man with thinning hair. "There's a party of merchants on the river road, coming this way."

"Is there?" Miles said. "Well, then, we should make their acquaintance. Show them forest hospitality." He raised his voice. "All right, lads! All but Oshere and Diote get your things and let's move out." He grabbed an apple from the sack, took a bite, and clapped Albinus on the shoulder. "Come, Father. Join the fun."

CHAPTER 19

*"Then back to camp
They did go,
And Brock treated his guests
To a feast the likes of which
Was ne'er seen in those parts . . ."*

THE FOREST. DEEP. Impenetrable.

The path. Winding. Narrow. The river road ran inland here, to avoid bad ground.

Four hired men, goading a string of laden mules. Ahead of them, two monks on good horses. One monk was Gervase, abbot of Huntley; the other, his cellarer, Sampson. Four guards armed with spears and swords attended the party—two in front and two in the rear.

Sampson, the cellarer, was well built, with dark hair and the barest trace of a tonsure. Women didn't like tonsures. He hadn't been in England long. His family, who were prominent in Normandy, had advised him that the quickest way to obtain advancement in the Church was to go to the wilds of England, where there was always a shortage of good men. From what he had seen of England so far, he regretted that decision. "A lot of adversity this trip, my lord, but we're almost there," he said to his companion.

Abbot Gervase had more tonsure than Sampson, but not much. He was fair and slender, and he wore a brown robe and hooded cowl of the finest cloth. "Praise God," he said. Gervase had once been Huntley's cellarer himself. He had

81

hoped for promotion to an abbey in Normandy, or France at the least. Something better than England, anyway, as befitting a distant relative of both Kings Henry of England and Louis of France. Still, he was young yet, and things could change.

"I pray we find shelter by nightfall," Sampson said.

"We'd better," said Abbot Gervase. "I'll not sleep in an English wood."

From the trees came a voice. "You may not have a choice, my lord."

As if by magic, figures emerged from the trees and brush, some with drawn bows, others with spears or knives, and one with a spiked club. Ragged figures, dirty and unkempt and smelling to Heaven. One of them had a badly burned face. Their leader was an older man, big and rugged. "Tell your guards not to try anything," this man told the clergymen. "We don't wish to hurt anyone."

The guards hesitated, looking to Gervase.

"Stand down," Gervase told them in a resigned voice. He threw back his head and squeezed his eyes in frustration. This wasn't the first time he'd been robbed in these woods. The so-called "Viking" and his gang had perpetrated an identical outrage years before. He cast a sour look at the grimy outlaw leader, then started when he realized who it was. "Well, well. It's the great Lord Miles, or Brock the Bugger, or whatever it is you call yourself these days."

The cellarer Sampson frowned. "Wait, this old man is Brock the Badger?"

"His real name is Miles of Redhill, or Miles of Ravenswell," Gervase said. "He's an English peasant, and he's been a thorn in the side of Huntley Abbey for years."

"I've always paid my rents," Miles reminded him pleasantly. Huntley Abbey owned land in Ravenswell Manor, and Miles's family farmed some of it.

Gervase was just getting warmed up. "He's rude and insolent, and he had the audacity to marry a Norman noblewoman." To Miles he said, "You're a traitor now, as well, so your days of insolence are drawing to a close. You and your pack of English thieves."

Miles put a hand to his heart, as though his feelings had been hurt. "Thieves, my lord? That's a bit harsh, don't you think? The ballads say we're free men, living happily in the greenwood."

"Damn your ballads," Gervase said. "It's not like anyone understands that gibberish you people speak."

Sampson noted one outlaw's tonsure and crucifix. "They have a priest with them, my lord."

"Damned right, sonny," Father Albinus said. "That's because we're good Christian men, not like your lot."

Sampson's eyes widened in umbrage. "What do you mean, we're not good Christians? Why, you imbecile, we're brothers of—"

"Argue theology later," Miles told them. "In the meantime, would you two gentlemen be so kind as to dismount? The rest of you, step away from those pack animals and surrender your weapons."

The two monks—Sampson still sputtering—their servants, and guards did as they were told. Miles said, "Bondo, check those packs, will you? Let's see what we've got." To Gervase, he said, "Any news of our old friend Joscelin?" Joscelin had been abbot of Huntley before Gervase. He was a well-known womanizer who had at one time been besotted with Lady Blanche.

"No," Gervase said, "We've no way to keep in touch. He got his bishopric and is presently attached to Chartres School, that's the last I heard."

Miles grinned. "He'd rather have been attached to a nunnery, I'll wager."

"Very funny," Gervase said. "Enjoy the jokes while you can, Miles. You won't enjoy them so much when Onfroi of Buchy places a noose around your neck."

"It's always uplifting when you're dealing with Churchmen, don't you think?" Miles observed to his fellows. "Bondo, how do those packs look?"

"They look good," Bondo said. With his one hand he rummaged through them, while the hapless servants stared at him. "There's fish packed in salt—cod and hake, it looks like. There's bolts of cloth, too—expensive cloth. And wine."

Patches had joined Bondo. "These look like French goods. Comin' from the wrong direction to be bringin' these, ain't you, Father?"

Gervase nodded gloomily. "We purchased those goods in Le Havre."

"With Church funds?" Miles guessed.

"Any profits will of course go toward the abbey's upkeep," Gervase said.

"Of course," Miles said. "Pray continue."

Gervase hemmed. "God in His infinite wisdom sent us contrary winds as soon as we left Le Havre. Blew us down the Narrow Sea and around what you call the Lizard. We tried to get into Bristol, but couldn't. We were lucky to make Liverpool. We purchased horses and pack animals there and hired these guards. We plan to sell the fish and wine in Badford, on market day next, and the cloth in Nottingham, at the Martinmas Fair."

"Those plans may have changed," Miles informed him. He turned. "Father, be so kind as to broach a cask of that wine, will you?"

"With pleasure," Albinus said.

Oswald and his brother Oshere lifted a barrel of wine from one of the mules. Albinus wasn't sure how to tap it, so he bashed in the top with his axe.

"Watch it!" Sampson cried. "That's expensive wine!"

"Don't worry, my son," Albinus said, "it's not yours anymore."

Patches swaggered over with a cup he'd found in someone's gear, and he dipped it into the broached cask. "Watch for splinters," Albinus warned him.

Patches looked into the cup and jolted his head back. "What sorcery is this? This wine has no color."

"It's hock," Sampson said patiently, as though speaking to a child, "from the Rhineland."

"Wherever that is," Patches said. "Why can't you Frenchies drink ale, like normal people?"

"Because we're civilized," Sampson told him.

Patches frowned. " 'Civilized?' "

"It's a big word," Bondo explained. "Means they talk funny."

Patches tasted the wine.

"Well?" asked Miles. It was late in the year, and wine didn't keep. "Is it still good?"

"A little vinegary," Patches said, drinking more, "but not much."

"It's been stored in a spring house in the mountains," Sampson said.

More cups were produced. Men drank, passed the cups around. The Cornishman Ioco tasted it, made a face, shrugged, and kept drinking. "It's sweet," said Scarlet, surprised.

Odda said, "Goes down smooth, too. You could drink a fair amount of this in a hurry, I'm thinking. Specially on a hot day."

Miles said, "Well, don't drink too much of it now, or you won't be able to make it back to camp."

Albinus indicated the clergymen and their party. "What do we do with them?"

Patches had refilled his cup. "String 'em up," he urged gleefully. "Watch 'em kick."

"No, no," said Miles, "we can't do that. They'd think we weren't civilized. No, we'll take the purses from our religious friends, here. We'll have those jeweled rings off their hands, as well."

Gervase said, "You can't take—"

"Be quiet," Miles told him. "We'll give you two an escort as far as Brightwood. The rest of your party we'll send back to Liverpool."

Gervase was surprised. "You're not going to rob them, as well?"

"Why would we?" Miles said. "They're not French. In fact, we'll give them coin from your purses to see them on their way."

The guards and servants exchanged pleased looks.

"What about all this expensive cloth?" Father Albinus asked. "What are we going to do with it?"

A smile crossed Miles's face. "I have an idea."

CHAPTER 20

October 8 – Feast of St. Keyna
34 Days Until Martinmas

𝔐ARKET DAY IN Badford Town. The church square filled with awning-covered stalls, with farmers' barrows loaded with goods for sale. Townspeople and villagers crowded the square, admiring, buying or bartering for goods. Market day was held on the second Saturday of each month, but this one was especially crowded. It was autumn, the harvest was in, and there was much to sell—horses and cows and pigs, bread, pies, fruits, grain, cabbages, leeks, peas and beans. Urchins tried to steal apples or pears from the barrows and were warned off or ran away with their plunder, laughing. Tanners hawked leather, saddlers displayed bridles and bits. Wandering preachers decried the evils of sin. Dogs and cats raced about, dodging the odd stray duck or goose. Beggars plied their trade. Musicians played, with blankets spread before them in the hopes that people would give them money.

Among the crowd was a tall, broad-shouldered man, stooped with age and with a patch over his left eye. He wore a ragged cloak of grey with a white cross sewn on the shoulder that marked him as a pilgrim. On his head was a wide-brimmed felt hat with one side pinned up. He carried a hawthorn staff with a knob at one end, and across his shoulder was a worn leather scrip. The cloak was decorated with tin badges from the many sites he had visited, as well as with an ampul of Durham water. The hat was pinned with the crossed keys of Rome. He shuffled across the bridge into town largely unnoticed.

Badford hadn't changed much since the pilgrim had last been here. The square in front of the church of St. Hugobert—renamed by the French after Galon burned most of the town—had been cobbled. Aside from that, the town was much as it had been before, just newer. The pilgrim remembered Morys Gretch's big house on Shitte Lane, and the strawberries he had eaten there. The house had gone up in flames, and Morys had long ago been chopped to pieces by Galon's men. *Tempus fugit.*

Miles's men entered the town separately from one another, leading the pack mules bearing the stolen goods. They couldn't bring Oswald, because his burned face stood out too much, and Miles didn't trust Ioco. So Patches had the wine; Scarlet, the cloth; and Frithric, the salt fish. They had scrubbed their faces and hands in a stream, and they wore clothes taken from Abbot Gervase's party in order to make themselves look more respectable. As sellers of goods, they had to pay a fee to enter the town. Father Albinus came along discreetly, to watch over them.

Miles's men established themselves at different places in the square. Patches improvised a plank table where he displayed, and let people taste, the wine, using wooden cups tied to nails on the table so that people wouldn't steal them. One man kept coming back for more. He was French by his dress, probably a steward or bailiff from one of the neighboring villages. "Hey," Patches finally said, "that's enough, friend. I ain't givin' it away. Buy some, or move on."

The Frenchman ignored him and poured another cup. Patches gave the man a shove. "Did you hear me? I said, move along."

The shove spilled wine down the Frenchman's shirt. The man swore and started forward, but before he'd taken more than a step, Patches backhanded him across the face.

The Frenchman was stunned. He couldn't believe what had happened. He swung a fist at Patches, who stepped back, avoiding it, then stepped in again and hit the Frenchman on the jaw.

The Frenchman dropped to the ground on his butt. He got up again, pulling his dagger. Patches knocked away the hand with the dagger and hit the Frenchman again. The man stumbled and fell once more.

Patches went after him, but cooler heads prevailed and held Patches back. Father Albinus appeared. "Calm down," he urged Patches. "Calm down."

Patches' anger was up. As the Frenchman struggled to his feet, Patches tried to wrest himself from Albinus's grasp. "Fucking French—"

Though Albinus was stronger, he had a hard time holding Patches back. "It's all right," he said. "All done now. We can't break the earl's peace." To the Frenchman, he said, "Move along, *monsieur*. We want no trouble."

Cursing, the Frenchman let himself be dragged away by some of his friends. He picked up a rock and threw it at Patches.

The rock hit Patches in the ear. Eyes wide with rage, Patches went after the Frenchman again, but once more Albinus held him back. He grabbed Patches' shoulder, shaking him. "You fool," he growled in a low voice, "you want to get us all hung? This place is crawling with the sheriff's men."

Patches struggled against Albinus's grip. "That French fuck—"

Two guards who had witnessed the commotion came over, shoving the pilgrim aside. "Out of the way, *grand-père*."

"What's going on here?" one guard demanded.

"What's it to you, Frenchy?" Patches snarled, on the balls of his feet, ready to fight.

"Nothing," Albinus interrupted, holding up his hands to the guards. "There was a disagreement about price. Everything's settled now."

The second guard turned to the pilgrim. "Did you see what happened, *grand-père?*"

In a wheezy voice, the pilgrim replied, "It's as the priest says, my lord. It was a disagreement about price. Could you spare a coin for a—"

"No," said the guard. He looked over the pilgrim's collection of badges, saw the crossed keys on his wide-brimmed hat. "You have been to Rome? How was it?"

"Magnificent, my lord. Grandest city as ever was, or ever will be. You can feel the spirit of Christ watching over you when you're there."

"I envy you," said the guard.

While this was going on, the first guard examined Patches's merchandise. The pilgrim watched and readied himself for action, picturing how he would kill the guards, plotting the most unobstructed route to the city gate for escape.

"You are English, and you selling wine?" the first guard asked Patches skeptically.

"Got the right do to it, ain't I?" Patches said.

The guard nodded agreement. "Still, it's odd. You English don't drink wine."

The pilgrim started his dagger from its sheath.

A prosperous-looking Frenchman had come over and was sampling the wine. "It's good wine, too," he told the guard. "Well preserved for this time of year." To Patches, he said, "How did you come by it?"

The two guards watched closely as Patches answered. He seemed to realize the potential trouble he was in and curbed his temper, all smiles now. "Shipwreck, my lord. Barrels washed ashore near Romney. I bought 'em off the folks what found 'em. They didn't have no use for 'em."

The prosperous Frenchman nodded again. The guards gave Patches a last look, then moved on.

The Frenchman came forward. "I am Othon, steward for St. Mary's Lodge. The lodge is crowded right now—the earl of Trent and his party are staying there—and I need food and drink for them. Is all your wine as good as this?"

"As good or better, my lord," said Patches, who could be quite winning when he chose to be. "You'll find none finer, guaranteed."

"Hmm," said Othon. "I'll take all of it."

Patches' eyes widened. "Why, thank'ee, my lord. Thank'ee. A pleasure doing business with you."

While Othon paid for the wine, his servants loaded the heavy barrels onto mules. When they were done, they followed Othon around the square as he searched for more things to buy. He ended up at the pack mule bearing the stolen cloth. Scarlet stood with his arms outstretched, bolts of the cloth layered over each one. As he stood there, he whistled a tune—it was "The Ballad of Brock and the Sheriff." Some of the townsfolk and villagers recognized it and grinned, but none of the French picked up on the insult.

Othon fingered the bolts of cloth, came back to the first one. "What is this?"

Scarlet remembered what Gervase's hired men had told him. "It's called silk, your lordship. Comes from the East."

"Hmm," Othon said. "I've never felt anything like it before. It's so smooth."

"Never had nothing like it to sell before," Scarlet allowed. "Picked it up in London, I did, off a fellow what died from plague, God rest his soul."

Othon fingered the silk again. "Earl Galon is looking for something special, for a present. I'll take this."

"Just the silk, my lord? What about the rest? Finest cloth of Milan."

Othon shook his head. "No. I've no need of it. Just the silk, if you will."

As it turned out, the rest of the cloth sold quickly. Even better, the buyer was from Huntley Abbey. Sampson, the abbey's cellarer, who would normally have been here, was too ashamed to show his face after being robbed. So, in his stead, came his young deputy, Mordecai, eager to show what he could do. "This is beautiful," he said, admiring the soft cloth. "Italian?"

Scarlet grinned and wagged a finger. "You know your cloth, my lord."

"Did you bring it from Italy yourself?"

Scarlet had no idea where Italy even was. He repeated the story about buying it from a plague victim.

"Poor fellow," Mordecai murmured.

Scarlet crossed himself. "I've promised a portion of any sales to his widow."

"How thoughtful of you. You're a good Christian."

"Aye," said the old pilgrim, looking on. With a shaky hand, he made a sign of the Cross in blessing.

Mordecai bought the cloth. He also purchased the casks of salt fish from Frithric, after satisfying himself that the fish was still fresh enough to eat. "This will see us through Wednesday and Friday of next week," he told Frithric. On those days, it was forbidden to eat meat.

After Mordecai and his servants left with the cloth and salt fish, the pilgrim and his men sold the pack mules. Then they gathered in a street off the square. The pilgrim remained bent over and kept the patch on his eye, lest a passerby recognize him. The men pooled their profits, and Father Albinus jingled the resultant sack full of coins. "A fine day," he said with a grin. "The Lord be praised."

"Aye," Scarlet said happily, "we stole from the abbot, then sold his goods right back to him. I'm going to make up a song about that. Already got it started in my head."

Albinus said, "Even better, we sold the rest to Earl Galon." He clapped Scarlet on the back. "There's another song for you."

Patches said, "Dunno about you lads, but all this sellin' and talk of ballads has got me thirsty. I'm for a drink."

As luck would have it, they were next to a tavern. The tavern door was open; a low roar of talk and laughter issued from inside. On the sign above the tavern door was the crude representation of what might have been a man's head, topped by some kind of headwear that might have been a helmet.

"Is that a Saracen, maybe?" said Frithric, scratching a flea bite and holding his head sideways as he studied the sign. "Is this the Saracen's Head?"

"I dunno," said Scarlet. "What's a Saracen look like? Are they like real people?"

"I can barely tell that it's a head," Albinus said.

Patches said, "Whatever it is, let's go in."

He hitched his belt and started in the door, but the pilgrim straightened and pulled him back. He pictured Patches getting in a fight, the bailiffs coming. "No, we've done enough today. No sense taking any chances. Let's get out of here before we're recognized."

"But—"

"There's plenty of drink back at camp," Miles told him, pulling off the eye patch.

"We're in town," Patches said, "let's have some fun."

"No. You nearly got us hung once already."

"That fellow deserved it. He—"

"No."

Patches glared at Miles. He was ready to fight.

At last Patches waved a hand. "Ah, it ain't worth beatin' up on an old man. Look here, I'm tired of taking orders from you. Rob the French and give to the English? Well, I'll rob who I please and keep it for myself, see? Who's with me?"

No one said anything.

Patches waved his hand again. "I'm goin' back out on my own, where I should've been all along. Give me my share of the take, and I'll be on my way."

Miles didn't argue. Patches was right; he would fare better on his own.

Miles counted out some coins and gave them to Patches. "The extra is from my share. Good luck to you."

Patches nodded. He turned and swaggered away.

Miles beckoned the others, and they headed out of town.

CHAPTER 21

Had patches gone into the Saracen's Head, he might have seen a hooded figure occupying a table in the corner. Had he observed that figure more closely, he might have realized that it was a woman. It was, in fact, Ediva.

Ediva had taken a room at the inn, using money she carried with her for an emergency. The inn's owner, Milo, had surmised she was a prostitute seeking work. He was a middle-aged fellow with a scarred face—maybe an ex-soldier, like a lot of tavern and inn proprietors. "I can always use a good whore," he said with a wolfish grin. " 'Course I'll need to try you out first."

"I'm not a whore," Ediva told him in a cold voice. "I just want a room."

"Well, now, we usually fit five to a room. I'll put you in a room with four men. Give you a head start in your line o' work—"

"I told you, I'm not a whore," she said. "And I want a room to myself."

Milo rubbed his greasy chin. "Single room, that'll cost."

"Do it," Ediva said, banging a silver coin on the bar. "I'll want meals, as well."

Milo hesitated.

"Oh, do it," said his shrewish wife, Helga, from behind. "Mayhap she'll add a bit o' class to the place."

Milo said, "Mayhap she'll be workin' on her own and not payin' my toll—"

Ediva leaned forward and stuck her face in Milo's. "You call me a whore one more time, and I'll slit you from stem to gullet."

And, thus, the arrangement was concluded.

"I'm here for my mistress," Ediva added, by way of explanation. Let Milo and his wife think they stood to make money from her presence. "She's looking to expand into Badford, and this is one of the properties she has an eye on. I'm here to see if it's suitable for her needs."

"Then *she's* a whore?" Milo said.

"That's not your affair."

Milo pursed his lips. "Say your mistress likes this place, but I don't want to sell?"

"You'll sell," Ediva said, "if you're chosen."

"I could take that a lot of ways."

"Take it any way you wish, but you'll sell."

The room was upstairs. It was dirty and ridden with vermin. The bed was a grimy sack of straw set on wooden slats, and the sheets and blankets looked—and smelled—as though they'd never been washed. Fortunately, Ediva had brought a small bottle of lavender water to use as insect repellent. She carried another bottle containing a mixture of vinegar, olive oil, mustard seed, garlic, and herbs with which to disguise the taste of food. She hadn't needed it at Garth's house, but she had an idea it would come in handy here.

Ediva spent her first night listening to drunken revelry punctuated by cries and moans of whores in the other rooms. To top it off, Milo sneaked in. He crossed the room on tiptoe, dropped his braies, and pulled back the bedcovers.

To find Ediva's dagger aimed at his engorged member.

"No need for that," Milo said, raising his braies hurriedly. "Just checkin' to see you're all right. It's a service we provide. No charge." He backed from the room with his hands up.

The inn's common room was furnished with long trestle tables, with benches for seating. There were a few smaller tables in the corner, and Ediva staked out one of those. She'd barely taken her place when a man approached her, a burly laborer, covered in filth.

"Upstairs," he grunted. He reached for her arm, but the tavern's guard grabbed his hand. "She's not to be disturbed," the bouncer said. "Owner's orders."

"Why not?" said the man. "That's the best bit of ass I seen in five years. Why shouldn't I—?"

"I don't make the rules, friend," said the guard. "I do as I'm told. You should, too."

"But—"

"Just move along, will you? I don't feel like breaking your arm so early in the day."

Ediva sat there, day after day, hood drawn over her head until only her eyes were showing, occasionally taking some drink or a meal—if one could call what the Saracen's Head served a meal. The stew came in dirty bowls. It was greasy and filled with God knew what—it was impossible to tell, and Ediva was afraid to taste it. The bread and cheese were little better. Her bottle of food flavoring was of no use here. She ended up purchasing her own supplies at the town market, though Milo and Helga insisted she pay for meals, as per the original arrangement.

Ediva watched, and waited, and wondered why she had come here. She had wanted an adventure. Was this an adventure? It didn't feel like one, sitting in this room all day, eating food unfit for animals, drinking watered ale. And the smell—God's mercy, why did people live in towns?

If this was an adventure, it certainly wasn't fun. It was dangerous, too. She might make bold with her dagger, but the men around her could take her at any time. She could be gang raped, beaten, even killed. It was only the presence of the tavern guards that saved her. They'd been instructed to keep her safe by Milo—no doubt thinking about the money to be made if he sold the inn—and she gave the guards extra money to keep them on her side. Of course, she couldn't trust them, either, not really, but it was the best she could do.

From time to time, Milo came over. "When's your mistress goin' to make me that offer?"

"When I decide whether this is the proper location for her business," Ediva told him. "Now leave me alone."

Ediva's vigil was proving fruitless. Would she even recognize anything untoward if she saw it? The inn was always crowded, even more so on Saturdays and Sundays. It was filled with townspeople, with men looking for whores, with traveling priests and monks and other clerics—most of them looking for whores, as well. With merchants and travelers of all types, all looking for whores. Ediva saw fights. She saw rats. She saw people fornicating on tables, saw men vomiting in corners. And still she sat patiently, her hood up, her dagger to hand.

Market day came, and the Saracen's Head was so packed that Ediva could barely see across the room. Money flowed freely, as was to be expected with villagers flush with the profits from selling their goods.

A lot of these villagers wanted sex, as well. The guards were kept busy fending them away from Ediva, for which she gave him an extra penny—she would have given more, but she was running low on funds. She would have to return to Redhill if she learned nothing this day. And though returning would mean that her adventure had been a failure, she looked forward to it, because she was eager to get away from this rat-and-flea-infested—

There. Across the room.

A face she knew.

He was hunched over the table with another man, an old man with a blue cap and deep lines in his cheeks. The two of them drank ale and talked in low tones.

Ediva watched. The noise around her subsided to a dull background roar as she concentrated on the two men, wishing she could hear what they were saying.

They got up and made for the door.

Ediva followed, hood drawn over her head.

She had to push her way through the crowd, drunken men grabbing at her breasts and bottom. When she got to the door, the two men were gone.

She looked both ways.

There, almost out of sight. They had turned left, heading deeper into town.

She followed, hurrying along the filth-laden street to keep them in view.

As she neared them, she slowed, not wanting to get too close.

A hay wagon with a broken wheel jammed the street, forcing Ediva through a narrow opening.

A stocky, blond-haired man stepped from the alley in front of her, grinning and blocking her path.

She stopped. Before she could turn and run, someone from behind threw a hood over her head.

Then she was struck on the head and felt nothing.

CHAPTER 22

October 10 – Feast of St. Paulinus of York
32 Days Until Martinmas

EDIVA'S HEAD HURT. No, it didn't hurt. It throbbed. It pounded like a drum. What had they hit her with?

She remembered being on a street in town, remembered a man blocking her path, then bright lights and pain, then nothing.

She smelled animals, manure, turned earth, crisp autumn air. She was in the country, then, no longer in town. Something simmering, smell of peas and beans and meat.

She opened her eyes, gingerly, as if the act might make her head hurt even more. Above her was a thatched roof. She was in a bed, scented with lavender, with a blanket over her. Her head was tightly wrapped. She turned her head, and the resulting pain made her eyes swim. She was in a house, a bit larger than most, well kept. There were no farm animals in the house, but a curious dog kept poking his wet nose into her hand.

She knew that dog . . .

"She's awake!" cried a girl's voice.

The girl came from the other side of the fire pit and plopped onto a stool beside the bed. She was about ten, with wavy brown hair. "We were afraid you wouldn't make it," she told Ediva. "You've been unconscious for over a day." She pushed the panting dog away. "Get down, King."

King.

To Ediva the girl said, "Have some water." She held Ediva's bandaged head and placed a wooden cup to her lips. Ediva drank gratefully. The cool water tasted wonderful. "I'm Turfrida," the girl said.

Turfrida had been the wife of Hereward the Wake. These people were obviously not friends of the French. "Where am I?"

"Ravenswell," said the girl

Ediva had a sinking feeling. "And this house?"

"It belongs to my Uncle Garth."

Him. Great.

"How . . .?"

Footsteps outside. King barking, jumping up and bouncing off the door. Garth entered along with another man about Garth's age and an attractive woman.

"You're alive," Garth said. It was a statement of fact. He didn't sound like he was all that thrilled about it.

"I think I am," said Ediva. "How did I get here?" She remembered the inn, what she had seen there, and her voice grew urgent. "There's something I have to tell you."

"Time enough for that," Garth said. "You need to take it easy, you've had a nasty bump on the head."

"No. Something I saw . . . in . . ." *What was the town's name?* ". . . Badford?"

"Later," Garth said.

Ediva was aware of people gathered outside, clustered at the door and looking through the windows, King barking madly.

"No, it's about . . ." *What was it about?* ". . . the plot. That's it. I saw something." *What had she seen?*

"Later. Get some—"

Ediva remembered. "I saw your brother."

Garth stopped. "You mean Aelred?"

"Yes. He was talking to an older man at . . . the Saracen's Head, that's what it was called. The Saracen's Head. They looked suspicious, so I . . ." *What did she do?* ". . .I followed them. Someone stopped me, and . . . and that's all I remember."

Garth's friend and the woman pushed people back from the door and barred it, the dog still barking. Garth gave Ediva a knowing smirk. "So you think Aelred is part of this plot?"

"He must be. He—"

"It was Aelred who saved you."

The room spun. Ediva struggled to understand. "What?"

Aethelwynn gestured for Turfrida to give Ediva more water as Garth said, "Aelred saw you at the Head—you were pretty obvious, he said. When he left, he realized you were following him. He turned to find out why and saw you being attacked."

None of this made sense . . . "No, Aelred had—"

Garth went on. "Apparently whoever it was had been waiting for you. They threw you into a hay wagon. They were probably going to sell you as a prostitute somewhere, or even as a sex slave. Aelred and his friend rescued you. If not for them, you'd be long gone from here, maybe on your way across the Narrow Sea."

"Who were the men?"

"Aelred didn't recognize them. They got away. Probably trolling market day for likely prospects."

Ediva felt a fool. "I . . . I . . . How did I get here?"

Garth's friend replied. "I was in town for market day. Aelred found me, and we put you in my wagon. I'm Peter, by the way. I'm Garth and Aelred's brother-in-law. My father, Leofric, was Lord Miles's best friend. This is my wife, their sister Aethelwynn. You've already met Turfrida, our oldest girl." To Turfrida he said, "Fri, get Ediva something to eat."

Turfrida brought a bowl of pottage. While Aethelwynn held the happily lunging dog by the collar, Turfrida put a spoonful of the pottage to Ediva's mouth. Ediva blew on it, swallowed.

"Well?" said Aethelwynn with an expectant brow.

"It's good," Ediva said. She added, "But your father's pottage is better."

"Ha!" Laughter all round, accompanied by a groan of exasperation from Garth.

Ediva went on. "He always has a pot of it going at Redhill Hall. Makes it himself. Always adding to it. Drives Lady Blanche crazy because she wants him to 'eat better.' "

More laughter. The door was unbarred and, admitted through the press of people, came Aelred. He smiled down at Ediva, and his blue eyes sparkled. "I heard you're alive. Thank God. You gave us a scare."

"She's not out of the woods yet," Aethelwynn told him. "She needs plenty of rest. And I'm still not sure her skull isn't cracked."

"Thank you for what you did for me," Ediva told Aelred. "Saving me, I mean."

"It was nothing," he said.

"It wasn't nothing. You saved my life."

He gave her a curious frown. "Why were you following me?"

Ediva looked down. "Forgive me, but I thought you were part of . . . you know."

"Ahh." Aelred grinned. "The mysterious Martinmas plot?"

"Yes," she said sheepishly.

To his brother, Garth said, "Like it or not, you're involved in all this now."

"I was involved in it before," Aelred said, his tone serious. "That's why I was at the Head."

Garth gave him a look. So did Ediva.

Aelred explained. "Thought I'd stop by there and ask around, while I was in town, see if anyone knew anything about your plot."

"Lucky for Ediva you did," Peter said.

"My friend and I were off to check another tavern when Ediva was attacked. I've been talking to some of my old contacts from the Beardmen, but no one has heard anything." The Beardmen were a society dedicated to driving the French from England. They hadn't been active for years. Aelred said, "If there is a plot, the French are the ones behind it. It's not us."

"What's this about a plot?" said an old woman, poking her head in the window.

Garth thought quickly. "I fear someone is plotting to disrupt my marriage," he told the woman.

The old woman looked over her shoulder. "Well, they're doing a proper job of it. Here comes Oli himself."

Garth swore mightily.

There was laughter and shouting from outside—this had become like a village holiday—and a man pushed his way through people trying to hold him back at the door. It was dour Oli. He wore the same clothes as last time, but then, so did Garth.

"What's going on here?" Oli demanded, looking around. "Where is Garth?"

Garth raised a hand above the crowd. "Here."

Oli got right to it. "I've re-thought your marriage offer, Garth, and I've decided to . . ."

He saw Ediva in Garth's bed, and his cheeks turned the color of a ripe apple. "What is this, sir! You have a woman staying here?"

"She's hurt," Garth explained. "We're taking care of her. I have more room than anyone else, so I—"

"Is she married?"

"No, she—"

"You're entertaining an unmarried woman? In your bed?"

"It's not what it looks like—"

"God's wounds, sir, you insult my daughter's honor. I'm treating with you for Mallette's sacred virginity while you harbor a woman in your house?"

Garth tried to explain. "Look at her, Oli. She's barely alive. We couldn't just leave her in that state. It would have been unChristian."

"What about the hospital, eh?" The chapter of the church of St. Hugobert ran a hospital in Badford. "Eh? You could have left her there."

"She belongs to my father's household," Garth said. "I'm obligated to—"

"You're obligated to fornicate with—"

"Nothing happened between us," Ediva interrupted hotly.

"Shut up, girl."

That was the wrong thing to say. Ediva struggled to get up, while Aethelwynn and Turfrida tried to hold her down. "You constipated old prune, don't talk to me that way, or I'll see you strung up by your floppy ears. I wouldn't come between this man and your hedge pig of a daughter if someone offered me a fortune to do it. If he's fool enough to marry into your bog-witted family—"

Garth pleaded with Ediva. "Stop—"

Oli fumed. "You insult my daughter? My family?"

"I'll box your ears, you slobbering old fart. Hers, too, if ever I see her."

Garth said, "Ediva, please—"

Oli turned. "We're done, Garth. Do you hear me? Done. I was going to give you another chance, but you bring this strumpet—"

Ediva threw the bowl of hot pottage in Oli's face.

The room fell silent. Even the dog stopped barking.

Oli stood there, thick, greasy liquid dripping down his face into his beard and onto his clothes, then to the floor. Bits of meat and onion and other things mixed into it. He spit something from his mouth.

Enraged, Oli started for Ediva with his hand raised to strike her.

"That's enough," Garth said.

There was a steely tone, a scary tone, in Garth's voice that Ediva had not heard before.

Oli stopped. He stared at Garth. Garth's eyes were cold, flat.

After a second, Oli lowered his hand. He turned and left the house, to laughter and catcalls from the crowd in the yard.

Ediva lay back down, exhausted and out of breath, her head exploding with pain. She had gone too far, she knew, but it felt good.

Turfrida gave her more water.

Garth's scary side disappeared. Now he was furious. "This is how you repay my hospitality?" he said to Ediva. "By destroying my marriage prospects once and for all?"

"You weren't married yet," Ediva said defensively.

"I was going to be!"

Ediva was breathing hard from her exertion, sweating. Her head was killing her. "Sorry," she said, "but you really could do better."

"What do you know about it? You're a spinster."

"I told you—"

"You've been nothing but trouble since you showed up here."

Ediva tried to look properly chagrined, but couldn't. Throwing pottage in Oli's face had been fun.

More noise outside. "Why is no one working?" a man yelled. "Move away, there. Christ's sandals, get to the fields. This isn't a holy day. Move."

Aethelwynn looked out the window. "It's Pierre," she told the others. Ediva remembered that Pierre was the manor's steward.

Pierre came in and petted King, who had jumped up on him. "This entire village seems to have lost its mind. God's breath, if Lord Stigand was here, he'd have the hide off your backs. What the Devil is—"

"Where is Stigand?" Garth asked.

"He's at St. Mary's Lodge with Lord Galon. I came to bring you news. The sheriff is fitting out an expedition against your father. They mean to put an end to him before more people rally to him."

Ediva swung her legs over the side of the bed and sat up. The blood drained from her head, and she fell back.

"What are you doing?" cried Aethelwynn, rushing to her.

Ediva tried again, staggering to her feet, holding onto Aethelwynn for support. "I have to warn Miles."

"You stay here," Garth told her. "I'll do it."

"The Devil you will," Ediva said. "Where's my horse?"

CHAPTER 23

October 4

BLANCHE SHOOK OUT her wet cloak as she entered the vintner's hut. She came here every day to see if Miles had left a chalk mark. Today, she also came because this was one of the few places on the manor where she could be alone to think. Normally she would have gone for a ride to do that, but the day was grey and drizzly. The sheriff's men always followed her, anyway, and she resented their presence. Her life seemed to have whirled out of control. She placed a veil of normalcy across it, attending to her family, her estates, and her staff as though nothing was wrong, but beneath that veil everything was falling apart. It wasn't just her husband's safety she feared for, but that of her children. Winter was fast approaching and—

A footstep.

She turned. "Galon!"

"That would be 'Lord Galon' to you," he said, "I'm earl now, remember?" In one of Galon's meaty hands was a bundle, tied with red ribbon.

"What are you doing here?" she said.

Behind his drooping moustache, Galon smiled, the way a wolf might smile in the presence of a lamb. "Why, I've come to see you, of course." He held out the bundle. "I've brought you a present."

Blanche took the bundle, though she didn't want to, and untied the ribbon. It was a headdress, white with red embroidery around the border. It was made from . . . "Is this silk?" she asked.

"It is."

She had never owned anything made of silk, had only seen the fabric once. She thrust it back. "I want no presents from you."

"It's by way of an apology," Galon explained. "For what I've put you through these past weeks."

"Still, I can't take it."

"You must. I had it made especially for you. I found the material at Badford on market day."

"I'm a married woman" Blanche said. "I cannot accept gifts from a man other than my husband."

"Oh, but you can," Galon told her. "I'm your lord, and if I choose to bestow a gift upon you, you cannot refuse without offering me insult."

That was true. Blanche was about to protest further when she noticed a chalk mark high up on the hut's door, and she went unsteady on her feet.

Miles was here.

How had she missed seeing that earlier? She fumbled for words, flush faced. "Um . . ."

Galon seemed to read her mind. "Have you heard from your husband?"

"What?" she said. "No. No, I haven't. Have you?"

"No, all I hear is the English singing songs about him and how he outwits the sheriff of Trentshire and the evil Earl Galon."

"You? Evil? Who would ever think that?"

Galon ignored the jibe. "The English used to sing about that Hereward fellow, now it's Brock this and Brock that. You'd think the bastard was running the country. I tell you, Blanche, your husband would do well to remember the business he's on for me and spend less time making himself a hero to these—"

"Oh, stop pretending that he's doing a job for you," Blanche told him. "He's not. This is your way of having him killed."

"You don't know what—"

"This way you can do it legally, with no questions asked. Of course, Miles is English, so there wouldn't be many questions, anyway. You, Onfroi—all of you will be happy to be rid of him. I've written to the king about this."

"I know," Galon said, leaning against the table and picking up an ink pot. "I read the letter."

Blanche had no comeback for that. Her stomach twisted.

Galon straightened, putting the ink down. "As for your husband's business with me, if he's successful, you'll find out soon enough. If he's not, it won't matter. Now, I'll take my leave." He paused. "Unless you'd prefer that I stay the night?"

She thought about the chalk mark, impossible Galon hadn't seen it. He wouldn't know what it meant; still . . . "I can manage without your presence, thank you."

"Pity," he said. "You could wear that new headdress for me. Perhaps wear it and nothing else?"

"I believe we're done here," she told him.

Galon laughed. "As you wish." He bowed deeply. "*A bientôt.*" Then he turned and walked away.

Blanche found herself shaking.

Where was Miles?

She turned, and he emerged out of the shadows, like a wraith.

They stared at each other for a long moment, then she threw herself into his arms, kissing him, biting his lip and neck, his hands running over her body. Still kissing, they staggered into the back room, among the barrels and casks and tools, where Miles spread his cloak and drew her to the floor.

* * *

After, they lay entwined in each other's arms, naked, heedless of the damp chill. Kissing and fondling, oblivious to any other presence. They weren't exactly hidden here, and there was a chance they would be discovered, but they didn't care. It had been too long.

"How did you get here?" Blanche asked.

"It wasn't easy," Miles said. "The sheriff's men are everywhere."

"Don't be offended, but I'm surprised Galon didn't smell you."

Miles chuckled. "Afraid there's not much bathing this time of year in the forest."

"Did you hear what Galon said?"

"I'm Brock the Badger. I hear all, know all."

She slapped him playfully. "Be serious, will you? So now what? Back to your life in the greenwood? You know, Galon was right about those songs. The common folk sing them all the time—not just in Redhill, but all over the shire, I'm told. Beyond, as well. Even the children know them. I heard a new one the other day that tells how you robbed the abbot of Huntley, then treated him to a great feast at your camp in the forest. After that, you went to Badford and sold the goods you'd stolen back to the abbot and to Lord Galon." She shook her head. "Who comes up with these tales?"

"I have no idea," Miles said. "We never treated the abbot to a feast."

She paused, raised those exquisite brows. "Then the rest . . .?"

Miles said nothing.

"Is true?" she asked.

"More or less."

"And that headdress Galon gave me . . .?"

"I sold him the cloth."

She laughed. "Then I shall cherish it always."

He nuzzled the nape of her neck and she twitched. "I'll have to leave soon," he said.

She nibbled his ear lobe. "How soon?"

"Not that soon."

She pushed his shoulders down and rolled on top of him.

* * *

When they were finished, they dressed, and Blanche said, "You may be taking this Brock the Badger business a bit too seriously. You need to be careful. Galon does *not* like to be made fun of; Onfroi, even less."

Miles shrugged. "I have to do something while I'm waiting for this so-called plot to unfold."

"Why do you still pretend there's a plot? I thought we decided it wasn't real."

"We did, but some things still nag at me."

"What things?"

"Galon," Miles said. "Why kill me now? He could have done it years ago. And why is he in England? He never comes here. Why now?"

"You think his presence has something to do with this plot?"

"I don't know what to think."

"I still believe Galon's plan is for Onfroi to kill you. That way, no guilt will attach to Galon."

"Maybe, but that's not Galon's style. He would have sent men—Stigand, probably, and a bunch of his mercenaries—and just chopped me up. Galon might even have done it himself. He's not one for subterfuge."

Blanche put on the new headdress and adjusted her gold circlet over it. "If he killed you outright, the king might be upset with him. Galon is an important personage now, he can't go around killing and torturing people the way he used to do. King Henry doesn't like that sort of thing, so subterfuge might be to Galon's benefit."

Miles sighed. "It doesn't make much difference. If there is a plot, there's no chance of my uncovering it while living in the forest. Unless Garth and Aelred can come up with something."

"Speaking of that," Blanche said, "Ediva still hasn't returned."

Miles frowned.

"What if she was waylaid?" Blanche said. "What if she was . . .?"

"I know," Miles said gloomily. "I'll have my men search for her. Meanwhile, Martinmas grows closer. I should have had you flee with me in the beginning like you wanted to. Now you're watched too closely. You'd never get away. You and the children are effectively hostages."

"While you stand up to 'Norman oppression,' " she said sternly. She moved close to him. "Really, we're not that bad, are we?"

He fondled her breast. "Some of you aren't."

"Such insolence," she said. "I should throw you in the dungeon and whip you."

"Sounds like fun," he said. "Next time, perhaps."

CHAPTER 24

October 11 – Feast of St. Ethelburga of Barking
31 Days Until Martinmas

GARTH AND EDIVA headed for Miles's camp. They rode double on Ediva's horse. The horse had been brought back from Badford by Aelred and Peter when they had rescued Ediva. Garth sat awkwardly behind Ediva, holding her in the saddle as she drifted in and out of consciousness, while he tried not to fall off the horse in the process.

"You shouldn't be doing this," he told her when she was in one of her lucid moments.

"You sound like my mother," she said. "I'm fine."

"You're feverish, I can feel it."

"It's a warm day, that's all."

That evening, they camped beside a creek. There was a village nearby, but Garth didn't want to seek shelter there and draw attention to themselves. Garth watered and fed the horse, then bathed Ediva's hot face and forehead. "Leave me alone," she fussed. "I'm all right."

"I know. That's why you feel like a charcoal furnace."

Delicately, he removed her bandage. The bandage stuck to her skin and hair, and she yelped in pain. "Be careful, will you?"

"I would, if you'd stop squirming," he said.

"I would stop, but you're ripping my head off."

When the bandage was off, he bathed her head. Aethelwynn had cut the hair around the wound. Blood and bits of the bandage had clotted on the wound, which went nearly to her skull. *Bastards.* He dampened the wound and worked the clotting off the wound and out of her hair, then he cleaned the wound with vinegar mixed with water. The back of her head was swollen, and beneath her hair, the skin around the wound was a blackish purple.

She struggled under his touch. "Would you stop? I said I'm—"

"Do as you're told for once, will you? You're no good to anyone dead. I told you not to go into Badford."

"You tell me lots of things, but that doesn't mean I have to pay attention to them."

"Maybe you should. Look where your little spying expedition got you. And for what? Nothing."

She harrumphed at that, as though she still couldn't accept that it had been for nothing.

"What?" he taunted. "Nothing to say?"

"Hurry up and finish what you're doing. If you're as good a farmer as you are a doctor, it's a wonder your family hasn't starved to death."

"Actually, I'm quite a good farmer."

"You think you're a good cook, too."

When Ediva's hair was dry, Garth changed the dressing with linen that Aethelwynn had given him for that purpose, binding it tightly. As he pinned the bandage in place, he said, "My father will probably have some of his magic pottage for you at his camp. That should heal you in no time."

"You're still upset because I said his was better, aren't you?" she said. "You're jealous."

"I'm not jealous. I don't see how his can be better, that's all. I make mine the exact same way. He taught me."

"Well, it doesn't taste the same," she said.

Garth shook his head. "You're just trying to stay on his good side. Get some sleep."

"How can I? You keep talking."

She slept fitfully. Garth held her at first, to comfort her, but she was hot to the touch, so he let her go, taking her cloak off her, hoping the night air would cool her. He had a hard time sleeping himself, worried Ediva might take a turn for the worse. There was no help out here; they were on their own.

The next day brought rain, which was the last thing Ediva needed in her condition. Garth pulled her hood up, to try to keep her head dry. She was on the verge of delirium, though she was more or less able to guide them. She shivered through her fever. At one point she had been unconscious for so long, Garth worried that she might have died, but she was still breathing, albeit faintly.

Of a sudden, she murmured, "I meant it when I said I'm sorry I broke up your marriage."

"You should be," Garth said. He spoke as though there was nothing wrong with her. It wouldn't help her spirits any to treat her like she was dying. He added, "Doesn't mean much now. We've got more important things to worry about."

She went on. "I shouldn't have thrown pottage in that man's face, either."

Garth shrugged. "He deserved it. Never liked the old goat, anyway." Then he said, "It *was* kind of funny."

Her voice was faint. "Is his daughter beautiful?"

"She's reckoned as such."

"Do you—did you—love her?"

"I barely know her," Garth said. "I married my first wife for love. This was business."

"Impressing your father means that much to you?"

"To be honest, I don't know if I was doing it for him or for me. To show I can accomplish something with my life. To make people look up to me like they look up to him."

"They look up to you," she said in a whisper. "You're hundred pledge."

"That's all going out of style. Like as not, I'll be the last . . ."

He stopped. She had lapsed into unconsciousness.

They rode on in the rain.

CHAPTER 25

October 11

"On a fair day in May
Jolly Brock the Badger
Set forth in search of adventure . . ."

𝕿HE COLD RAIN poured down.

"What news?" Miles asked Hugh Middewynter.

Hugh claimed to be fifteen, though his real age was probably less. The men called him Shadow, because of his attempt to grow a beard, which so far looked like—well, like a shadow. Miles hadn't wanted someone that young in the band, but Hugh had talked him into it. "My parents are cottars. They have no land or money," he'd pleaded in a voice that had barely broken. "They kicked me out of the house, and I have nowhere else to go."

Hugh was of average height and looks. A lad with no distinguishing marks or habits, the type no one notices or remembers. He was also the type who avoids drawing attention to himself. All of which made him a perfect spy. He'd come from St. Mary's Lodge, where he'd mingled with the crowd at the gates, collecting information. "The sheriff has raised the price on your head," he told Miles. "A herald announced it while I was there. Three silver marks it is now."

They, like many others, huddled in the comparative shelter of the rock outcropping. Standing next to Miles, shivering with his arms folded, Father Albinus whistled. "That's a fortune to most of us. Every time Onfroi raises the price on your head, it's more likely someone will betray you. I hope Lord Galon knows what he's doing."

"Maybe Galon hasn't told Onfroi that I'm working for him in uncovering the plot," Miles said. "Or maybe the plot is a ruse, and Galon is using Onfroi to kill me. That's what Blanche thinks."

Albinus took that in. "And what do you think?" he asked Miles.

"I think what she says makes a lot of sense."

Albinus raised his woolly brows. "Meanwhile, new men keep rolling in."

"That they do," Miles said.

Miles had close to thirty men with him now. Bondo led one section; Oswald had been promoted to lead Patches's old section; and Frithric headed a new, third, section. The damp days and chill nights were having an effect on the men, especially the one who'd been there the longest. Many were sick, and almost all suffered from the flux. Two new graves had been added to the makeshift cemetery, making three in all.

After a while, the rain slowed. Frithric's men were out scouting; Oswald's were hunting. Coughing and sneezing, some of Bondo's men cut wood or resumed work on their shelters in the ever-expanding camp. Others, including Oshere's wife, Diote, dressed a deer and a sheep to be roasted on spits. Miles had obtained a larger pot, a kettle, for his pottage—it had been donated by friendly villagers—and it simmered on the edge of one of the cookfires. He removed the cover. To the peas and beans and water already in the kettle, Miles added oats, to make the pottage thick, as well as garlic and leeks, carrots and cabbage, herbs, and almond milk for flavor, stirring and tasting as he worked. Bits of the roasted deer and sheep would go into it when they were ready.

A cry came from the guard at the edge of the camp. "Frithric's coming in! He's got people with him."

Moments later, Frithric entered the camp, leading a horse. On the horse were a man and a woman. The man was Garth, wet and tired. The woman was Ediva. She looked more dead than alive, slumped over, her face chalky white, her head wrapped with a thick bandage.

Miles said, "What the—?"

He and Albinus rushed to them, along with some of the others. The new men didn't know Garth or Ediva, and there was a buzz of conversation as they tried to figure out what was going on.

"Get her off the horse," Miles said. To Frithric, he said, "Steady her."

Bondo held the horse. Miles and Albinus eased Ediva from the saddle, aided by Frithric. "She's burning up," Albinus said.

Miles said, "Take her to my hut."

While Bondo handed off the horse to one of the men, Miles, Albinus, and Frithric lifted Ediva and carried her to Miles's hut. "What happened to her?" Miles asked Garth, who followed them.

"She was attacked," Garth said, "in Badford."

"What the Devil was she doing in Badford? She was supposed to—"

"She was in the Saracen's Head, looking for your plotters."

"The fool girl. Why did you let her travel in this condition?"

"I couldn't stop her." Garth ran ahead and held the hide door open. "I told her not to come, but she wouldn't listen. Said I'd never find your camp again on my own."

"Garth couldn't find his shoes if they weren't on his feet," Ediva murmured with her eyes closed.

They got her inside. "Put her on my bed."

They placed Ediva on the bed, removed her wet cloak and hood. The hut was smoky and stuffy from the fire in the pit. Ediva began coughing.

"This won't do," Father Albinus said. "Take her next door to my quarters. My fire isn't lit."

They carried Ediva to Albinus's hut. While Miles and Garth turned their heads, Albinus removed the girl's soaked clothes and wrapped her in a warm blanket. "You can turn back now," Albinus said.

"What can you do for her?" Miles asked him.

"Not much, I'm afraid. Had I some chamomile or comfrey, I could make her an infusion. I could use propolis on that head wound, but we've none of that, either. As it stands, all we can do is make her comfortable, then pray and trust in the Lord."

Frithric brought an armload of cloaks donated by the men to use as blankets.

"Not yet," Albinus told him. "She's too hot. Let her cool down a bit."

Miles motioned Garth back outside. "Now, what happened in Badford?"

"Ediva saw Aelred in the Head," Garth said, "reckoned he was involved in the plot."

"Aelred's not involved in any plot. He gave all that up."

"I know," Garth said. "Anyway, she followed Aelred when he left the tavern, and got jumped by some men trying to kidnap her. For slavery or prostitution, I expect. The idiots— as hard as they hit her, I don't know what good she'd have been to them."

Miles hung his head and shook it sadly.

Garth went on. "We came to warn you that the sheriff is organizing an expedition against you."

"Shadow just came back from St. Mary's," Miles said. "He said nothing about an expedition."

"The expedition is coming from Brightwood Castle. They may not know about it at the lodge yet."

"They may want to get it under way before Galon finds out about it, lest he try to interfere somehow," Miles said. He added, "The sad part is, you needn't have come. The sheriff and his men won't find us if they look for ten years. Like as not, they'll blunder about in the forest for a few days, declare some kind of victory, and go home. Still, we'll send out extra scouts, to be on the safe side."

He sent Scarlet and Oshere as additional scouts. Then he and Garth went back into Abinus's hut. Albinus had propped Ediva against a pile of rolled-up cloaks. She was grey faced, breathing shallowly. Albinus knelt beside her, praying and using his thumb to make the sign of the Cross on her forehead with improvised Holy Water.

Miles's stomach turned.

He was giving her Last Rites.

Miles stumbled back outside, followed by Garth. Miles couldn't imagine Ediva dead. After the events of a decade earlier, he thought Ediva had a charmed life, thought she would live forever. Blanche would be devastated; she'd become quite attached to Ediva. The entire manor would be devastated. Ediva was regarded as a hero, a legend—a saint almost—for her work during the struggle against Aimerie; and Miles suspected some people were secretly glad she had never wed because they thought no one was good enough for her.

"This is my fault," Garth said, distraught. "I should never have let her go to Badford. I should have kept her away from there by force if I had to."

Miles agreed, but it would do no good to say so. It was too late for that. He rested a hand on Garth's shoulder. "You couldn't have known—"

"Of course I could," Garth said. "A girl alone? In Badford? In a place like the Saracen's Head? What did I think was going to happen to her? *You* wouldn't have let her do it."

That was true. Still . . . "Ediva is hot headed. She does as she pleases."

"Miles!"

Ioco and Wighelm, Frithric's long-ranging scouts, came running into camp from the east. Wighelm was breathing hard but Ioco had scarce broken a sweat.

"There's armed men headed this way," Ioco said in his deep voice.

Wighelm caught his breath and added, "The sheriff himself is at their head."

CHAPTER 26

"HOW FAR OUT are they?" Miles asked. Miles's scouts searched for travelers to rob. They also watched for the sheriff's men, bailiffs, or bounty hunters. The long-range scouts, like Ioco and Wighelm, went further afield than the others, staying out overnight.

"Day, day and a half, maybe," said Wighelm, who had largely recovered his breath. Both men were covered from head to foot with mud and grime. "They can't travel fast on account o' their horses and their pack train."

"And they're coming from Brightwood?" Miles said.

"Aye. We picked 'em up not long after they left the castle."

"So they'll take the road that passes through Edsworth."

"Like as not," Wighelm said. He and Ioco both nodded. Ioco's dark, hooded face betrayed no emotion. Miles wondered if it had ever betrayed emotion.

Miles went on. "But they'll never find us, surely?"

"Oh, they'll find us, all right," Wighelm said.

"They got a guide," said Ioco.

"Guess who it is?" Wighelm said.

Miles and Albinus looked at one another and answered at the same time. "Patches."

"None other," said Wighelm.

"That bastard," Bondo said. "After all we done for him."

Odda said, "Judas is lookin' to get his three pieces of silver. He must've gone straight to the sheriff after he left us."

"He'll lead 'em right to us," Frithric said.

"How many are there?" Miles asked the scouts.

"Maybe a hundred," Wighelm said.

Talk and low whistles around the glade.

Wighelm went on. "It ain't just the sheriff. Theobald and Gautier of Haverham are with 'em, too."

"The Three Wise Men," Scarlet cracked, and that got a few laughs.

Ioco went on. "They got knights and footmen both. With a few crossbowmen, for fun."

Miles looked at the sky reflexively, though clouds hid the sun. "Time enough to prepare," he said, "though just. I want to hit them as far out from camp as possible tomorrow. There's a spot this side of Lost Cow Creek that should do."

"Surely you're not going to fight?" Albinus said.

"I am."

"Thirty men against a hundred? That's madness. We can't beat those odds."

"The Devil we can't." Miles's blood was up. He knew they should run, but he didn't want to. He didn't want to give the French the satisfaction. Especially after what had happened to Ediva. He said, "Wiggy, you and Ioco rest. Bondo, pick two men to replace them. Have them find that column and track it."

"If it's all the same, I'm good to go back out," Ioco said.

"You're sure?" Miles said.

"Aye."

Miles hesitated. It was asking a lot, but Ioco looked fresh.

"I'll go with him," Odda said.

"Very well," Miles told them.

Ioco got a drink and grabbed something to eat. While he did that, Odda fetched his gear. Then the two men set out.

Miles said, "Bondo, take two men and guard the camp."

"Why me?" Bondo complained. "Just 'cause I got one hand don't' mean I can't—"

"Next time," Miles said, "I promise. Get the rest of your men together to go with me. We'll wait for Oswald's hunters to come in, then leave. We'll hope to pick up most of the scouts on the way. You and the camp guards send the rest to join us when they get back."

Albinus pulled Miles aside. "This is risky, Miles."

"Life is risky," Miles said.

"What about Ediva?"

"You'll have to stay here with her," Miles told him.

Albinus looked crestfallen. He didn't like to miss a fight.

"I'm sorry," Miles said, "but you're the only one we have who can treat her. If there's any chance at all that . . ."

"Aye," said Albinus, nodding in the realization that what Miles said was true. "Poor child. I'll make her comfortable as I may, until she . . . you know."

Garth had stood off to one side, absorbed in guilt over what had happened to Ediva. Now he spoke to Albinus in that flat, hard tone he seldom used. "I'll borrow your bow, if I may, Father."

"And welcome to it," Albinus said. "Get one of those heathens for me."

The three of them went into Albinus's hut. Ediva's eyes were closed. Miles knelt beside the bed and took her hand. She was as hot to the touch as if a bonfire had been lit inside her. "We have to leave," he told her in a soft voice. "The sheriff's men are coming, and we have to stop them."

Ediva's eyes fluttered open. She tried to roll her legs off the bed. "I'm going with you."

Miles put a restraining hand on her shoulder. "No, you stay here. You need to rest. Father Albinus will look after you."

"But—"

"No but's," Miles said, and his eyes were wet because he knew what awaited her. He sniffed and wiped his nose. "If anything happened to you, your mistress would have my hide."

She inclined her chin toward Garth. "You're making me stay, but you're letting him go with you?"

"Aye."

She shook her head in despair and lay back. "God help you."

"Rest easy," Garth told her. "I . . . I'm sorry."

"Good luck," she breathed. "You'll need it."

Miles and Garth went back outside. Oswald and the first of his hunters had returned, carrying a deer slung on a pole. Bondo was telling them what had happened.

"Patches is mine," Oswald said to Miles as he came up.

"Worry about that when the time comes," Miles said. "For now, leave that deer with Diote and the men staying here."

Miles raised his voice so that everyone in the clearing could hear. "All of you—get ready to move out. Take as many arrows as you can, plus water and food. Hurry, we'll need time to set up."

CHAPTER 27

October 12 – Feast of St. Edwin of Northumbria
30 Days Until Martinmas

"Lo, in the greenwood
Did Onfroi set forth
Onfroi the Fat,
With Theobald Hack-Ear,
Guibert the Greedy,
and their retainers,
Brock the Badger for to seek . . ."

THE SHERIFF'S EXPEDITION made its way through the forest. Dense fog obscured vision, turning trees and brush ghostly, like looming spectres, in this heathen wilderness. The trees crowded right up to the path, making it difficult to see under any circumstances, but the fog rendered vision nearly impossible. It was as if the expedition had been transported to a different world.

The men were quiet for the most part. The fog didn't lend itself to talk. They swiveled their heads right and left anxiously, as though expecting demons to materialize before them. The previous day's heavy rains had made the track muddy, boggy in places, so the going was slow. The wet tramp of feet and clop of horses' hooves seemed to rebound off the mist and to be swallowed by it at the same time.

Leading the column was a man on foot. He was a shortish, thick-built Englishman, his dimpled chin half hidden by an untrimmed beard. His shoes and lower legs were caked with mud. His clothes were better made than the patched rags he had formerly worn, but perhaps his most distinguishing feature was the rope around his neck, the end of which was held by the horseman behind him.

"Do you have to keep this damn rope on me?" Patches asked in broken French.

"We want to make sure you don't get up to any tricks," the horseman told him, while keeping a sharp lookout in the mist. "If you do, you will be the first to die."

Patches waved a dismissive hand. "I'm not getting up to any tricks, Frenchy. I need that money. I got a family to take care of, back in Lower Wynchecombe."

The horseman was unimpressed. "Tell me, English. Are you proud of yourself for betraying your friends this way?"

"They're not my friends. They're robbers, outlaws. I'm doing my duty to the crown, that's all."

The horseman snorted. "Of course you are."

Behind Patches and the horseman came ten footmen with spears. They walked two by two; there was no room for more on the path; and most of the time two by two was an effort, men slipping in the mud, slowing the column's progress and causing it to be strung out. After the first group of footmen came the sheriff, Onfroi of Buchy, accompanied by his squire, Arnot. Arnot was in his twenties, old for a squire. He hadn't been knighted yet because he couldn't find a sponsor. He'd gotten a place with Onfroi when one of Onfroi's squires died from illness. If he did well, maybe he would finally be made a knight.

Behind Onfroi and Arnot were Theobald of Jumièges and Guibert of Haverham. They were followed by a cherubic priest named Nicholas and six knights, then by the main body of footmen and archers. The pack animals and another ten footmen brought up the rear. Onfroi and the knights wore only leather coifs and padded gambesons. They would not don their heavy armor until they were near the outlaw camp and ready for battle.

Onfroi hunkered in his saddle, wishing he was anywhere but here. He adjusted his hood over his shaved head. That was the trouble with shaving your head; it got cold. Onfroi had gone bald at an early age, and he shaved his head out of vanity. Also, it made him look scary, and he liked that. "I'm sheriff of four shires in this benighted land," he grumbled to no one in particular, "and d'you know which one I hate the most? Trentshire. More trouble comes out of this shire than all others combined. And a lot of that trouble involves Miles of Redhill, or Brock the Bunghole, or whatever he calls himself."

Gautier laughed at that. A hedge knight trying to curry favor with his betters, Onfroi thought.

Onfroi lapsed into moody silence. The other reason he hated Trentshire was because of its earl, Galon of Monteaux. Onfroi despised that arrogant bastard, despised the way he had made himself chief councillor to the king, a position Onfroi desired for himself. While Galon and King Henry spent most of their time in Normandy, Onfroi was stuck in godforsaken England, among people who spoke gibberish and who were little better than pagans. They were good only to work the land, and even then they acted like they were doing their lords a favor.

Onfroi wanted to return to Normandy. He wanted lands and titles. But how? He couldn't rise any higher here in England. He seemed to be stuck here, with no way out.

Now if Galon were gone . . .

That would open up a lot of opportunities. With Galon out of the way, the earldom of Trent would be open, and Onfroi might well get it. Onfroi might take Galon's place as the king's councillor, as well. The future of Henry's kingdom would be decided in Normandy, not in England. And if Normandy were to swallow the weak kingdom of France, which seemed possible, perhaps even likely, England would return to being a backwater, albeit one with a handsome treasury.

"Can't see a damned thing in this fog," said Theobald of Jumièges, Brightwood's battle-scarred castellan.

"It'll burn off soon," Gautier said, wrapping his cloak around him. "I hope."

Onfroi looked over his shoulder. "What shall we do with Miles when we catch him, d'ye think? Kill him, or bring him back for trial?"

"Cut off his head and be done with it," Theobald said. "A trial could be fun, especially if torture is involved, but Miles is too dangerous to be kept alive. For all we know, the king might step in and set him free."

"It's the king he's accused of treason against," Onfroi pointed out.

"No matter," said Theobald. "His wife has King Henry wrapped around her finger. She'll talk him into letting Miles go."

"Let me have the honor of killing him," Gautier begged. Perhaps because he'd never left England, Gautier's accent was different from those of Onfroi and Theobald. "I hate that English bastard. That he should possess three rich manors is an insult to us all, one that I would happily avenge. What was King Henry thinking, making a villein like that a baron?"

"Miles did kill the traitor Aimerie," Theobald reminded him.

"So?" said Gautier. "The king could have just given him a pig or something. Something more suited to his station."

The three men laughed at that.

Theobald, who was not married, said, "Miles will leave behind a damned attractive widow. Marriage to her would solve a lot of problems for me. I would finally have lands."

"Galon's already laid claims to her," Onfroi said, "so I'd tread lightly there. Very lightly."

"I'm not afraid of Galon," Theobald told him.

"The graveyards are full of men who weren't afraid of Galon," Onfroi said.

Ahead of them, barely seen in the fog, the English guide stopped and turned his head, as though he had heard something. As he did, there was a thudding sound, and an arrow embedded itself in the Englishman's chest. As the column ground to a surprised halt, more arrows flew out of the mist.

CHAPTER 28

ARROWS WHIPPED INTO the column. Some missed, some clattered off shields and helmets, but others struck home. Cries of pain. A man fell. The knight Blaise was struck in the thigh. A squire's horse reared in panic.

A second volley of arrows, all from the left side of the path. Not many, Onfroi thought—a dozen, maybe?

"There!" someone cried.

Onfroi saw movement in the dense fog. Figures running away? His archers loosed arrows at the fleeing outlaws, but there was little chance of hitting moving targets in this murk. The crossbows hadn't been loaded, and the men who carried them were still winding their bowstrings.

Onfroi turned to his main body. "Left-hand file—after them! Theobald, you're in charge. Right-hand file—turn and face the wood. Be ready for an attack from that side. Gautier, you're in command of them. Pass the word—the van and rearguard are to stay where they are. Squires—bring up the shields."

Chivvied by Gautier and their vintenars, the men on the right turned and faced the wood, weapons ready. This left them vulnerable to the occasional arrow that still fell from the rear, one of which struck a spearman in the back.

Theobald of Jumièges jumped from his horse. He drew his sword and took his place in front of the left-hand file. "Follow me!"

Theobald set off in pursuit of the outlaws, his men behind him. Theobald had commanded footmen in battle before. Some of the men on this expedition were from his garrison at the castle; a few had served on campaign with him. A bold deed during the Anjou rebellion had won Theobald command of Brightwood Castle, but he held no lands, and this might be a chance for him to acquire some. Killing or capturing Miles would do that—assuming Miles was one of their attackers.

Theobald led the footmen into the fog, dodging trees and brush that loomed out of nowhere, tripping over rocks and unseen folds in the ground, slipping and falling in the mud. The spearmen went as fast as they could, but they were hampered both by the fog and by their cumbersome weapons. A number of them threw down the spears and drew their swords.

"See anything?" Theobald asked a nearby spearman. It was one of his men from the castle, Reynard.

"No, my lord," Reynard said.

They pushed on. "Keep some sort of line there!" Theobald called out, and his cry was echoed by the vintenars. The damned trees blocked their vision as much as the fog did, making pursuit difficult.

An arrow slammed into Reynard's chest, and he dropped to his hands and knees with a groan, crawling around in the mud and fallen leaves, blood from his wound dripping on the ground.

More arrows.

"There they are!" someone yelled.

More movement in the fog ahead. The English leaving the cover of the trees? Running away again? *Cowards.*

"Shoot them!" Theobald cried.

The archers loosed arrows. Crossbowmen fired.

Some of the arrows and crossbow bolts bounced off trees and branches. At least one of the fleeing English shuddered and stumbled, but kept going.

"Come on!" Theobald shouted.

* * *

In the path, Gautier and the men of the right-hand file faced the trees, waiting to be attacked. Onfroi donned his helm and slung his shield, as did the wounded Blaise and the rest of the knights. The knights moved calmly. They were trained soldiers, used to acting under pressure.

"Nothing yet, my lord," Gautier said.

"I can see that," Onfroi snapped. His squire Arnot snorted derisively at Gautier. To Gautier, Onfroi said, "Move your men into the trees. Take cover." He wondered if Gautier had ever been in a real fight.

Onfroi couldn't take cover, of course; nor could the knights. Onfroi was in command and must be seen to be so, and it would be unseemly for the knights to seek protection from peasants. Besides, their horses would be difficult to maneuver in the trees. To Arnot, Onfroi said, "Go down the line. Tell the men of the rearguard they must protect the animals at all costs."

Arnot wheeled his horse and picked his way back down the path, knocking aside men who were in his way.

Gautier's head darted right and left at every perceived sound. He heard muffled noises and shouts from the direction in which Theobald had gone. Had Theobald and his men routed the outlaws? Or were they all being killed? He ran a hand across his mouth. "Why don't they come? They must be out there."

Onfroi didn't answer. He walked his horse forward, acutely aware of how alone he was, how vulnerable. He halted beside the body of their guide. The Englishman's eyes were open wide, the arrow in his chest. The man who'd been leading him by a rope was down, too, hit in the side and moaning.

Onfroi studied the dead Englishman for a moment. He would have said that the Englishman had led them into a trap, but the Englishman had been the first to die, so who knew?

Around him, the men of the van had taken shelter in the trees. They looked to Onfroi nervously.

"Steady, men. Steady," he said. "Eyes front, not on me."

* * *

Theobald led the charge after the outlaws. He would catch these bastards and roast them alive. Save for Miles, of course. They'd take their time with Miles. Too bad Miles's pretty wife wouldn't be there to watch. Too bad Theobald wouldn't be able to marry her afterwards. *Damn Galon.*

They moved as fast as they could, crashing through the forest. "Keep a sharp eye!" Theobald cried.

As he said that, an arrow bounced off a nearby tree trunk. There was a cry from farther down the ragged line as another arrow struck home.

More arrows. There couldn't be many of the English ahead. One of Theobald's archers fell. The rest of his archers shot back. One or two of the crossbows replied, as well, but crossbows were difficult to reload on the move, and most of the crossbowmen held their fire, waiting for better targets.

Theobald ran faster. He was breathing hard, glad he wasn't wearing his hauberk. Around him, shadows drifted in and out of the fog, yelling, impossible to tell which side they were on.

He stopped abruptly. He had almost tumbled into a rock=strewn gully. Indeed, one of his men was down there, moaning and holding a broken leg. Theobald heard vague sounds in the fog to his front, and he knew the English were atop the unseen rise at the gully's far side. That was where they intended to make their stand, hoping to pick off Theobald's men with arrows while they were climbing the gully's side.

Theobald's men had stopped beside him. "Spread out," he ordered.

"They'll be waiting over there." The speaker was a grizzled spearman from Brightwood, a vintenar named Jacques, who struggled for breath after the run.

Theobald grinned at him. "Too much garrison duty for you, eh, Jacques?" He slapped the man's gut. "You need a few long marches to toughen you up."

"Could say the same about you, my lord," Jacques replied.

Theobald laughed. Talking that way to a noble would get a footman flogged, or even hung, back at the castle, but discipline was relaxed in the field.

Theobald raised his voice. "Give them a volley from the crossbows." He motioned to a vintenar. "Get that man out of the gully."

The crossbow bolts flew. Theobald was no great advocate of crossbows. They took no skill to operate—the lowest peasant could learn to operate one in the course of a morning—and the iron bolts were expensive even if you had a good source of supply. But they did have their uses.

Jacques said, "Don't fancy climbing the other side of that gully, my lord."

"Nor do I," said Theobald. "That's what they want us to do. How many of them do you think there are?"

"Fifteen, maybe. No more'n that."

"That's what I was thinking. Take five men. Go down this gully about a half-furlong and cross. Come up on their flank. I'll do the same from the right side. We'll catch the bastards between us. With any luck, Miles will be with them." He turned to another vintenar, one of the sheriff's men. "Phillipe, keep them pinned down with arrows and crossbow bolts. When we hit them in the flanks, you cross the gully and attack."

"*Oui*, my lord," said Phillipe.

"Move out," Theobald told Jacques.

Jacques nodded and turned to go. At that moment, three blasts on a horn sounded from behind them.

"That's the recall signal," Jacques said.

"I don't care," Theobald told him. "Move out." They were too close to victory to give up now.

The horn sounded again, and there was a sense of urgency to it.

"We'd best get back, my lord," Jacques said. "They might be in trouble. This bunch might be a diversion and the real attack coming from other side."

Theobald was so angry he was on the verge of tears. He had Miles in his grasp, and he was about to give him away.

The horn sounded again.

"Fall back," Theobald told his men at last. "Retrieve the wounded as you go. Make sure you don't leave anyone behind. I'll stay with the archers. We'll provide cover in case the outlaws attempt to follow us. All right, get going. And hurry. I'm tired of hearing that damned horn."

CHAPTER 29

ⓄNFROI'S SQUIRE, ARNOT, sounded the horn yet again. "Where are they?" he muttered. "Those fellows are slower than English servants."

The column waited for Theobald's men to return. Gautier and his men still faced the trees on the right, still waited to be attacked from that direction. The fog had settled in as though it never meant to leave, its damp chill penetrating men's bones.

The wounded had been seen to, the dead carried off the path and left in the trees. Blaise's squire had removed the arrow from Blaise's leg and wrapped a bandage around it. Blaise held the wound and grimaced in pain.

"Are you fit to ride?" Onfroi asked him.

"I'm fine, my lord," Blaise said through gritted teeth.

Guibert of Haverham had recovered some of his bravado. "Christ on the Cross," he swore, keeping his eyes on the trees. "The forest is meant for hunting, not fighting. These damned English can't do anything right. I wish my grandfather had stayed in Normandy instead of coming here."

"You've never been to Normandy, have you?" Onfroi asked him. It was a statement, not a question.

"No," Guibert replied sheepishly. There were a lot of knights like him these days. "Usually I'm sent to the Scottish border for my forty days of knight service, which is even worse than Trentshire, if you can imagine that."

"So you don't know it at all? Normandy, I mean."

"No," Guibert said. "Only what I've heard."

Onfroi had been born and raised in Normandy, had spent his entire life there—when not on campaign in Flanders and France and Anjou—until he came to England to be sheriff. "It's wonderful country, much prettier than England. People speak properly there, and the peasants know their place."

Guibert went on. "Speaking of peasants, my lord, what the Devil was Lady Blanche thinking, marrying Miles? Is his dick that big? She should be put to death for carrying on with a villein, and her lands confiscated by the crown."

Or by the crown's representative, Onfroi thought, who, in this case, would be me.

And that thought made Onfroi think some more. Perhaps Blanche could meet with a fatal accident. Because her husband was outlawed, her lands would automatically be forfeit to the crown. But doing that brought the problem of Galon, who desired Blanche's hand. If Blanche met with an accident, and if Galon suspected that Onfroi was behind it, he would retaliate.

Galon would have to be dealt with in any case, but Onfroi had planned that for later. Back to Blanche. There had to be a way to dispose of her without the blame coming back on Onfroi. A riding accident? Poison? Onfroi knew of someone who could make poisons that left no trace. A fall, perhaps, from a height—the way Baron Aimerie was supposed to have killed his wife? Onfroi doubted that was what really happened. He believed Aimerie's wife was drunk and fell, and that Miles and Blanche made up the other story to justify their killing him.

"Finally," Arnot said. "Took their damned time."

Onfroi came back to the present. Theobald's men appeared in ones and twos out of the fog, gathering spears and other equipment they had thrown down in order to chase the outlaws. Some assisted or carried the wounded. A handful of archers and crossbowmen moved from tree to tree, covering the party's rear. Theobald was with them, sword in hand.

Theobald was last man back to the column, and he approached Onfroi angrily. "Why did you summon us back, my lord? We were about to flank them—"

"For all his faults, Miles is an experienced soldier," Onfroi said. "That's probably what he was expecting you to do. He and his men would have just fallen farther back into the forest, leading you on."

"Miles is no soldier, he's a villein. We had him—"

"You were gone too long. The column can't stay in one spot, exposed like this, all day. It's too dangerous." To Arnot, Onfroi said, "How many casualties?"

Arnot had been counting; it was one of his duties, and he was good at his job. "Altogether, I make it eight dead and ten wounded, my lord, three of them still able to fight."

Theobald was still fuming. "That's not so bad," he said. "All the more reason we—"

"It's almost one-fifth of our force," Onfroi pointed out.

Arnot went on. "Two of the wounded are hurt too badly to move, my lord. What should we do with them?"

Onfroi swore. This was the part he hated. "You know what to do. We can't leave them to the tender mercies of the English."

"Yes, my lord," Arnot said, and Onfroi knew that Arnot would take care of that duty himself. He wasn't one to shirk unpleasant jobs.

Onfroi raised his voice. "Squires of the three knights with the least seniority will give up their horses to the wounded."

There were grumbles and complaints from the squires. One of the squires had already been unhorsed when his mount was killed by an arrow. This meant four squires on foot.

"Now!" Onfroi snapped.

The squires dismounted. Arnot kicked them and boxed their ears to make them hurry. Onfroi said to the knights, "Don your hauberks and helmets, in case the outlaws strike again."

"So," Theobald asked Onfroi, "do we move forward or go back?"

Onfroi motioned to where their guide lay dead in the path. "Our guide is dead. How will we find the outlaw camp without him?"

"We can't go back," Guibert protested. His wounded pride had him close to tears.

Theobald's anger had subsided to resignation. He knew this was a great defeat, knew he had suffered humiliation. He could already hear the English singing their imbecile songs about it. Fortunately, he had an alternative plan in place in case things went badly. And, even as he thought of that, another plan suggested itself. Maybe a better plan, and certain to be more fun . . .

"We had our chance and lost it," Onfroi said. "If you want to keep pushing ahead blindly through this forest, Guibert, go ahead and do it. We could tramp around here for weeks without finding anything, except more ambushes."

Onfroi raised his voice. "Knights to the rear! The rest of the column prepare to turn. We're returning to Brightwood."

CHAPTER 30

October 13 – Feast of St. Comgan the Monk

29 Days Until Martinmas

MILES AND HIS men were on their way back to camp. Yesterday's fog was a memory, and rays of sunlight filtered through falling autumn leaves. The men were in good spirits, though they had lost one of their number, Ulm, a cottar from Thornton, who had succumbed to a crossbow bolt. A few more men bore wounds, but all were minor.

After the sheriff's men had retreated, Miles's men had plundered the bodies of the dead for money, weapons and clothing. The sheriff's men had beat them to the money, though, robbing their dead comrades themselves. They'd left behind the clothing and most of the weapons.

"No matter about the money," a man named Legwulf had said, while pulling on a new wool shirt. "It'd just get stolen in camp."

Mutters of assent. One or two few men glanced furtively at Ioco.

A couple of the outlaws now sported steel caps on their heads, though these were impractical for a life in the woods and would soon be discarded or used as drinking bowls. Others, like the fire-scarred Oswald and Ioco had acquired heavy jacks, which would prove useful with winter coming on. The lucky ones, though, the lucky ones had shoes. Shoes had been taken first—shoes wore out fast, and new ones were more valuable than gold in the forest. Legulf, who had been a shoemaker, managed to get two pairs. He'd keep one and trade the other.

"Think you'll get a song out of this, Scarlet?" said Frithric. Frithric was one of those with a helmet.

"Already working on it," Scarlet said.

> *"Now listen to the deeds*
> *Of Brock and his men*
> *When against the sheriff they did come.*
> *Full attired was Onfroi,*
> *In all the panoply of war . . ."*

"Why do you call yourself Scarlet, anyway?" Oshere interrupted.

"Got to call myself something, don't I?" Scarlet said.

"What's your real name?" Oshere said.

"Kettlebern."

"I'd stick to Scarlet, was I you," Oshere said to laughter.

Odda was another who had a helmet, and Wighelm rapped his knuckles on it playfully. "Hey, Odda, you still never said why you was outlawed."

Odda was tight lipped about his past. "Killed a man," he replied, readjusting the helmet. "Bastard lay with my wife."

"You should've killed your wife, too," said Ioco.

"I did."

The attack on the sheriff's men had gone according to plan, which surprised Miles, because military operations rarely did. The outlaws had shot arrows into the sheriff's column, then fallen back to positions which had been scouted and prepared in advance. The plan was to keep shooting arrows and falling back to these positions until the sheriff's men gave up the chase and returned to their column. At that point, Miles's men would have regrouped, run ahead, and attacked the column again a mile or so further up the path, repeating the process. The afternoon of two days ago had been spent locating positions.

Miles had expected the sheriff's men to flank his position at the gully, and he had been readying his men to retreat when the horn sounded. With his guide, Patches, dead, Onfroi had decided to turn around, avoiding further loss of life.

"You said you'd get Patches, and you did," Oshere told his brother, Oswald, thumping him on the back as they tramped along.

"Aye," Wighelm said, "good job. He was a traitor."

"Wish it had taken him longer to die," Odda said.

"Buggers won't be coming at us again for a while," Frithric boasted.

"Not till spring, at least," added Wighelm.

"D'ye think we'll still be here in the spring?" asked Hugh Middewynter. Despite his youth, Hugh had acquitted himself well in the fight.

"Where else would we be, Shadow?" Frithric said. "I'm an outlaw. I go back, that fuck Gautier will have my hand for poaching."

"That's if he don't hang you for runnin' away from the manor," Oshere said.

Hugh looked despondent, and Miles guessed he missed his home, despite the circumstances under which he had left it. As for Miles, he reckoned he would be here this winter, and every winter thereafter, until he died. Some of these men, those who had not been outlawed, might be able to sneak home for the winter. Maybe they would return, maybe they wouldn't. Maybe new men would take their place when the weather warmed. But Miles would stay here year after year, until he was dead and his name remembered only in old songs.

* * *

As the men neared the camp, they quieted.

"This is the part I've been dreading," Garth said to his father.

"So have I," Miles said.

"Poor girl," Garth said. "She was only trying to help."

Miles nodded.

They purposefully made enough noise on their approach so that Bondo and the camp guards knew they were coming. The nearly empty camp was quiet, funereal, though Diote threw her arms around Oshere and kissed him in greeting.

Miles and Garth went to Father Albinus's hut. They moved slowly, afraid of what they would find. Garth held back the deer hide door and they went inside.

The hut stank of sickness. Albinus stood beside the makeshift bed, head bowed in prayer, blocking their view of its occupant.

Miles whispered, "Is she . . .?"

Albinus stood aside.

Ediva was propped against the piled cloaks. Her eyes were open.

"The fever broke," Albinus said.

"Praise God," Miles breathed.

Garth closed his eyes and sighed with relief.

" 'Twas a miracle," said Albinus, "truly."

Ediva's face was wan. She croaked, "Father Albinus put Holy Water in your pottage and gave it to me."

Miles and Garth stared at the priest.

Albinus hemmed. "Well, I may have added . . . a little."

Miles crossed himself. "Whatever you did, Father, it worked."

"She's too weak to travel," Albinus went on. "Will be for some time, I fear."

"She'll stay here, then," Miles said.

Garth stepped forward. "I'm glad you're all right," he said to Ediva.

"Thank you," she replied. "I'm surprised to hear you say that."

"Just because I don't like you doesn't mean I want you dead," Garth told her.

"You have a way with compliments," Ediva said in a weak voice. "No wonder you're having such a hard time finding a wife."

Garth rolled his eyes and turned to Miles. "I need to get home. Alfstan and the others need me. I'll stop at Redhill and let Blanche know about Ediva. And I'll see if Aelred's learned anything about the plot."

He returned Albinus's bow and quiver. "Thank you, Father."

"I trust you put them to good use," Albinus said.

"I did," Garth told him. He turned to Miles. "The sheriff won't let this go, Father. You've made a fool of him, and he'll want you dead. Now, more than ever."

"I know," Miles said, "I wonder what he'll do next."

CHAPTER 31

October 15 – Feast of St. Thecla of Kitzingen
27 Days Until Martinmas

HERSENT WAS SUPPOSED to be picking the last of the apples with her youngest daughter. After that, there was cider and perry to be made. Instead, she stood outside Redhill's manor house wall, lost in thought and staring across the fields toward the distant forest. She was tall, sturdy, and attractive, with strands of grey creeping into her curly red hair.

She didn't hear Wada come up behind her and was startled when he spoke. "Wish you could be with Miles, don't you?"

She recovered and sighed. There was a chill in the air, and Wada wore his wolf-skin cloak. He was so proud of that cloak. "Aye," she said. "There's times I miss the old life of the Brotherhood—the freedom, the excitement."

"Wish you were still with them?"

She patted his arm and smiled. "No, I'm happy here. I'm happy with you. It's just that, with Miles in trouble the way he is, it feels like we're letting him down by being here instead of out there with him."

Wada wrapped an arm round her shoulder. "I know. We have a duty to Lady Blanche, though. Plus, there's our children to look after."

"But if it wasn't for Miles, we wouldn't be here," she said. "He made all this possible for us."

"Miles will get it tended to, you'll see. He'll be home soon enough."

"You really believe that?"

Wada hesitated. "I like to think I do. But . . ." His voice tailed off.

"Look," said Hersent.

Wada turned. Riders approached the manor house from the east. Two nobles and an armed escort. Workers in the fields stopped what they were doing and stared.

Hersent squinted at the distant riders; her vision wasn't what it had been when she was younger. "Isn't that Onfroi, the sheriff?"

"Aye," Wada said, "and the one in black is the earl's steward, Stigand."

"What do you think they want?"

"I don't know, but it can't be good."

"I'll warn Lady B," Hersent said and departed.

Wada retreated across the bridge and onto the manor house grounds. He waited until the sheriff's party had crossed the bridge and entered the gate, then approached them. "Greetings, my lords."

"Who are you?" Onfroi demanded.

"Wada, my lord. The steward."

Onfroi frowned at Wada's accent. "You're English?"

"Aye, my lord."

"Christ save us," Onfroi said. He added, "That's an expensive cloak for a steward, especially an English one."

Wada said nothing.

"Where is Blanche?" Onfroi said.

"*Lady* Blanche is in the kennels, I believe," Wada replied. "One of the bitches has whelped, and—"

"Get her!"

"Aye, my lord," Wada said calmly. He turned and started away, taking his time and making sure the French knew he was doing it.

He met Blanche coming from the kennel, dusting straw from her hands, Hersent behind her. He said, "You heard, my lady?"

"I did," Blanche replied.

They went back and approached Onfroi, who had dismounted and waited impatiently in the yard, Stigand beside him. The other members of their party, knights and spearmen, sat their horses truculently, like they had hoped for a fight. Blanche's children, Richard, John and Alice, had gathered there, as well. Richard and John wore padded gambesons from sword training.

Blanche was cool and polite. "I presume this isn't a courtesy visit?" she said to Onfroi.

He inclined his shaved head in what might have passed for a bow. "You presume correctly, Lady Blanche. It is my duty to inform you that you have been placed under arrest."

Richard, the oldest child, started forward, but Blanche motioned him to remain calm. To Onfroi she said, "Really. On whose authority?"

"On authority of the king, my lady, as vested in me."

"And is there a reason for this arrest?"

"You know the reason," Onfroi told her. "Your husband has been outlawed, and I believe that he was behind a recent attack against me and my men."

"That's doubtful," Blanche said. "If Miles was behind the attack, it would have been fatal." She smiled.

Onfroi's cheeks reddened.

She went on. "So perhaps this attack was carried out by someone else whom you've unjustly outlawed."

Hersent and Wada were watching. Hersent began sliding away, and Wada knew she was going for her bow. He put a hand on her arm and shook his head. "Not with the children here," he whispered.

Onfroi controlled himself and went on, his tone less polite than it had been. "I also have reason to believe that you are in communication with your husband. It is because of this—you'll no doubt be surprised to learn that aiding an outlaw is a crime—that you are to be arrested."

John balled his fists. Richard said, "You can't—"

"Am I to be imprisoned in the castle?" Blanche said.

"No," Onfroi said. "You will be restricted to your manor at Brightwood, where we may keep watch on you. You will not be permitted to leave the manor without my permission. That permission, I might add, will not be forthcoming, so you needn't bother to ask for it."

"Even for hunting?" Blanche said.

"Even for hunting."

Blanche turned calmly to Stigand. "And your part in this, Lord Stigand?"

Stigand said, "I'm looking out for the earl of Trent's interests, my lady. I'm here to make sure that you aren't mistreated."

"How thoughtful of the earl," Blanche said.

Blanche's maid, Estrild, had appeared, and she berated Stigand, wagging a finger at him. "I understand this Frenchy acting the way he does, but you, an Englishman, taking part in such a travesty. You should be ashamed of yourself."

Stigand cast her a baleful look.

Blanche said, "That's enough, Estrild. It's all right."

"But they have no reason—"

"It will all be straightened out," Blanche said.

Alice threw her arms around Blanche's waist. "Mother, will you be safe?"

"I'll be fine, dear. Don't worry."

Onfroi was tired of talk. "Gather what you need," he told Blanche. "We must make haste if we are to make Brightwood by dark."

"Of course," Blanche said. "Estrild, get some things together. Wada, see to horses for myself and Estrild."

"Aye, my lady," said Wada, hurrying off.

"We're going, too," Richard said. John and Alice nodded vigorously in assent.

"No," Blanche told them. "I want you to stay here."

Alice said, "But—"

"Mind what I tell you," Blanche said.

Stigand looked around sharply. "Where's your other maid, the one with the big mouth? What's her name—Ediva?"

"I've no idea," Blanche said. "Wool gathering, I expect. She's a dozy girl. She can catch up to us."

"Enough banter," Onfroi said. "Ready yourself, my lady."

With Estrild's assistance, Blanche gathered clothes and other belongs. She hugged her children in turn. "I'll be back soon." Then she and Estrild mounted and rode away with their captors. Blanche was next to Onfroi, with Stigand behind them. Estrild rode a distance back and, behind her, came the knights and mounted spearmen.

As they started down the path that eventually led to Brightwood, Stigand noticed a broad-shouldered figure making his way toward the manor on foot from the opposite direction. He left the little party and rode over to the man. "Garth," he said, "what are you doing here?"

Garth bowed his head. "My lord. I've come to see how Lady Blanche fares."

"Lady Blanche has been arrested," Stigand told him.

Garth was jolted. He looked toward the departing riders, to whom he'd paid little attention before, and recognized Blanche among them. "Why, my lord?"

"To appease Onfroi's wounded pride," Stigand said. He added, "Why are you not at Ravenswell?"

"With my father gone, I need to help Blanche with the children—"

Stigand's eyes narrowed. "Are you sure you haven't come from seeing your father?"

"Quite sure, my lord," Garth said.

"And, of course, you have no idea where he is."

"No, my lord."

"That's a pity, because Lord Galon wishes to meet with him."

Garth said nothing.

Stigand regarded Garth evenly. "I'll be at Ravenswell. Get back to me with a time and place for that meeting. And make it soon."

"But I don't know where he is," Garth protested.

"Find someone who does," Stigand told him. He rode away, his black cloak billowing behind him.

CHAPTER 32

𝔍T WAS LATE afternoon when they arrived at Brightwood. In the distance, Blanche saw Belot, Brightwood's steward, waiting for them in front of the manor house, which lay at the opposite end of the village from the castle. No doubt, he had been alerted to their coming.

Blanche and Miles rarely stayed at Brightwood. It was too close to the castle for their liking. Buildings were springing up like toadstools outside the castle bailey—inns for travelers, taverns, brothels. In addition, warehouses were being built for the trading boats that plied the river and docked at the castle overnight for protection. All these buildings, of necessity, infringed upon the manor's lands. Their owners paid rent to the manor, but the manor's fields were being nibbled away, as though by some implacable caterpillar, their tenants granted new lands by Blanche or leaving the manor altogether in search of better opportunities. Blanche could imagine a distant future when the manor's farmlands had disappeared and this area had simply become Brightwood Town.

The manor was in capable hands with Belot. He was half French and married to the daughter of another steward. He got along with those at the castle, especially Theobald, much better than did Miles or Blanche. More importantly, his father had been steward of Brightwood before him, so he knew the manor intimately and ran it at a good profit. And if he pocketed the occasional extra coin, it was nothing other stewards didn't do. As long as he didn't overdo it, it was tolerated.

Now Belot stood respectfully, but obviously puzzled as to what this sudden appearance portended. He was a stocky man of medium height, with thinning hair and a broken front tooth. He bowed. "My lords. My lady. *Mademoiselle* Estrild."

Onfroi and Stigand acknowledged him with curt nods of their heads, while Blanche said breezily, "I've been placed under arrest, Belot. It seems I'll be staying here for a bit."

Belot struggled to hide his surprise. "Yes, my lady. I'm sorry to hear that, my lady. That you've been arrested, I mean—not that you'll be staying with us. We're always glad to see you."

Nicholas, the manor's cherubic young chaplain, was there, as well. He doubled as chaplain for the castle, where he spent most of his time, as he found the company more to his liking. "I'll pray for you, my lady."

"You'd do better to pray for my husband," Blanche told him, though that was unlikely to happen because Nicholas didn't approve of Miles. "He's the one they're trying to kill with their false accusations of treason."

"They're not false," Onfroi snapped.

"Of course they are," Blanche said dismissively, as though this were a game they were playing, which in a way, she supposed, it was.

The party dismounted, Belot holding Blanche's reins. "Take Lady Blanche's things," he told a servant. To Blanche, he said, "Where is *Mademoiselle* Ediva?"

"She'll be along presently, I expect," Blanche replied.

Brushing dust from their clothes, the party entered the low-ceilinged hall. The hall was old and dark. It smelled of smoke and mold and wet dogs. The heavy wooden beams were mildewed and warped. The main door was at the southern end, instead of in the building's center, as it was in most newer houses. A brace of hams hung from the roof near the glowing fire pit. The hall would need to be rebuilt soon— which would cost a deal of money. Blanche felt guilty because it would have been rebuilt already if she and Miles spent more time there.

As Blanche neared the head table, Estrild sidled close to her. "Where *is* Ediva?" she whispered.

"With Miles, I hope," Blanche murmured.

Refreshments were set out, and as they were, Theobald, Brightwood's castellan, bent his head at the low door and entered the hall. He stalked to the head table as though he were the lord here and not Blanche. He halted opposite Blanche and bowed. "My lady." He spoke politely, but his smile resembled a sneer. He acknowledged the steward, "Belot."

Belot bowed and handed Theobald a cup of wine, heavily spiced at this time of year to hide its vinegary taste.

Theobald nodded to the chaplain. "Nicholas."

"My lord," said Nicholas with a bow.

Onfroi smiled at Blanche, obviously pleased with himself. "Theobald will check on you every day, Lady Blanche, so don't get any ideas about running away to join your husband."

"That would be hard to do, since I don't know where my husband is," Blanche said.

"Ah, but we believe you do know."

"You believe a lot of things that aren't true," Blanche said. "All I know about my husband these days is what I hear in the villagers' songs." She raised a forefinger "There's a new song, by the way, a rather amusing one. It tells of your recent adventures—or should I say, misadventures—in the forest. Shall I sing it for you?"

Onfroi's face reddened. Theobald looked like he wanted to hit Blanche. Father Nicholas glowered.

"Amusing?" Onfroi said at last. "Perhaps, *madame*, for the moment. The amusement will be mine, however, when I have your husband at the end of a rope."

"My husband is a noble. If he's to be executed, it must be by beheading."

156

"He's not a noble," Theobald said, "he's English. And a rope is too good for him."

Blanche smiled. "If you say so."

Onfroi said, "You and these peasants with whom you associate may find this funny, but I'll have the last laugh. I've already seen to that."

"What do you mean?" Blanche said sharply.

Onfroi had the look of a man who'd said too much. "You'll learn soon enough." He stepped forward. "And if you mock me again, I'll—"

"I believe we've heard enough, Lord Onfroi," Stigand cut in. He had one hand on his sword. "You border on discourtesy."

"I'll say when she's heard enough," Onfroi told him.

"As you wish," Stigand replied. "But I don't think you want to get on Lord Galon's bad side." He could have added, "Or on mine," but that part came through quite clearly.

Onfroi huffed. "We'll be leaving now," he said to Blanche. He bowed. "Good day, my lady."

Theobald bowed, as well. "Good day, my lady." He smirked. "I shall see you on the morrow."

"I look forward to it," Blanche said brightly. "You being such an engaging conversationalist. Perhaps we can discuss theology—St. Augustine, perhaps? *The City of God*?"

Theobald's jaws clenched and he turned. Stigand watched the two men and their retainers leave the hall. He turned to Blanche, "If there's anything you need, my lady, don't hesitate to let me know."

"You're being awfully kind," she said. "That's not like you."

"Lord Galon wished nothing to happen to you, in case . . ."

"In case . . .?" In case my husband fails in whatever 'mission' he's been sent on, and I have to marry Galon? But she couldn't say that with the others around.

Stigand understood what she meant, and he smiled. "Exactly, my lady. And now, I bid you good day."

He bowed deeply and left the hall.

The chaplain. Nicholas, left as well. "There are things I must attend to. I'll be back soon for your prayers at vespers."

Estrild watched Nicholas leave the hall. "I don't trust that one."

"Nor do I," Blanche said. She beckoned Estrild and Belot close. "Onfroi has sent someone to kill Miles."

Belot and Estrild stared at her.

"How can you be certain?" Belot said.

"He seemed too confident when he said he'd have the last laugh, like he knew something. I can't think of what else it could be. His expedition against Miles failed, so he's hired a killer."

Estrild said, "We must warn Miles. We can send—"

"I'll do it," Blanche said.

Belot said, "But you heard them. You're not allowed—"

"I'll not tolerate that oaf Theobald looking over my shoulder every day. I need to get away from here as soon as I can."

CHAPTER 33

October 13 – Feast of St. Luke the Evangelist
25 Days Until Martinmas

GARTH APPROACHED THE mill, and Aelred's cottage beyond. The mill wheel creaked as it had done for centuries, driven by the stream. It was such a part of the villagers' lives that they didn't notice it. It was always there, in the background, like the wind.

The trip from Redhill had taken longer than expected. Bad weather had rendered the roads nearly impassable. Garth had been given a good meal and lodging at the Priory of Mt. Carmel last night, but he'd spent the previous night in an abandoned charcoal maker's hut. Today was clear. Most of the leaves had fallen, plucked from the trees by the storm's heavy winds. It was cold. In the distance, a cart headed from the forest, piled with firewood. Garth felt guilty because he should be with the wood gatherers, not leaving the job for his sons. He hoped all this running around didn't result in his family freezing to death this winter for lack of wood.

At the mill, the usual line of people waited with grain to be processed. Aelred was weighing a sack of grain before loading it onto the platform to be hauled to the mill's upper floor. He saw Garth coming and waved. He handed the work off to his assistant, Wat, the swineherd's son, then came forward and shook his older brother's hand. "You look tired."

"It's been a long few days," Garth admitted. "Cold, wet ones."

"Aye, I'm not looking forward to winter," Aelred said. "Here, have something to eat."

From the side table, Aelred cut Garth a hunk of good rye bread and slathered it with fresh-churned honey butter and some damson jam. "Have you been home yet?"

Garth bit into the bread gratefully; it warmed him. "No. I came straight here to find out if you'd learned anything more."

Aelred shook his head. "Nothing. I've contacted everyone I could think of from the old days—sent messengers to the nearby manors. No one knows or has heard anything about a plot. Not so much as a whisper."

Garth said nothing, munching the bread. Aelred gave him a cup of ale to wash it down with.

"So Blanche was right," Garth said at last. "This 'plot' is an excuse to kill Father."

Aelred nodded gloomily. "How is he?"

"As well as can be expected, for being an outlaw with a price on his head. I never thought I'd live to see this."

"I did," Aelred said. "The French have always wanted to take him down. It was only a matter of time till they did it." He cut himself a piece of the bread. "He's becoming famous, by the by. Those songs about him and the sheriff of Trentshire are all over Badford. They've spread to Leicestershire, Derby, Cambridge. To the North, as well, I hear. He's becoming a hero."

Garth finished the bread, sucking jam from his fingers. "There was a time he'd have liked that," he said ruefully. "No longer. He just wants to live in peace now."

"As do we all," Aelred said.

Garth gave him a look, and Aelred added, "Seriously, Garth, you and I can't afford to be tainted by Father's notoriety. If we are, before you know it, we'll be on the run as well. All we can do for him is pray."

"Can't afford . . ." Garth grew angry. "If you were outlawed, Father would move Heaven and earth to save you, no matter what the cost to himself. He's done it before, which is why you're still alive, which is why you have this mill."

"What would you have me do?" Aelred shot back. "If I could think of something helpful, don't you think I'd already be doing it? It's out of our hands. Father's a noble now; he's playing by a different set of rules. French rules. Rules we're not a party to."

Garth let out a long breath. "You're right. It's frustrating, that's all. I feel . . ."

"Helpless?"

"Aye."

"I feel the same."

There was a pause. "And Ediva?" Aelred said. He looked afraid to finish the question. "Did she survive the trip to Father's camp?"

"She did, but it was touch and go. We thought we'd lost her."

Aelred let out his breath. "I'm glad. I like her. It's a shame what happened to her. I feel responsible for it—her thinking I was involved in the plot."

"She's still at Father's camp. 'Twill be a while before she's fully recovered."

Aelred nodded, as though that were to be expected. "What will you do for a wife now that Oli's daughter is no longer available?"

"I'll have to put my own marriage aside for a bit, I'm afraid. Mallette was my best chance, and I've lost her. I need to find a husband for Cecily by next year. She's fifteen—I should have found her a husband already. And Alfred's sixteen—he'll be wanting a wife."

"I've a while before I have to worry about that," Aelred said somberly.

There was an awkward pause. Aelred had lost his oldest boy, Edmund, a few years back. Edmund had been playing follow my leader with some friends when he'd fallen out of a tree. He'd suffered internal injuries, and had died a week later, in great pain.

"We grow old quickly, don't we?" Garth said at last.

"That we do. It seems like yesterday we were lads, dodging work to hunt in the forest or play Hereward fighting the French."

"Those days are long gone."

"Aye." Aelred lifted his brows. "Not the French, though. I've come to believe they'll never be gone."

Garth nodded. "I fear you're right."

"So, are you ready to get back to work?"

"For a bit," Garth said. "Then I must arrange a meeting."

CHAPTER 34

October 25 – Feast of St. Jude (Martyr)
14 Days Until Martinmas

𝕿HE OLD OUTLAW camp smelled of filth and cooking and unwashed humanity, though that might have been Galon's imagination. Ten years should have got rid of all that. The remains of huts, stone firepits, bits of cloth, cracked pottery, a few animal bones—a few human bones, as well. All of it overgrown with weeds and grass and new trees.

Galon drew his plain cloak closer about him as he and black-clad Stigand rode through the camp. By their dress, one might have thought Stigand the master and Galon his servant. There was a bite in the air; the breeze carried the tang of the distant sea. Fallen leaves blew into corners and recesses. In this deary, late autumn weather, the camp seemed filled with ghosts. Galon could almost hear the lilt of a pipe, the thump of a drum, the cries and laughter of men and women and children.

"Lived in worse places when I was young," Stigand muttered, looking around.

Galon grunted; he expected that was true. Stigand had spent his early years as a refugee, after King William had destroyed the North of England.

Galon, who had spent much, if not most, of his life in army camps, said, "Remember the siege of Coutances? When the plague struck? That was bad."

"Aye," said Stigand. So many had died among the besiegers, of whom Galon and Stigand had been part, that they'd been forced to abandon the siege and go home. There'd been so many dead, they'd burned the bodies in piles, rather than bury them. "These outlaws lived here for years, I heard. It's a wonder disease didn't carry all of 'em off."

"It probably did carry off a lot of them," Galon said. "They're long gone now, that's certain."

The two men halted in the center of the deserted camp and dismounted. There was a large stone fire circle here, along with the remains of a larger hut nearby that might have belonged to the outlaw leader, whoever he had been. "Why'd he pick this place to meet?" Stigand wondered.

Galon shrugged. "Why does Miles do anything?"

Stigand eased the sword in his scabbard and looked around slowly. "Good place for an ambush."

Galon was unconcerned. "You know Miles. He's so honest, he'd probably let us know in advance if he intended to ambush us. And where he was going to do it, and with how many men."

"Greetings, my lords!"

The cheerful voice startled Galon, though he was careful not to show it.

As always, Miles seemed to appear out of nowhere, a grin on his rugged face. He looked worn down, and he'd lost weight since Galon had last seen him. He was filthy and his clothes were patched with deerskin. To say he smelled was an understatement.

"Stop playing the jolly outlaw," Galon told him. "You've no audience to impress here."

The three men faced each other. Galon and Stigand had swords and daggers; Miles had only a short sword at his belt.

Galon said, "I assume you have men hidden nearby in case there's trouble?"

"You mean, in case you try to kill me?" Miles said. "Yes, I do. I presume you've taken the same precaution?"

"We have."

Miles turned to Stigand. "You don't seem happy to see me, Lord Stigand."

Stigand glowered. "I'd prefer to see you dead. I've never forgiven you for breaking my nose." His long nose was skewered to the right.

"If it makes things any better, I've never forgiven you for hanging me," Miles told him brightly. "Besides, the broken nose makes you look tough."

"I was already tough," Stigand said.

"Tougher, then. Like a man who chases spies, even if they are imaginary ones."

"What are you japing about?"

"Come, come, gentlemen, let's not play. There is no plot, you know that, no plot save to kill me and seize my lands."

Galon said, "You imbecile, if I wanted to kill you, I could have done it any time in the last ten years. Trust me, I thought about it enough. 'Twould have been easy to arrange. No, there's a plot, all right, one that you have obviously made no headway in uncovering."

"It's hard to uncover things when I'm being hunted by the sheriff," Miles pointed out. "By the by, have you told the sheriff about this plot?"

"No," Galon said. "For all I know, he's part of it. Onfroi's ambitious. He'd do anything for land and power. That's why I chose you for the job. You hate us. You wouldn't join us for an apple pull, much less for a plot against the crown."

"You're right there," Miles admitted. "By the way, how do I know that you're not part of the plot?"

"You don't," Galon told him. Patiently, he added, "What would it avail me, having you investigate something I'm a part of? You'd probably muck it up, and then where would I be?"

"And why are you so—?"

165

"I am the king's chief councillor. A plot against the king is a plot against me, and I take unkindly to that. Now stop yapping and tell me if you've learned anything."

"I have learned one thing," Miles said. "Assuming you're right and this plot actually exists, we English aren't involved in it. My son Aelred—remember him? you tried to hang him, too—has investigated. He was a Beardman, and none of his sources are aware of anything happening."

"Which leaves the nobles," Stigand told Galon. "High ranking ones, too, I'll wager."

"Don't forget the Scots," Galon said. " 'Twas through a Scot we learned about this. How do they figure into it?"

Miles said, "Perhaps someone promised them the northern part of the kingdom in return for their assistance. They've always claimed it."

"Hmm." Galon considered that. "You're not as stupid as you look, Miles."

"But why Martinmas?" said Stigand. "Why that day?"

"That's obvious, I should think," Miles said. "Day of slaughter. Someone's idea of a joke. Or of being prophetic."

Galon said, "So to sum up, we little more than we did to start, and Martinmas fast approaches. That's not very helpful."

"I've done what I could," Miles said.

"You'll need to do more than that if you wish to see your wife and family again," Galon told him.

Miles visibly struggled to control his anger. "I understand you intend to marry my wife should I not survive this."

"Just being practical," Galon said. "Somebody has to do it, might as well be me. She could do a lot worse, you know, especially if the king puts her up for auction. Who knows what kind of brute she'd end up with?"

"As opposed to the brute she'll get if she marries you?" Miles said.

Galon was unfazed by the insult. Miles added, "Promise me one thing."

"I'm not in the habit of making promises to Englishmen," Galon said.

Miles waited.

Galon growled, "Go on."

"If something happens to me, promise that you won't kill my children."

Galon thought it over. At last he sighed. "Fine, I won't kill your children. Blanche would be vexed with me if I did that, anyway. Not the ideal way to start a marriage. Your children won't inherit your lands, though. Fairleigh will be held in dowry for my daughter Beatrice; and the rest will go to my son Pons. Blanche will be free to make whatever arrangement she likes for your children, but I won't kill them."

It was the best Miles could hope for. "Thank you, my lord."

"Now get busy," Galon said, "Send any news you get to Stigand. He'll be at Ravenswell. Use your eldest boy—Garth, isn't it?—as a conduit."

Miles said, "And if there is no plot? What happens to me then? A pardon?"

Galon laughed heartily. "Not likely. No, in that case I go back to Normandy with your wife, and you get to live out your miserable life as an outlaw. There will be a plot for you then—a plot of earth."

"Inspiring words, my lord, as always. I'll take my leave then."

Miles turned and, like that, he was gone, seemingly vanished into the trees.

"Think he'll come through, my lord?" Stigand asked Galon.

Despite his bluster, Galon felt this Martinmas plot bearing down on him like an oncoming storm, and he feared he would be swept away by it. "No," Galon said, "but he's all we've got."

CHAPTER 35

October 28

𝕿HE TWO-WHEELED cart trundled out the gate of Brightwood's manor house. The cart was piled with hay, covered with a protective tarp. The horse pulling it was led by the young groom Mody. The glowering beadle Simon walked alongside him for protection, carrying a carved hawthorn club. They were watched from the gate by Wada and Hersent, who had come to Brightwood to help Lady Blanche settle in.

The cart was no sooner across the bridge than it was stopped by two of the men the sheriff had left to guard the manor and see to it that Blanche did not escape.

The guards were beefy Flemings. "Does Flanders produce anything but mercenaries?" Hersent whispered to her husband.

"Shhh," said Wada.

"What have you there?" the first guard asked Mody.

Mody peered over his shoulder and scratched his cheek thoughtfully. " 'Pears to be hay."

The guard did not find this funny. "And where do you go with this hay?" he said.

"It's under contract to St. Mary's Lodge," Mody said. "You know, where the earl of Trent is staying?"

"Hmmph," said the guard.

He walked round to the back of the cart. He looked the cart over, then thrust his spear into the hay.

"Stop that!" cried Mody.

"Just making sure hay is all that's here," said the guard.

Hersent started forward, but Wada put a hand on her arm.

The guard thrust his spear into the hay again. Some of the hay spilled from the back of the cart. Again. Yet again.

Simon the beadle stepped between the guard and the cart. "That's enough, Frenchy. Are you trying to ruin the hay? Because I don't think Earl Galon would like that. Or are you just playing with your little pig sticker?"

"Watch your mouth," the guard said.

Simon tapped the club in the palm of his hand. "Make me."

"Enough! Enough!" Wada cried, hurrying toward the group. "We want no trouble here. Not over a cart load of hay."

The second guard did not want trouble, either, especially if Galon of Trent was likely to get involved. He pulled the first guard back. "Let them go," he said. He motioned to Mody with his free hand. "Proceed."

Mody touched the horse's rump with his goad, and the animal moved forward. Simon glared at the first guard and fell in behind Mody.

The cart left the manor house and rumbled through the fields. "You all right, my lady?" said Mody over his shoulder.

No answer.

"My lady?"

Still no answer.

Mody and Simon shared a glance.

"Hurry," Simon said.

They entered the forest. They turned off the path and down a pre-selected side track—the woods were busy at this time of year, and they didn't want to be seen. Satisfied that no one was around, Mody and Simon rushed to the cart's rear. "My lady?" Mody called, while Simon looked underneath the cart for blood dripping through the boards.

There was a muffled sputtering, then the hay twitched from inside. Simon and Mody scooped handfuls of it aside. More was pushed away from the inside, and soon the outline of a woman was revealed.

Blanche emerged, spitting pieces of hay from her mouth, her clothing and headdress stubbled with it. She bore a wound across the back of her left shoulder; her cloak and kirtle were torn. Blood tricked from the wound down her back.

Mody examined the wound. "You're lucky, my lady. Another inch or so and . . ."

"I know," Blanche said. Mody and Simon helped her down from the cart.

"Does it hurt, my lady?" Simon said.

"No," she said, though the look on her face said the opposite.

"Better let me tend to it," Mody told her.

"No," she said. "I must get to my husband. I'll have Father Albinus look at the wound when I get there. I never thought I would have to wait so long to get away from the manor. I only hope I'm in time. Do you have my horse?"

"Aye," said Mody. He whistled toward the trees. After a moment, another groom led forth a black mare. The mare was not one of Blanche's regular mounts, and it had been brought from the manor house earlier that morning so as not to attract attention.

Mody helped Blanche into the saddle. "Thank you, gentlemen," she said. "Now put that hay back in the cart and get it to the lodge. Get rid of any with blood on it."

"Aye, my lady," Mody said. "Are you sure you don't want me to—?"

"I'll be fine," Blanche told him, and she rode way.

CHAPTER 36

October 29 – Feast of St. Narcissus of Jerusalem
13 Days Until Martinmas

MILES AND HIS men headed back to camp after the meeting with Galon.

Wighelm waved his bow angrily. "You should have let us kill that bastard, Miles. I had an arrow aimed right at him."

"We could've had him and that traitor Stigand, too," said Odda.

This was not the first time they'd had this conversation. "It never would have worked," Miles told them patiently, as he had before. "They had men on hand in case we tried anything. Just like we did. All we would have accomplished was getting a lot of people killed."

"Why did Galon want to talk with you?" Oswald said.

Miles couldn't tell them the truth, that he was supposedly working for Galon. They'd feel themselves betrayed. "He wants to see if there's any way I can return to my old life."

"Galon?" said Scarlet. "Why would he do that?"

"He's the one preferred charges against you," Frithric said.

"Those charges were false," Miles said. "Now he thinks Onfroi is plotting against him, and he's decided he needs me on his side."

"You?" Oswald said. "On Galon's side? That's rich."

"Damned Frenchies don't know what they're doing from one day to the next," Scarlet said.

The group came to a stream. A log had been thrown across it for crossing. "Poor man's bridge," cracked Scarlet.

Albinus sighed. "Aye. Where are the Romans when you need them?"

Young Hugh Myddewinter said, "Did the Romans build bridges?"

Albinus sputtered. "Did they . . . Now you listen, boy, those Romans could build anything. Why, they built a wall clear across Scotland. And their roads? We're still using them."

Stubbornly, Hugh said, "If the Romans were so great, why'd they leave England?"

"Didn't like the weather," Scarlet said.

"Or the cooking," said Frithric.

"If they'd had some of Miles's pottage, they'd have left a hundred years sooner," Albinus jested.

"Hey," laughed Miles.

"Where *is* Rome?" Hugh asked.

"Italy," Albinus told him.

"Where's that?"

"Boy, you ask too many questions."

Wighelm and Oswald ran nimbly across the log. Then it was Miles's turn. "I'm getting too old for this kind of thing," he said.

"You're not the only one," Albinus groused. "I should be sitting in front of a roaring fire right now, warming my feet and nursing a cup of good ale."

Miles started across the log, Father Albinus behind him. It really wasn't much of a drop if someone fell off the log. Still, Miles thought, this had been a lot more fun when he was—

"Miles!" shouted Albinus.

Albinus grabbed Miles from behind and twisted him around. This made both men lose their balance, and they fell into the icy stream. Miles heard yelling from his men.

Miles hit the stream bed hard, rocks banging into his back and head, cold water flooding his clothes. Albinus lay atop him, moaning.

Miles pushed his head out of the frigid water. "What the—?" He struggled to sit up and to get Albinus's head out of the water because Albinus was face down and he seemed to be hurt. Then Miles saw the arrow in Albinus's back.

Footsteps and shouting as men slid down the bank to the stream bed. "What happened?" Miles said, trying to hold Albinus out of the swift-flowing water.

"I don't know," Frithric said as he splashed toward them. "I saw Father Albinus grab you, then he was hit by an arrow."

"Who shot the arrow?"

"No idea. Whoever it was ran off. Wiggy and Oswald went after him."

Frithric, Hugh, and Legulf lifted Albinus off Miles. "Careful, there," Frithric said.

Gently, with Miles's assistance, the men carried Father Albinus out of the water. With help from Odda and Scarlet, they lifted him up the steep stream bank back to the path, where the log was. They laid him on his side and caught their breaths, Miles shivering as the chill breeze hit his wet body.

The arrow was embedded deep in Albinus's back; it must have been shot from fairly close range. Miles snapped the arrow at its base, causing Albinus to shudder, and he held the priest in his arms. Albinus's once ruddy face was already going grey.

"Who did it?" Miles asked him gently. "Did you see?"

Albinus gripped Miles's hand. He opened his mouth to speak but no sound came forth.

The grip weakened. The light in Albinus's eyes faded.

He let out a long sigh and lay back.

Miles made the sign of the Cross over Albinus and closed the priest's eyes. There was suddenly a great void in Miles's life, in the life of the outlaws, in the life of the manor. It was hard to picture Redhill without bluff, hearty Father Albinus.

He was the glue who had held the manor together, the one constant in all their lives, always there when he was needed.

Frithric crossed himself, as well, as did the others. "He was a good priest," Frithric said. "And a better friend."

"A good friend to us all," added Hugh Myddewinter, whose eyes were moist.

"He was," Miles said. "He gave up his life for mine."

The others looked at him for explanation. He said, "Whoever put that arrow in him was trying to kill me."

Just then, Wighelm and Oswald came back. Miles rose. "Any luck?" he asked them.

They shook their heads. "Fucker's fast," Wighelm said. "There's no trackin' him with all them dead leaves."

"Which way were the tracks headed when you lost them?" Wighelm waved his arm. "West."

"Toward our camp?"

Wighelm nodded. "General direction."

Miles shared a glance with Frithric. "Could he be one of ours?" Miles said.

"Christ's blood, that's all we need," Frithric said.

The men cut some sturdy branches and, using Albinus's cloak, they rigged a litter and carried the priest's body back to camp. As they came in, everyone stopped what they were doing. Some of the men were out hunting or scouting, but there were about forty in camp. Ediva and a stocky, broad-hipped young woman had been stirring bread crumbs and freshly picked berries into the pottage. Diote, wife of Oswald's brother Oshere, was helping to dress a fresh-killed deer. She wiped her bloody hands on her apron and joined the others around the priest's body, crossing themselves and murmuring prayers. Ioco hung at the back of the group, expressionless. Ioco hadn't gone with the group that met Galon. He'd said he was incapacitated by the flux.

"What happened?" one-handed Bondo asked Miles.

"He was shot from ambush with an arrow," Miles said. "Whoever did it was aiming at me."

"You?" said Bondo. "Why? For the reward?"

"I expect," Miles said. Ediva brought blankets. She removed Miles's wet cloak and wrapped the blankets around him.

Shivering and holding the blankets close, Miles spoke to the assemblage at large. "We'll bury Father Albinus as soon as it gets dark. I'd like to take him back to St. Michael's Church in Redhill. That's where he was baptized, and that's where he'd want to be buried, but we can't do it."

Scarlet spoke up. "How 'bout that glade near here, where he used to pray? It's peaceful there, he'd like that."

"Good idea," Miles said.

"I'll make a cross," Hugh Myddewinter said.

"I'll start a grave," Ioco said in his heavy voice.

"I'll join you," Wighelm said, and he and Ioco started off.

Just then, a cautionary voice said, "Miles."

Miles turned as Blanche rode into camp on a lathered black horse. Men rushed to take the horse's reins. As Blanche dismounted, Miles saw her torn cloak and bleeding shoulder. "You're hurt."

"Albinus can take care of it later," she said. "I came to warn you. The sheriff has hired a killer to—"

She stopped when she saw Albinus's body. "Sweet God. What's happened?"

Suddenly, everything made sense. Miles said, "It appears your killer has already struck. Only he got the wrong man."

Blanche crossed herself and stood over the body in disbelief. "Father Albinus. Anyone but him." Tears welled in her eyes. "Did you get the man who did it?"

Miles shook his head ruefully.

Ediva's broad-hipped companion tapped Ediva on the arm. " 'Oo's the Frenchy, then?" she whispered.

In the sudden silence, everyone heard her, including Blanche.

Ediva cleared her throat. "The, uh, 'Frenchy' is Lady Blanche, Miles's wife."

"Oops." The woman grimaced. "Reckon I put my foot in it, didn't I?"

Ediva gave her a look that said "yes."

Blanche saw Ediva. "Ediva, there you are. Where have you been? And what happened to your head?"

"Got a bit of a knock on it, my lady. I'll tell you about it later."

Blanche turned to Ediva's companion. "And you are?"

"Gytha. I mean, Gytha, my lady." The woman made an awkward attempt at a curtsy.

Blanche wiped tears from her eyes. "How do you come to be in this group, Gytha?"

Gytha toed the ground, looking down. "I was a . . . a whore, my lady. In Badford, that is. Got tired of getting beat up, so I run away. Reckoned bein' an outlaw couldn't be much worse'n what I had."

"She's fit in well, my lady," Ediva said. "She's a good cook."

"It seems you've made friends with my maid, Ediva," Blanche said.

"Yes, ma'am, my lady. She's, like, helped me out, sort of. Showed me around."

"Good," Blanche said.

"Sorry for calling you a Frenchy, my lady," Gytha said.

"Apology accepted." Blanche said. Coolly, she added, "I'm not French, I'm Norman."

Ediva said, "Let me take see to that wound, my lady."

"In a bit," Blanche said. "I need to speak with Miles."

Blanche took Miles's elbow and led him a ways off, where they couldn't be heard. "So Onfroi's hired a killer to do away with me?" Miles asked her.

"I believe so, yes."

"This gets worse and worse," Miles said. "We've lost one of our best friends—more than that, we've lost the heart of Redhill Manor. And for what? A plot that doesn't exist."

Blanche said nothing. What could she say? He was right.

Miles went on. "None of this is worth it, Blanche. Look at these men. There's over fifty here now altogether. They're here because they think I'm some kind of savior, most of them. They think I can right the wrongs the system has imposed on them and improve their lives, when in reality I can do none of those things. They think I'm Brock the Badger, dashing outlaw of the greenwood, when the truth is I'll probably get them all killed."

"And the killer the sheriff hired?" Blanche said. "Do you think he'll be back?"

Miles looked her in the eye. "I think he's still here."

Her eyes widened. "He's one of you?"

"I believe so. Before Wiggy and Oswald lost his tracks, they were headed in the direction of this camp."

Blanche stood straighter. "Did you recognize the arrow that killed Albinus?"

Miles nodded. "It belonged to Oshere, but like as not, the killer stole it to do the job. He's a professional, remember, he wouldn't use his own."

"And now?" she said.

"If he's here, he'll try again."

CHAPTER 37

"WHICH IS WHY," Miles continued, taking Blanche's hand, "you must leave."

She wrenched her hand away. "I'm not leaving. I just got here."

"It's not safe," Miles told her. "I won't have you—"

"You 'won't have?' " Blanche's almond eyes flashed. "Just because we're married doesn't give you the right to tell me what to do."

In point of fact, it did exactly that, according to both Church and civil law, but Miles knew better than to say so. He stepped back and took a deep breath. "I'm asking you— begging you—to leave the camp. For your own protection." He paused. "I couldn't bear to lose you, Blanche. If the killer can't get me, he may well take you, instead."

"Why would he do that? Killing a woman would make the people hate the sheriff even more than they do now."

"Onfroi doesn't care about that," Miles said. "He wants to hurt me, and he doesn't care how he does it. Killing you would do that. This has gotten personal for him. It's not about the law anymore. And if something happens to you, it will get personal for me, as well."

"Meaning?"

"I'll kill Onfroi, or die trying."

He went on. "I won't lie to you, Blanche, there's a fair chance I won't live through this. I can't have something happen to you, as well. What would become of the children if we were both dead? Galon has promised me that he won't kill them, but I doubt Onfroi would be of the same mind. Garth would take them in, of course, but would they live long enough to reach Ravenswell? And even if they did, what's to stop Onfroi from coming after them there? He's the king's representative; he can do as he pleases in this shire."

Blanche knew Miles was right. Onfroi wouldn't hesitate to kill the children, or to throw them in some prison where they would languish for the rest of their lives. "I still can't go back," she said at last. "I escaped detention. I'll be wanted now, like you."

"Tell Onfroi you were playing a joke on him. Tell him you went back to Redhill, you'll think of something. Beg his forgiveness. You'll be safer at Brightwood than you would be here. Onfroi can't do anything to you—not yet, anyway. Not with Galon around. Galon likes you, as much as he can be said to like anyone. He'll protect you to spite Onfroi, if nothing else. Also," he hesitated, "also, there's too much disease in camp. Men are dying at a rate I don't like to think about, and it's only going to get worse as winter comes on. I don't want you exposed to it."

Blanche shook her head in frustration. "It's hard to picture myself on the same side as Galon."

Miles nodded. "We live in strange times. If you want, go to St. Mary's Lodge and seek Galon's protection there."

"I prefer Galon at a distance, thank you—the Antipodes, for instance, though I don't suppose I could persuade him to go there." She sighed. "Very well, I'll return to Brightwood. I'll stay the night here and be on my way in the morning."

Miles took her hands. "I'm sorry, Blanche, but it's best this way."

"I know," she conceded. Mischievously, she added, "You just don't want me staying here and playing with your pottage."

"There's that, too," Miles acknowledged. "You might add something French to it, like wine."

Her eyes gleamed. "That might actually make it edible." She grew serious again. "If you get yourself killed out here, I'll never forgive you."

Miles bowed his head. "Understood, my lady."

They returned to the bustling camp. Ediva waited there, and Blanche approached her. Ediva took in Blanche's blood-stained cloak. "Now may I—?"

"Let me look at your head first," Blanche told her. She unwrapped Ediva's bandage. "How did this happen?"

"I was in Badford—"

"Badford! Why in the name of all that's holy were you in Badford?"

"I was trying to get some evidence about that plot, my lady."

Blanche turned on Miles. "You let her go to Badford?"

Miles spread his hands. "I had no idea she was there. I thought she'd gone back to Redhill."

Ediva went on. "I went on my own, my lady. Some men tried to kidnap me there and gave me this knock on the head. Miles's son Aelred saved me."

Blanche examined Ediva's bandage. No blood or pus had seeped through. She sniffed the bandage, was satisfied. "Do you clean the wound every day?"

"I do, my lady."

"Does it still hurt?"

"It does, but not so much as before," Ediva said.

"Are you well enough to return to Brightwood with me?"

Ediva hesitated, and Blanche sensed—without surprise—that Ediva enjoyed the outlaw life. "I suppose so, my lady."

"Good," Blanche said. She added, "That was a brave thing you did, going to Badford."

"Thank you, my lady."

"Brave, but foolhardy."

Ediva looked her in the eye. "You'd have done the same in my place."

Blanche hemmed, saw Miles grinning. "That's different," she said at last.

Ediva led Blanche into Albinus's hut to tend her shoulder. While that was going on, Diote and Gytha washed Father Albinus's body and wrapped it in a shroud. Albinus was buried after dark, by torch light, in a small glade about a half-mile from the camp. Blanche, whose confessor Albinus had been, led the prayers over his grave, and Hugh Middewynter hammered the cross he'd made at the grave's head. As Hugh finished and stepped back, the moon came out, and a shaft of silver light shone onto the grave.

"It's an omen," breathed Frithric.

Bondo murmured, "Speakin' to us from Heaven, he is."

Some men crossed themselves; some, like Hugh, cried; others, like Miles, watched with hooded eyes and set jaws. Blanche and Ediva cried, especially Ediva, and Blanche put a comforting arm around the girl's shoulder. Albinus had been there for Ediva's birth; he had baptized her. There had never been a time in her life when he wasn't around. Until now.

After a while, they went back to camp, where they toasted Albinus's memory with wine stolen from a Flemish merchant. That night, Blanche slept in Miles's hut. They wrapped their arms around each other, but that was the extent of their physicality. Miles didn't want to do anything that would open the stitches Ediva had taken in Blanche's shoulder.

The next morning was frosty with a thin sun and hard ground. A couple of 'liberated' pigs wandered the camp grounds and nearby woods, snorting and snuffling.

Gytha had found a nearly flat stone, which she used for baking bread by the fire, and breakfast consisted of fresh, thick flatbread covered with pottage. When the pottage was done, they ate the soaked bread, sopping up the remains and licking their fingers clean. Then Blanche's and Ediva's horses were saddled and made ready for the journey to Brightwood. They were taking Miles's sad-faced sumpter horse, Maurice, back with them. "I think he'll appreciate a warm barn for the winter," Blanche said, patting the old horse's neck.

"I'd appreciate one myself," Miles said. He felt tired. He felt tired all the time, anymore.

Before they left, Ediva went to Gytha. "You're in charge of the pottage when Miles is away from camp," she told the girl. "That's a big responsibility. Miles loves his pottage almost as much as he loves his children." She glanced back at Miles, who was watching her with his brows raised in amusement.

"I'll do my best," Gytha promised.

Miles hugged Blanche and held her in a lingering embrace, kissing her. As Blanche and Ediva prepared to mount, Bondo, who had been on scouting detail, jogged into camp. "Travelers," he told Miles, "comin' from the east." That was the direction in which Blanche and Ediva would be heading, so their departure would have to wait until it could be determined that there was no danger to them.

"How many?" Miles said.

"Half-dozen, maybe. All men."

"Armed?"

"Daggers and the like."

"Could it be the sheriff's spies?" Blanche said.

"Too many for that," Miles said.

"Could be men comin' to join us," Bondo ventured.

"Either way, we can't have you seen out here," Miles told Blanche. "If you are, people will guess you've been at our camp, and if the sheriff finds out about that . . ." His voice tailed off and he turned. "Frithric, bring a dozen men."

Frithric told off his men and had them get their weapons. Then Miles said, "All right, Bondo, let's go meet these travelers."

CHAPTER 38

October 30 – Feast of St. Aethelnoth the Good
12 Days Until Martinmas

𝕿HE OUTLAW PARTY followed the narrow path. Bondo
and Frithric had gone ahead. After a bit, they hurried back.
"Half a mile," Bondo told Miles.

Miles picked a spot where the path went down a short,
steep slope, then took a sharp bend to the right. He stationed
his men in the trees and brush. He picked out a spot for
himself just past the bend, beside a large oak. He leaned
against the tree nonchalantly, the way Brock the Badger of
the songs would do.

In the distance, footsteps crunched dead leaves hardened
by frost. Miles heard voices. Someone laughed.

The party scrabbled down the hill and rounded the bend.
They saw Miles and stopped. In their lead was an old man
with a blue cap and a deeply furrowed face.

Miles stepped into the path, beaming. "As I live and
breathe, it's Grugan the pedlar."

The old man inclined his head. "You have a good
memory, my lord."

Grugan was accompanied by four younger men, two of
whom looked familiar. These younger men were fit and alert;
they looked more like guards than anything else. One wore a
linen coif. Miles said, "And this is your nephew . . ."

"Brand, my lord," said the man with the coif.

"Brand, that's right," said Miles, snapping his fingers. To a well-built blond, he said, "And you're Hugh, aren't you?"

"I am, my lord," said Hugh. He grinned because Miles had remembered his name and not Brand's.

"And these other two are your friends?" Miles asked Grugan.

"After a fashion," said the old man.

Miles's men revealed themselves, moving in from all sides with bows and other weapons. "Relax, lads," Miles told them. "These fellows are English. We won't be robbing them."

Bondo, Frithric, and the rest of the men lowered their weapons.

To Grugan, Miles said, "Where are your packs, your horses?"

Grugan rubbed a hand across his mouth. Miles wondered how old he was; his crinkled skin was like vellum. Some enterprising monk could make pages for a book out of it. "Truth is, my lord, we didn't come this way for trading," Grugan said.

Miles lifted his brows in question.

Grugan continued, "We come to see you."

"Me?"

"Aye. We bring you a message. Well, more of an offer, really."

"A message from who?"

"I'm not allowed to say, my lord. Not just yet."

Miles looked at his men, who seemed as bewildered as he was. "Very well, what is this message?"

Grugan cleared his throat. "How would you like to lead an army?"

CHAPTER 39

MILES FROWNED. "WHAT kind of army?"

"An army of Englishmen," Grugan said told him. "Loyal and true."

Miles might have laughed at that, but Grugan looked dead serious. "And what is this army to do?" Miles said.

"Drive out the French, of course."

There was muttering among Miles's men, along with a few chuckles. Brand, Hugh, and Grugan's other two companions were silent, so presumably they knew about this plan already.

Miles motioned Grugan to walk away from the others with him, where they could not be heard. "Is this a joke?" Miles asked Grugan. "Because if it is, it's not—"

"It's no joke," said the old man.

"Who's behind it? Not you."

Grugan shook his head. "Told you, I'm not allowed to say yet."

Miles took a turn back and forth. "Why me?"

Grugan shrugged. "It's obvious, isn't it? You're famous, and you're English—the last English lord."

"Stigand is a lord, and he's English."

Grugan made a deprecating gesture. "Stigand's gone over to the French. He's not English anymore."

Miles heard running feet, and Ediva burst into view. The wrapping around her head had come loose. The little fool must have followed them here, when she should be resting. Why hadn't Blanche stopped her? Ediva looked excited. "Miles—"

"Not now," he said.

"But—"

"Not now. Wait over there with Bondo and the others."

She looked put out. "There's something I have to—"

He stepped forward and led her away by the shoulders. "Later." She started back after him, but Frithric and Oswald held her, while some of the men laughed.

Miles turned back to Grugan, who waited patiently, sitting on a fallen tree branch. "This army," Miles said, "how is it to be equipped and supplied?"

"You'll have to do most of that, I'm afraid."

"Great." Miles couldn't believe he was wasting time talking to this fool. "And what will the French be doing while I'm raising an army? Sitting by idly and watching?"

"The French will have their hands full with other matters. That's all I'm allowed to tell you now."

"You realize this scheme sounds insane," Miles said.

"It's very real, I assure you."

An idea began to form in Miles's mind. "You're not really a pedlar, are you?"

"Once," Grugan said. "No longer." He looked calm, not insane at all; but that was the way with a lot of madmen.

Miles summarized. "So, I'm to raise an army, more or less on my own; equip them, more or less on my own; and lead them to victory against the French. More or less on my own."

"Not on your own," Grugan said. "You'll have help."

"Who?"

"The Scots."

The idea that had been forming in Miles's mind took better shape. "Who's to be king when the French are gone?" he asked Grugan.

"The throne of England will be offered to Alexander of Scotland. He has English royal blood, as you know. Also, his becoming king would eliminate the constant warfare on our northern border."

186

Grugan stood. "As for the French and their knights. You can expect the French to be in disarray, a very great deal of it, if things work out as planned. You raise your banner, and men will flock to it. The country has been waiting for this for fifty-one years."

Aelred had told him there was no plot among the English. How had he missed this? Miles gave that idea in the back of his mind full voice. "Let me guess. This is to begin on Martinmas."

The old man paled. "How did you know that?"

Miles didn't answer. "Not the best time to start a revolt, is it? With winter setting in?"

Grugan recovered from his surprise. "Perhaps, but it will be harder on the French than it is on us. They'll have to raise an army and cross the Narrow Sea, and the Narrow Sea is treacherous in winter. Like as not, they won't be able to start till spring. By which time, England will once again be securely in the hands of the English."

"And the French who are already here? What of them?"

"If things go as planned, there won't be many of them left. Now what do you say?"

Miles turned away. A few leaves drifted to the ground around him, blissfully unconcerned by talk of war and death. This plan might sound insane, but it was what Miles had dreamed about since he was a boy. Leading an army to drive the French from England. And here was that dream come true, handed to him on the proverbial platter. The offer before him was the chance to fulfill his destiny. It was as if God had planned it this way.

What had Galon said? "I believe the plotters will come to you."

And so they had, but not in the way Galon had envisioned. This was not a group of French nobles plotting against the king, as Galon imagined; it was Englishmen plotting to drive out the French.

This was the moment Miles had waited for all his life. His father, Edwulf, would be proud, as would his grandfather, Wulfstan. Miles would revive the glory of his house. Miles could lose his life, he could lose his family, but could he turn this offer down?

He looked at the niello-inlaid ring on his hand, the symbol of his house, then he looked at his waiting men. If they stayed in the forest as outlaws, half of them would be gone by spring—dead of disease or exposure to the elements. This way they had a chance to achieve something positive, to throw off the yoke that bound them.

Miles turned back to Grugan. "I'll do it."

"Good," said Grugan. "Thank you, Lord Miles."

"And my reward?"

Grugan spread his arms expansively. "What do you want?"

What he had always wanted. "To be earl of Trent."

"I think our future king will agree to that, and more. You'll be hearing from us shortly." Grugan strode over to his men, his brisk gait belieing his years. "We're set, lads. Let get moving. Lots to do."

The four men each shook Miles's hand. "Congratulations, my lord," said Brand.

"God be with you, my lord," said Hugh. "I'll be there when you raise your banner."

Then the party started back the way they had come, Grugan at their head.

Miles was left to marvel at what had just happened. His life would never be the same after this.

He went over to where Frithric and Bondo held the struggling Ediva. "Now what is it that's so infernally important?" he asked her.

"That man, the old one?"

"Grugan? What about him?"

"He's the man Aelred was talking to at the Saracen's Head in Badford."

CHAPTER 40

"WHY DIDN'T YOU tell me this before?" Miles said.

"I tried to, but you didn't give me a chance," Ediva told him.

"And why did you leave camp? You're too sick to be running around in the woods."

"I didn't want to miss anything," she said.

"Was it worth it?"

"I reckon," she said with a bit of a shrug. "Though my head does hurt a bit from all the running."

Miles swore to himself. "Let's get you back to camp before we end up having to bury you."

Frithric spoke up. "You want we should go after those fellows and bring them back?"

Miles thought. "No, let them go. It's Aelred I need to speak with, not them."

They returned to camp to find Blanche worried. "There you are," she cried when she saw Ediva. "I turn my back on you for the blink of an eye, and you're gone."

Ediva lowered her eyes. "Sorry, my lady."

"Don't compound the situation by telling lies," Blanche snapped. "You're not sorry at all."

"No, my lady," Ediva said.

"You're entirely too willful."

"Yes, my lady."

"Don't just stand there saying 'Yes, my lady' and 'No, my lady.' Tell me what you learned."

When Ediva was finished, Blanche said, "You're sure this Grugan was the man you saw with Aelred?"

Robert Broomall

"I'm sure, my lady" said Ediva. "I watched the two of them long enough at the tavern. I followed them after that—till I got knocked on the head. And Grugan's nephew, the blond one? I'm pretty sure it was him that blocked my path before I got hit."

Miles said, "Aelred must know about the plot, but he's chosen not to reveal it. Why? What the Devil is he up to?"

"Maybe Grugan is just someone Aelred knows," Blanche said. "Or someone he met in the tavern that night and started drinking with. It doesn't necessarily follow that Aelred is part of the plot."

"I hope you're right," Miles said. "There's still the matter of his nephew Hugh blocking Ediva's path, though. Either way, I need to get in touch with Aelred."

"I'll do it," Ediva said.

"No!" said Miles and Blanche at the same time.

"You're hurt too badly," Blanche added. "You need to stay here and rest."

"I'm fine now, my lady," Ediva protested. "Mostly. Anyway, who else would you send?"

"Anyone but you," Miles said. "It's too dangerous."

"You been telling me that for more than ten years," Ediva said, "and I'm not dead yet."

"God knows, it's not for your lack of trying," Miles said.

Miles let out a long breath. This part was going to be difficult. To Blanche he said, "Galon was right. There really is a plot, and it really is to start on Martinmas. Except it's not the plot Galon thought. It's not a conspiracy of nobles against the king, it's a revolt of the English against the French."

Blanche frowned. "Why did this Grugan fellow want to speak with you about it? Do the plotters want your support?"

"They want me to lead their army."

Blanche stiffened.

Miles went on. "The Scots will help, and the crown is to be offered to the Scottish king."

"You're not going to do it, are you?" Blanche said.

Miles said nothing. Activity in the camp had come to a halt. Everyone was watching, listening.

A warning note entered Blanche's voice. "Miles . . ."

"It's my duty, Blanche. Maybe it's my destiny. Either way, I'd be remiss if I didn't do my part."

"You've always said you didn't want to be a soldier again," she told him. "Now you talk about some crazy scheme for a revolt, with you at the head of it. You'll be fighting Normans, the best soldiers in the world. You'll be killed."

Miles shrugged. "Some things are worth dying for."

"Is it worth destroying your family so that one group of aristocratic leeches can be replaced with another?"

"Except the ones replacing them will be English."

"That doesn't mean they'll be any better," Blanche said. Her face hardened. "I'm against this."

"Why?"

"Because it will bring endless war and suffering to the country, that's why. There's enough of that in Normandy; we don't need it here."

Miles said, "Is it that, or do you not wish to see your countrymen deposed from their stolen lands? Do you not wish us to have our country back?"

That got her back up. "You can't deny we've been a civilizing force here," she said.

"I can deny it quite easily. You Normans, as you choose to call yourselves, are barbarians, no better than the Danes. Before you arrived, art and trade flourished in this land. That's all gone now."

"What about slavery?" she shot back. "That flourished in this land, as well—or it did before we 'barbarians' put an end to it."

"So you've done *one* good thing," Miles said. "The North of England will need another hundred years to recover from your destruction of it, maybe more."

"So we've done one *bad* thing. The Church thrives now, and is bound to the Pope once more."

"Thrives? You call being filled with blood-sucking French clerics thriving? Endless tithes upon our people? When the clerics were English, we've didn't have all this corruption."

Their voices had risen. Ediva tried to stop them, but Blanche went on. "I'm serious, Miles. I don't want you taking up arms against my people. You're so blinded by pride and ambition that you don't see how foolish this is. You'll end up dead."

"Is that what you're afraid of? Or are you afraid we'll win? Because I will take up arms against the French."

"And what about me? What about the children?"

"You're my wife, no harm will come to you or our children."

"We'll be safe from your English friends?"

"I am to be earl of Trent when this is done. No one will act against you."

"And what if you lose?" she said.

"I don't intend to lose."

Blanche took the reins of her horse and got ready to mount. Miles moved to assist her. "I'll do it myself," she told him.

She swung onto the horse. "Ediva, are you coming?"

Ediva hesitated. "With your permission, my lady, I'd like to go to Ravenswell first, to tell Garth what we've learned and to see what Aelred knows about this, like Miles wants. Then I'll come straight back to Brightwood."

Blanche gave her a sour look.

To Blanche, Miles said, "I'll get word to you as soon as I can."

"Don't bother," Blanche told him.

She wheeled the black horse and rode off.

CHAPTER 41

MILES WATCHED BLANCHE disappear into the forest. The rhythmic thumping of her horse's hooves could be heard long after she was out of sight.

Miles turned away.

He wasn't searching out some plot for Galon now. He *was* the plot, or a large part of it, anyway.

He didn't know how he felt about the English crown being offered to the Scots, but in a way it made sense. King Alexander shared the royal blood of Wessex. There was no English noble who could say that, no English noble to offer the crown to, in fact; because, save for Miles and Stigand, there were no longer any English nobles. They were all dead, or fled abroad, or subsumed into the peasantry. Only by sheer luck had Miles risen as far as he had, and now it looked as though the reason for that luck—Blanche—might be leaving him.

Where did his duty lie? To his wife and family, or to his country? He loved Blanche more than he had ever imagined he could love anyone, but if there was a chance to take England back from the French, that chance had to be taken. Miles was son of a thegn, descended from nobles, with a distant connection to the royal house of Mercia, or so he'd been told. He had a responsibility that outweighed family. He had been called, and he meant to answer that call.

Blanche was right—there would be war, blood, destruction. But it would be worth it if they succeeded. And they would succeed.

"Miles?" It was Ediva, standing by his side. "Are you all right?"

"What?" he said, as if snapping out of a dream. "Yes. I'm fine."

"They're waiting for you to say something."

He looked round the camp. Every face was turned toward him.

"Yes," he said. "All right." He cleared his throat and raised his voice. "Everyone! Gather round."

The men obediently clustered round. Miles mounted the large tree stump that stood in the center of the camp—there was a time he would have leaped up on it. He was older now, tired, and he needed to regain the toughness of body and mind he'd had as a young soldier in Wales. Could he do it? Had he grown too soft for campaigning in all weathers? Did he still have the drive to lead men in battle even when the battle seemed hopeless?

He would soon find out.

He looked at his men, at Frithric and Bondo and Odda. At Hugh Middewynter and Wighelm, Ioco and all the rest. They were ragged and lice ridden, all of them, and so was he, and no amount of wood smoke could hide their smell. With the coming of cold weather, some had wrapped deerskin leggings over their hose, or coverings of sheepskin. Some had made sleeveless jacks out of sheepskins, and they wore these over their shirts and beneath their cloaks. On their heads were knit caps or sheepskin coifs. Some wore two cloaks, one over the other, made from the thickest wool they would find. They had red noses and cheeks, runny noses they wiped on their arms. Sores. Coughs.

Miles began. "All right, lads . . ."

"And lasses," yelled Oshere's wife, Diote.

"That's right," added Gytha to laughter.

Miles grinned and motioned for quiet. "I expect you heard me and my wife. I expect you heard what we were arguing about."

There was silence. They had.

Miles went on. "There's going to be a revolt against the French."

A low murmur.

"And I'm to command an army."

The murmur grew louder. A few cheers.

"I would like you men—and women," he made exaggerated gestures toward Gytha and Diote, to some laughter, "to join me in this undertaking, but I won't think badly of you if you don't. This won't be a traditional army, and it won't be a traditional war. We're going to fight the French in the forests, where their knights do them little good. It's going to be hit and run, and take what we can."

"Like bein' an outlaw," shouted Scarlet, "only more fun."

"That's right, Scarlet, like being an outlaw, though I don't know how much fun it will be. Supposedly the French are going to have other troubles, but we can't count on that. Supposedly we'll have help from the Scots, but we can't count on that, either. We'll wear the French down. If they retreat into their castles, we'll starve them. We'll raze their crops. If they burn our villages, we'll burn their manor houses. And if they hide in those manor houses, we'll burn them there. It won't be pretty, but war isn't pretty."

The men looked at each other. There was low talking.

Miles went on. "Don't worry if you've never done any soldiering, because this isn't going to be like any soldiering we've known, and we'll learn how to do it as we go along. One thing I promise you, though—we'll win. No matter how long it takes, we'll win. And those of you who survive will be outlaws no longer. You'll be heroes who'll see this land returned to its rightful owners. Now, are you with me?"

"Aye!" they shouted, waving fists in the air. "Aye!" shouted Ediva and Bondo and Frithric. "Aye!" shouted Hugh and Scarlet and Gytha. "Aye!" shouted the rest.

Miles went on. "We'll need to recruit men, that will be our next, and most important, task. There's little time to waste—we raise the banner of revolt on Martinmas."

"What is our banner to be?" asked Scarlet.

Miles hadn't thought about that. "Is there anyone here who can sew a banner?"

Gytha raised her hand. "I can."

Miles took off his niello-inlaid ring with the figure of a lion on the bezel. He tossed the ring to Gytha, who caught it deftly. "Use this as a guide."

Then he raised a fist. "Death to the French!" he shouted.

"Death to the French!" they roared back.

CHAPTER 42

As THE CHEERING died, Ediva turned to Miles. "So, I'll be off to Ravenswell, then."

Miles was skeptical. "Are you sure you're well enough to travel?"

She shrugged. "Who else are you going to send?"

She was right. If Father Albinus were still alive, he could have gone, but there was no one else. Miles let out his breath. "Very well, but no going off on side adventures. Tell Garth what's happened. Find out what Aelred knows about it, and get back to me. After that, you'll go straight to Brightwood and stay there."

"I'll leave now," Ediva said.

"Will you need an escort?"

"No, I prefer being on my own."

"That's what worries me," Miles said.

"I do better that way," Ediva said.

"Last time, you got your head broken," Miles pointed out.

Ediva had Gytha clean her wound with vinegar and water, then rebandage it. She went to her horse and mounted.

"Be careful," Miles told her.

She laughed. "I'm always careful." She waved and rode off.

Miles turned to the rest of the group. "All right, we need to get organized." He walked around, tapping men on the shoulder, "Frithric, you're second in command. You, Bondo, Scarlet, and . . . Wighelm will be vintenars to start. There's not enough of us for a centenar yet. Divide the men equally amongst yourselves. Add new ones as they come in. When you've done with that, send men to the manors, to our contacts there. Try and get recruits. If men can't leave their work now, tell them to be ready to join us on Martinmas. Have them pass the word on to other manors—but only to men they trust. All right, get—"

From the distance came a plaintive lowing.

Men looked at each other.

More lowing, the sound of a large animal lumbering through the trees and fallen leaves. "Come on," a voice coaxed.

Miles said, "Now what?"

More lowing and coaxing.

Into the camp plodded an ox, led on a rope tied to one of its horns by Oshere and prodded from the opposite side by Oshere's brother, Oswald. "Look what we found!" Oshere cried.

There were cheers and slaps on the back as the brothers led the animal into the center of the glade. The ox looked around, curious, probably glad not to be pulling a plough.

"Where did you get that?" Miles asked.

"Haverham," Oshere, the younger brother, said. "From Lord Gautier's home farm."

There was a loud cheer at that. No one liked Gautier.

Bondo pointed out the obvious. "We've no place to keep an ox here. Plus, there's no grain to feed it."

"Might be time for a feast then," Oshere said.

More cheers.

Gytha cried, "I claim the tail, to use in the pottage. If it's all right with you, Miles."

Miles nodded his assent.

Oswald didn't join in the good mood. "Why is everybody gathered in one spot like this?"

Frithric told him briefly what had happened.

Oswald glanced at his brother and whistled. "Looks like we're just in time, then." He patted the ox's head. "Sorry, old friend."

Miles studied the animal. "Haverham, you say?"

"Aye," said Oshere. "Went there special, to torment old Gautier."

Oswald added, "Amazin', ain't it, the things you find sometimes."

Miles said, "It's not branded."

The brothers looked the ox over. "You're right," Oshere said. "Maybe Gautier don't brand his animals."

"Maybe," Miles said. A lot of lords didn't.

While the men led the ox off to be butchered, Gytha studied the figure on the ring Miles had given her to copy. "You sure this is a lion?"

Miles shrugged. "That's what I was told."

"If you say so," she said. "What color d'ye want the banner to be?"

"Well . . ." Miles hadn't thought about that. He had no idea what the colors of his house were. "White for the figure, I suppose, on . . . what colors do we have?"

"There's bolts of red and green. Red's prettier, but the green's better quality."

"Use the green then." He waved a hand, indicating the trees. "It can represent the forest."

Gytha nodded and slipped the ring into her purse. She started off to claim her ox tail.

Miles watched the activity in the ever-growing camp. He still couldn't believe this was happening. After all these years, his dream was coming true.

He felt like he had somehow grown, become bigger. Taller and wider and stronger. Like the world was his. He knew there needed to be preparation, but he was eager to get on with the task, eager for battle. He would march on the French right now if he could. This would be the undertaking of a lifetime. It would, in fact, define his life. It was what he would be remembered for, successful or not, though he had no intention of being unsuccessful.

There were two shadows over the enterprise. One was Blanche, and the way she had departed. The second was Onfroi's hired killer. Who was it, and when would he strike again?

Unless the killer deserted the camp to warn Onfroi about the plot, Miles thought. But why desert when he could kill Miles and end the plot right here? And probably earn himself additional money by doing so.

No, he would strike again. And soon.

CHAPTER 43

BLANCHE RODE BACK to Brightwood. The sky was the color of hammered copper. The air was crisp, on the verge of being cold, the path hard beneath the black horse's hooves.

Miles could be such a fool at times. He was stubborn, and he had an unlimited belief in himself and his abilities that was about to get him, and a lot of other people, killed.

Blanche had always known that Miles dreamed of driving the Normans from England. But she'd thought it was just that—a dream. She'd never imagined he would act on it. This scheme for revolt was insane. Either Miles would be defeated outright, and his supporters would be executed; or he would plunge the country into a period of vicious warfare with unknown consequences.

She should take the children and leave while there was still time, but there was nowhere for them to go. Anyway, Onfroi wouldn't let her leave. Galon would, but the price to pay for that was too high.

The whitewashed keep of Brightwood Castle came into view. Seeing it always brought back bad memories for Blanche, memories of being kept prisoner there when Baron Aimerie attempted to marry her by force.

She turned down the rutted lane that led to the village. Men, women, and children waved to her, called greetings. They knew she had escaped confinement, but pretended all was well to avoid any awkwardness.

"Afternoon, my lady."

"Fine day, my lady. Feels like rain comin', though."

Blanche responded in kind, as though she hadn't a care in the world. "It's England, Hannah. There's always rain coming."

As the lane entered the open field before the manor house, two of the sheriff's mounted guards appeared and blocked her path. "Halt," said the first. He was one of the ubiquitous Flemish mercenaries that populated the country and were so hated by its inhabitants. "Lady Blanche?"

"You know who I am," Blanche replied.

"Surprised to see you back, my lady," said the second guard, a Norman by his accent.

Blanche said nothing.

The Norman went on, as though admonishing a recalcitrant child. "You escaped, my lady. You violated your word. Some of us got in a lot of trouble because of that."

"I didn't escape," Blanche said. "I went for a ride. That's not against the law, I believe?"

"Buried in a wagon load of hay?"

"It was the only way I could get out."

"You were gone two days," the Fleming pointed out.

"It was a long ride."

"Sorry, my lady," the Norman said, "but you'll have to come with us." He reached for her horse's bridle.

As though it had appeared from nowhere, Blanche's dagger was in her hand. "Touch my horse, and I'll have your eye," she told the Norman. She turned to the other guard. "That goes for you, as well."

The two guards looked at each other, backed their horses away. "We'll inform the sheriff," the Fleming warned.

"Please do," Blanche told him. She rode past them.

Residents of the manor house had seen what was happening. Belot, the steward, hurried onto the bridge; so did Wada.

"We've been worried about you, my lady," Belot said to Blanche as she drew near.

Wada nodded his chin toward the two guards. "I was wishin' I'd brought my iron bar with me."

Blanche laughed, evincing a lightness of spirit she did not feel. "You still have that thing? Isn't it rusted through by now?"

"I keep it oiled, my lady. Never know when it'll come in handy."

Alerted by the commotion, Hersent hurried though the gate, bow in hand and a quiver of arrows at her hip. She feigned frustration. "I was hoping I'd get to shoot one of those buggers."

Estrild was there, as well. "Are you all right, my lady?" she fussed. "Did they hurt you?"

"I'm fine," Blanche assured her.

"Any word of Ediva?"

"No," Blanche lied. "I've no idea where she's got to."

Estrild tisked. "Rattle-headed child."

A groom took Blanche's horse, and she entered the smoky manor house. She started up the stairs to the tiny solar, Estrild behind her. "Leave me for a bit," Blanche told Estrild. "I wish to be alone."

"Yes, my lady," said Estrild, bowing and retreating down the stairs.

Blanche sat in the seat that had recently been built into the window, copying the window seats that were becoming fashionable in castles. She pushed open the shutters and looked out on the chilly landscape, and tears ran down her face. She was on the verge of losing Miles, of losing everything.

She straightened and wiped her eyes. Crying wasn't going to help anything. She had to think.

What was she going to do? Miles was about to ignite a fire that had no foreseeable end. War, terror, the land laid waste. It could go on for years, decades even. Blanche would be sucked in. So, eventually, would their children. She couldn't permit that. But how could she stop it?

The Normans should never have come to this land, she thought. They were not wanted, would not be accepted no matter how long they stayed. It was all because of King William's pride and ambition, which struck her as funny because now Miles's pride and ambition threatened to unleash new horrors upon the land. Miles and King William had a lot in common, though Miles would let himself be pulled apart by horses before he'd admit that.

A disturbance in the hall below. Raised voices.

Estrild appeared at the top of the stairs. "My lady, it's the sheriff."

Blanche collected herself and descended into the hall. Shaven-headed Onfroi of Buchy and Theobald of Jumièges warmed themselves by the fire pit, watched by Wada, Hersent, and Belot. Hersent still had the bow and looked eager to use it. A dozen armed men, two of them knights, waited by the door.

Onfroi bowed deeply to Blanche. Too deeply. "Lady Blanche."

"My lord sheriff," Blanche acknowledged.

Onfroi went on, his tone formal. "Blanche of Redhill, you have abetted the traitor Miles. You are to be taken to Brightwood Castle, where, at a date to be determined, you will be put on trial for your life."

CHAPTER 44

BLANCHE WAS DEFIANT. "I won't go."

"Then we'll carry you," Onfroi said. He motioned, and one of the bigger armed men started forward. "Throw her over your shoulder," Onfroi ordered. Behind Onfroi, Theobald grinned, only too happy to see the haughty Lady Blanche treated like a sack of turnips.

Wada and some of the manor's men edged forward, as well. Hersent fitted an arrow to her bow.

Blanche didn't want this to end in bloodshed. She signaled to her followers. "Stop." To Onfroi, she said, "Very well."

Estrild ran forward and took a place beside her mistress. "I'm going, too," she said in a voice that was unusually bold for her.

"No," Onfroi told her. "We have enough servants, we don't—"

"Try and stop me, you egg-pated—"

"Oh, let her do it," Theobald told Onfroi. "Norman servants don't want to be with Blanche. She's not one of us anymore."

Onfroi considered, then indicated that Estrild could come.

Onfroi, Theobald, and their men escorted Blanche and Estrild from the hall. They mounted, Blanche being given a fresh horse, and started through the village toward the castle.

Word had spread about what was happening, and villagers lined the street, calling support to Blanche despite menacing looks from the French soldiers guarding her. "We're with you, Lady Blanche."

"God bless you, my lady. We'll be praying for you."

"Don't let them Frenchies get to you."

Onfroi, riding beside Blanche, regarded the villagers with amusement mixed with disdain. "Your villeins seem to forget that you are also a 'Frenchy,' " he told Blanche.

"How does that make you feel, Blanche?" laughed Theobald from behind.

"It makes me feel proud," Blanche told him.

Blanche should have remained in the outlaw camp. Miles had been wrong. She had tried to tell him that, but he was too thick headed to listen, too caught up in his grand scheme of freeing England from its masters, of fulfilling his lifelong dream.

They passed through the stone curtain wall and entered the castle bailey. Blanche wondered if she'd have to share the third-floor living quarters with Onfroi. Onfroi was the senior noble in residence, so he had taken possession of them, while the former resident, Theobald, now slept in the hall.

Blanche remembered the two-storey arched hall, remembered fighting Aimerie and his men there with Miles, Albinus, Blackie, and the others. She was scared as Onfroi led her and Estrild up the curving stairs. She was at Onfroi's mercy, and Onfroi was not renowned for his mercy. Blanche was accused of abetting a traitor, an English traitor, and no one here was going to stand up for her.

Onfroi ushered her into the living quarters. He paused, sensing her distress, relishing it, almost visibly rolling it around on his tongue, tasting it as one might taste a fine wine. At last he said, "I'll leave you for now."

Blanche tried not to let her relief show as Onfroi added, "Fortunately for you, I'm loyal to my wife, Lady Blanche. I have moved my quarters to the hall. It's warmer there, anyway. I'll send you up some servants." He bowed and took his leave.

When the servants came, Blanche motioned to the curtained bed. "Get this cleaned and aired out, and change the straw in the mattress." To Estrild, she said, "Thank you for coming with me, Estrild. It means a lot."

"I've been with you a long time, my lady," Estrild said. "I'm not about you let you go off by yourself now. Wish I knew where that hare-brained Ediva had got herself to, though. We could use her."

"She'll turn up," Blanche said. "She always does."

Blanche said that, but she wasn't sure. Ediva was firmly on Miles's side. She might well decide to accompany his 'army' in their attempt to liberate England.

Blanche heard hammering outside. She looked out the window to see workmen building a platform in the bailey. "Wonder what that's about?" Estrild said.

Blanche didn't care. Onfroi was using her as bait to trap Miles. He knew that Miles would try to rescue her.

"We have to get out of here," she told Estrild.

"How?" Estrild said.

"There's only one way." Blanche inclined her head toward one of the shuttered windows.

Estrild's eyes went wide. "That's a long drop, my lady."

"We'll make a rope," Blanche explained. "We'll use bed sheets. Knot them together, tie one end to the bed, and climb down."

"You could get killed," Estrild said.

"We'll get killed if we stay here, I'm certain of that. We'll have one advantage—they won't be expecting it. They think escape from here is impossible."

"Probably because it is," Estrild said.

Blanche was business like. "You'll need to get more sheets. Bring them from the manor house, smuggle them under your dress or cloak." Estrild would be allowed to go to the manor to fetch things for her mistress. "Get lots of sheets—we'll need two ropes."

"You will?"

"Yes."

"Is that all?" Estrild said. "Just sheets?"

"We'll need men's clothes, too—clean, if possible, free from lice, at least."

"Begging your pardon, my lady, but why do you keep saying 'we?' "

"Because you're coming with me," Blanche said.

Estrild shook her head vigorously. "Oh, no, my lady, I can't—"

"Do you wish to stay here and be put to torture?" Blanche asked her.

Estrild crossed herself.

* * *

The rest of the day passed quietly, but it was tense. If Blanche left the third floor, even to go onto the roof, she had to be escorted. And though none of the castle staff acted overtly hostile, Blanche felt threatened. She was to be put on trial for her life, but she could just as easily 'disappear' first. It happened to prisoners all the time. She slept little that night.

The following morning brought rain, as the villagers had predicted. Estrild was brushing Blanche's lustrous black hair, with that grey streak forming on the left side, when they heard voices from the keep's entrance. "That sounds like Galon," Blanche said. There was no mistaking his throaty growl.

"He came all that way quick," said Estrild. "Must have left St. Mary's Lodge soon as he heard what had happened."

Estrild put down the brush, Blanche drew on her linen headdress, and the two women went down the stairs, followed by their ever-present guards.

It was indeed Galon, wet from the rain. He strode impatiently to the head table, where Onfroi and a priest attended to a pile of papers. The castellan, Theobald, was not present, nor was Onfroi's squire Arnot. Galon was followed by a trio of capable-looking squires, but his seneschal, Stigand, wasn't with him. He must be in Ravenswell.

Galon stood before the table. When Onfroi didn't acknowledge his presence, Galon smacked the stack of papers away, scattering them. A pot of ink went over, as well, the ink dripping over the papers and onto the table and the floor.

There was a pause. At last, Onfroi looked up, as if noting Galon for the first time. "Lord Galon. Good day to you, sir." He saw Blanche on the stairs and inclined his head. "Good day to you, as well, my lady. I trust you slept well."

Galon got right to the point. "I've come for Lady Blanche."

Onfroi rose from the table. He walked to the hearth and warmed his hands by the fire. "I'm afraid I can't permit that."

Galon's jaw clenched, the muscles working. "I'm afraid you have no choice."

Onfroi turned. "No."

Galon's hand went to his sword hilt. His squires faced the guards. Galon started to draw the sword. "You insolent weasel, I'll—"

Onfroi raised a hand. "I may be a weasel, as you say, Lord Galon, and I may be insolent, but *I* represent the king in this shire, not you. I am the law."

Galon sneered. "Then I'll break the law and take her by force."

"Lady Blanche is a prisoner of the crown. If you take her, there will be a charge of kidnapping brought against you. You won't be the king's councillor, or much of anything else, after that. And if you kill me, as you're plainly considering, it will go a lot worse for you."

Galon seethed, but Onfroi was right.

"Now," Onfroi said to Galon, "was there anything else?"

"Nothing else," Galon said. He slammed the partly drawn sword back into its sheath.

Onfroi chided him. "You really should address me as 'my lord,' you know."

Galon leaned forward. "Don't push your luck, Onfroi. Treason or no, I'll jam this sword so far up your ass it'll come out the top of your shiny head."

Galon turned and bowed to Blanche, who was still on the stairs, Estrild behind her. "This isn't over, my lady," Galon told Blanche. Then he swaggered away, followed by his squires.

Onfroi addressed Blanche, as well. "You may return to your chambers. You will be informed when a date has been sent for your trial."

CHAPTER 45

November 1 – Hallowmas
10 Days Until Martinmas

GARTH WALKED DOWN the muddy lane that led to the village, sucking his thumb and spitting out blood. It was a Holy Day. No work was supposed to be done on a Holy Day, but the men had agreed to work till noon, anyway. Garth, Peter, Gilbert the reeve, and some of the others had been clearing wasteland for cultivation. They'd been removing a stubborn tree stump when Garth's hand slipped and he got the splinter in it. Peter had dug the splinter out, but Garth's thumb was bleeding.

The lane became the village street. People cast sideways glances at Garth as he passed. Some waved or said, "Garth," in acknowledgement of his presence; but most said nothing. A few smirked. It was like something was going on that he didn't know about.

Still sucking blood from his thumb, he passed the remains of the All Hallow's Eve bonfire in front of the stone church of St. Wendreda. The air still smelled of smoke and burnt wood. He came to his house, and there he stopped.

A horse was in his yard, a dappled palfrey, grazing on what remained of his grass. The horse raised a bored eye to Garth, decided he was nobody important, and went back to what it was doing. A saddle and bridle lay on the table beneath the roof eaves.

"What the . . .?"

Garth looked behind him. People were watching. In the next toft over, old Osbert, who used to be the reeve, regarded him with an amused expression.

Garth pushed open the door and stepped inside.

Ediva sat at the trestle table, her cloak and dress travel stained, her head still wrapped with the bandage. "There was no one here, so I made myself at home," she said.

She had restarted the banked fire and warmed the kettle of pottage. She was eating a bowl of it with a spoon made from cow's horn. A wooden cup of cider was on the table before her. King lay at her feet, and she warmed a bare foot in his fur. The dog looked ecstatic and ignored Garth.

Garth stared. "What are you—?"

"Did you put honey in this pottage?" she said.

He wasn't expecting that. "What? Well . . ."

Her eyes widened. "You did, didn't you? You put honey in it."

Garth stammered. "I was trying something different." He attempted to sound gruff. "No one's forcing you to eat—"

"No, I love it. It's excellent."

"Really?" He was taken aback. "You think so?"

"Yes. You've finally outdone your father." She scooped another spoonful. "I'm surprised he's never thought of this. Do you mind if I have more? It was a wet, cold ride."

"Help yourself," Garth said.

Putting her shoe back on, she ladled more pottage into the bowl. She dipped her finger in it and let the dog lick it off. "Don't worry, I'll pay for it."

"Nonsense, I have plenty. I'll have some myself."

"Where are your children?" she said.

"Alfred and Alfstan are working. They'll be home soon. Cecily is probably at Aethelwynn's house."

Garth fetched a bowl and went to the kettle. Ediva saw his thumb dripping blood. "Stop!"

Garth looked over.

"You'll get blood in the pottage. Mary's milk, you finally make it good, then you're going to ruin it."

Garth looked at his thumb. "It's just a little—"

"God's breath, you're worse than your father. Sit down and let me fix that."

She put down her bowl and stood. She got a fresh bowl and filled it with water from the bucket. "Soak your thumb in that. Got any cloth I can use for a bandage?"

"Look on the work bench," Garth told her, irritated.

She rummaged around the work bench, found some old cloth and cut a strip from it. Also a needle and thread. She located vinegar on the sideboard and poured some over the needle. Threaded it. Pulled Garth's thumb from the now-bloody water and patted it dry. Poured vinegar on the thumb, Garth hissing because it stung, and patted it dry again.

"How did you do this?" she asked him.

"I slipped on a—ow!"

She took three stitches with the needle.

"Who the Hell taught you how to sew? A blind man?"

"Oh, stop it," she told him. "That doesn't hurt."

When the stitches were tied off, she poured more vinegar on the thumb, dried it, then wrapped the strip of cloth around it. "There. Now you can eat."

Garth shook pain from his thumb. "What are you doing here, anyway? You didn't come all this way just for a free meal."

Ediva went back to her pottage. "Grugan visited your father's camp."

"Grugan?" Garth said. "The old pedlar?"

Ediva washed down the pottage with cider. "The same. Good cider, by the way."

Garth held out his arms. "And?"

She told him what Grugan had said.

"You mean there really *is* a plot?" Garth said.

"Yes," she said, "and now Miles is part of it. A very big part."

Garth sliced some cheese, handed Ediva and King a piece and took a piece for himself.

"That's not the best part," Ediva went on, starting on the cheese.

He stared at her.

"Grugan is the man I saw with Aelred with at the Saracen's Head."

Garth frowned. "You're sure?"

"Certain."

"Which means . . ."

"Which means Aelred was lying. He's involved in all this, and Miles wants us to find out what he knows."

Garth crammed the rest of the cheese into his mouth. He ran a piece of bread around the inside of his bowl, soaking up as much of the pottage as he could, and put the bowl on the floor, leaving the rest for King. He grabbed Ediva's arm. "Come on."

CHAPTER 46

ᴱDIVA GULPED AT her cider as Garth dragged her to her feet. "I'm not finished—"

"Come on," he repeated. He pointed at the dog. "King, stay here."

King whined in protest, then happily padded over to the bowl of pottage. Garth led Ediva out the door, closed it, and started down the village street, eating his pottage-soaked bread as he went. A thick cover of fallen leaves acted as paving for the muddy street. This time people were more open in their stares, more disapproving—especially the old women—of the widowed Garth and Lady Blanche's winsome young maid.

"What is the world coming to?" one said.

"It's all because of them Godless French," said another.

"Never saw nothing like this in the old days."

Thorild, the Dane Asmundr's middle son, leaned against his fence, munching an apple. "Nice piece you got there, Garth," he said as Garth and Ediva approached. "If me and the boys scrounge together a few coins, d'ye think we can take turns with—"

Without breaking stride, Garth moved the bread to his left hand and hit Thorild on the jaw, knocking him through the top two rails of the fence and onto his back.

Ediva gave a look back at the fallen man. "You don't have to defend my honor. I can look after—"

Garth flexed his hand and shook it, inspecting the bandage on his thumb to make sure it hadn't come loose.

"I've wanted to hit that bastard for a long time. You were just an excuse."

"You'll get fined in manor court."

Garth finished his bread and wiped his mouth on the back of his hand. "It'll be worth it."

They turned down the lane that led to the stream and the water mill. The mill was shut down for the day while Aelred, the apprentice Wat, and Aelred's two young sons performed maintenance on it, replacing some of the wheel's slats that had rotted. The millrace had been dammed so that no water could get through.

"Aelred!" Garth cried.

Aelred looked up from his work. "Garth. What happened to your thumb?"

"Termites," Garth said.

Aelred made a puzzled face, then turned. "Back again, Ediva? So soon? How's your head? Shouldn't you be—"

"We need to speak with you," Garth told Aelred.

Aelred frowned, then motioned for Wat and the two boys to carry on. He led Garth and Ediva to the trestle table and bench upstream from the mill. Fishing rods and hooks were laid on the table—one of the perquisites of being Ravenswell's miller was the right to fish the lord's stream.

"Is something wrong?" Aelred asked as they sat.

"Grugan visited Father's camp," Garth said.

"Grugan? You mean the pedlar?" Aelred laughed. "Don't tell me he wants to be an outlaw at his age?"

"Don't play ignorant, Aelred. Ediva says Grugan was the man you were talking to at the Saracen's Head the night she was hurt."

Aelred regarded Ediva. "She's mistaken."

"I'm not mistaken, and you know it," Ediva told him.

Aelred turned sullen. "What if it was him? I've known Grugan a long time. Is he in trouble?"

"You don't know?" Garth said.

"Know what?"

Ediva said, "He wants Miles to lead an army in a rebellion against the French."

"What! Grugan? That old coot is organizing some kind of rebellion? Don't be absurd."

"You know nothing about this?" Garth said.

"No, I—"

"He's never mentioned it to you? You who are famous for hating the French, who almost got hung for it?"

"No, he never said a word. I don't do that sort of thing anymore, you know that. Just like I don't poach anymore."

"I don't believe you," Garth said.

"It doesn't matter what you believe," Aelred said in a raised voice. Wat and Aelred's sons looked over, then went back to work. Aelred lowered his voice. "Look, Grugan's a friend, I don't want to see him get in trouble. But whatever he's involved in, I'm not part of it."

"Father doesn't want you getting hurt," Garth said.

"You mean he doesn't want me serving in this 'army' of his?" Aelred said.

"That's different. If the time comes, we'll all have to do our share."

Garth let those words hang.

"Aelred?" A sturdy, dark-haired woman came over, a worried look on her face. "Is everything all right?"

"It's fine, Til," Aelred said.

"Can I get your guests something to drink?"

"Thank you, Til, but no," Garth said. "We won't be staying."

"Are you going to introduce me to your friend?" the woman asked Garth with a knowing smile.

"She's not my friend," Garth said emphatically. "She's— this is Ediva, Lady Blanche's maid. You know, my father's wife."

"I know who Lady Blanche is," the woman said.

"Ediva, this is Aelred's wife, Matilda."

"Hello, Ediva, it's so nice to finally meet you. I've heard stories about you. From when Baron Aimerie was at Brightwood."

"Don't believe all that you hear," Ediva said with a dismissive wave of the hand.

"I heard about what happened to you in Badford, too." She indicated the thick bandage under Ediva'a headdress. "Are you all right?"

"It hurts a bit. Nothing to worry about."

Matilda went on. "They say Lady Blanche has been arrested."

"Just detained," Ediva said. "That's why I'm here, actually." She lied smoothly, unsure of how much Matilda knew. "My lady bids Miles's—Lord Miles's—family not to worry about her. She says she'll be home soon."

"I hope so," Matilda said. "I've always heard good things about her."

"She's a good person," Ediva said.

Matilda didn't look to be going away, so Garth said, "Well, we've delivered our news. We best be on our way. Ediva must return to Brightwood."

"The sheriff has confined Lady Blanche to the manor there," Ediva explained. "I need to be with her."

"Of course," Matilda said. "But it's getting late in the day for travel, don't you think?"

Ediva looked at the sky and sighed. "You're right. I'll have to wait till tomorrow."

"Where will you stay the night?" Matilda asked her.

"The church?" Ediva ventured. "It's uncomfortable, but I stayed there once—"

"You can stay at my house," Garth said. "There's extra beds." He added, "Plus, the food's better."

Ediva rolled her eyes.

"Is that wise?" said Matilda. "People will talk."

"They're already talking," Garth said. He glanced at his swollen right hand involuntarily. "My children are there. Nothing untoward will happen. We'd best be going now."

"Again, it was a pleasure meeting you, Ediva," Matilda said with a wave.

"The pleasure was mine," Ediva said.

As Garth and Ediva started back up the lane, Ediva said, "Do you believe what Aelred told us?"

"Not a word of it," Garth said.

CHAPTER 47

GARTH AND EDIVA approached Garth's house. The pale gold of the late October sky tinted the village, the trees, and the puddles in the lane, turning them gold as well. Smells of the dying year. Smoke issued from eaves under Garth's angled rooftop.

King barked and ran up to greet them. Ediva bent and petted him. "Your house is bigger than the one I grew up in," she observed. "You even have a separate building for the animals."

Garth grunted. "Our neighbors burned the house down eleven years ago. We had to rebuild. Father made it bigger and moved the animals out."

Ediva frowned. "Burned it? Why?"

"Aelred was suspected of killing the old earl of Trent. Lord Galon threatened to destroy the village—destroy the hundred—if the killer wasn't produced. Many people had no qualms about sacrificing Aelred to save their homes and livelihoods, but Father defied Galon and worked to find the real killer. Father eventually got the killer, but not before they burned us out."

"How awful," Ediva said.

"They helped us rebuild—some did, anyway—but there's still bad feelings. On both sides. That fellow I hit, Thorild? His family are Danes. His father and some of the other Danes instigated the burning. But plenty of others were only too happy to join in."

Ediva gave him a questioning look.

"Some of them resent us because we're free, and because my grandfather was a thegn. They think we put on airs. It got even worse when Father married Blanche and became a lord. Some called him a traitor for that. They still do." He stopped. "Sorry, don't mean to be running on."

"No, it's fine," Ediva told him. "I never knew. Miles doesn't talk about it."

Garth shrugged. "Village life. You know what it's like."

They went inside, the dog barging in front of them. Two boys sat at the trestle table, while a dark-haired beauty of a girl chopped chives and hyssop and added them to the pottage. They all looked up, and the boys stood respectfully.

Garth grinned. "That strapping fellow who's staring at you like he's never seen a woman before? That's Alfred, my oldest. The skinny one with curly hair is Alfstan. And the lovely young lady is Cecily," he smiled wistfully, "who gets her good looks entirely from her mother."

To the children, Garth said, "This is Ediva, Lady Blanche's maid."

Garth's children didn't know Ediva, but they all knew of her. They said hello, and Garth added, "Ediva is staying with us tonight."

That set off a flurry of excited speculation, but Garth raised a hand. "*Only* because it's too late for her to get on the road home."

"So you're the famous Ediva," said Alfred, on the verge of being a man and puffing out his chest.

Ediva smiled. "I'm not famous. I just did some things when I was younger. Things I had to do."

"Were they fun?" asked the younger boy, Alfstan.

"Some of them." She remembered Blackie, and Hugh, and how they died. "Not all."

Cecily laid bowls on the table. "And now you have a glamorous life with Grandfather and Lady Blanche."

"I'm just a lady's maid," Ediva said.

"Yes, but you don't have to feed the pigs," Cecily said, "or milk the cow, or stand ankle-deep in mud trying to get the cart out of a rut."

"I'd forgotten about all that," Ediva said with an wry smile. "Maybe being a lady's maid is rather glamorous, at that." Funny how easy it was to detach yourself from your old life, she thought, to pretend it had never existed.

Cecily added, "Plus, you get to meet the lords and ladies of the shire."

"Not really," Ediva said. "Save for Guillame of Edsworth and his wife, they avoid us."

"Why?" Cecily asked.

"Because Miles—Lord Miles—is English."

"You're pretty," Alfstan said with the guileless boldness of a thirteen-year-old. "Why are you a spinster?"

"Alf!" cried Cecily.

"It's all right," Ediva said. To Alfstan she said, "It just kind of happened, I guess. So far, anyway."

"You'll find someone," Cecily assured her.

Garth changed the topic. "Shall we eat?" He rubbed his hands together in anticipation. "Ediva has praised my pottage, by the way."

"Does he always go on like this about his cooking?" Ediva asked while Cecily ladled pottage and Garth broke bread.

"Always," said Cecily. "Grandfather's just as bad, but I expect you know that."

"Oh, yes," said Ediva. "My mistress never hears the end of it."

While they were eating, Garth's sister, Aethelwynn, and her husband, Peter, came to the house. They brought with them a pot of ale they'd bought from old Gunhild the alewife. Ediva sipped at the ale. It was a lot better than the ale they served at the Saracen's Head, but—

"Is the ale not to your liking?" Aethelwynn said, concerned.

"Oh, no, sorry. It's excellent. I'm afraid I've got used to drinking wine. Part of my 'glamorous' life."

Peter and Aethelwynn quizzed Ediva about Miles and his new life in the forest. "Enjoying the life of an outlaw, is he?" Peter said.

"He pretends to, for the sake of the men, but I don't think he does, really, especially with winter coming on."

"He's not getting any younger, either," Aethelwynn said.

Ediva didn't know how much she should tell them. Garth hadn't mentioned the rebellion to them, so she didn't either. It occurred to her that, should the rebellion come to pass, Peter would have to serve. So would Alfred—he was sixteen. And if it lasted long enough, Alfstan would be drawn into it, as well.

Aethelwynn shook her head. "And now Lady Blanche is arrested and is to be put on trial for treason."

"What!" Ediva said.

"You didn't know?" Aethelwynn said.

"No," Ediva said.

"I thought that was why you were here. We just learned it from the neighboring manor."

"I was here on another matter," Ediva said. "I've been away from Redhill for some time. When is this trial to take place?"

"Martinmas Day is the rumor. She's been taken to Brightwood Castle."

Ediva swore to herself.

"Sad times," Peter observed, pouring more ale.

"Poor Father," Aethelwynn said, "and now Lady Blanche. I pray it all works out."

"None of it should have happened in the first place," Ediva said. "Miles is no traitor. Nor is my mistress."

"Miles seems to be a pretty good outlaw, though," Peter said. They all laughed at that, because laughing was all they could do at this point. It was their only means of protest.

Garth agreed. "God knows, he gives the sheriff fits. And those songs . . ."

More laughter.

With the coming of darkness, Peter and Aethelwynn left. After everyone used the latrine, Garth banked the fire, while Cecily cleaned up, and Alfred and Alfstan saw to the animals. Then Garth barred the door, and everyone retired for the night. Each of them had had a curtained bed against the wall, a luxury that had been reserved for Ediva's parents back in Redhill.

Ediva drew her linen curtain shut, then stripped to her shift and climbed onto the straw bed. The straw was fresh and the blanket clean and warm, but she felt ill at ease. Partly because she was worried about Lady Blanche, and knew she should be at Brightwood with her. Partly because she was in a strange house. Garth's family tried their best to make her feel comfortable, but she knew they were judging her. She missed the familiarity of the manor house at Redhill. Beyond the curtain, and on either side of her, she heard movement, then snores. The bottom of her curtain rustled, and King jumped onto the bed with her, curling himself against her. She put an arm across the dog, so of course he immediately sat up and began licking himself. Ediva sighed and lay there, staring at the thatched roof, and at some point she fell asleep.

The next day was Sunday. Ediva accompanied Garth and his children to Mass. Well, it wasn't really Mass. "Father" Michael wasn't a priest and not entitled to serve the Sacraments. While most of the congregation stood and talked amongst themselves in a low hum, Father Michael recited what prayers he knew, then told stories from the Bible—some of which he made up, Ediva guessed—and implored the congregation to obey God's law.

Ediva stood with Garth and his family, along with Peter and Aethelwynn. She felt the eyes of the congregation on her and wondered if some of them had come today just to see her. There was no sign of Stigand, lord of the manor. Maybe he had his own chaplain, or maybe he just didn't go to church. From what Ediva had seen of Stigand, that seemed possible.

After Mass, they went back to Garth's house. While the others prepared to eat, Ediva saddled her horse. "Back to Brightwood?" Garth asked.

"Yes," she said.

"Fancy stopping somewhere else first?"

"That depends," she said warily. "Where?"

"Badford. The Saracen's Head."

CHAPTER 48

November 2 – Feast of St. Winifred of Wales (Martyr)

9 Days Until Martinmas

GARTH AND EDIVA headed to Badford Town. Ediva rode and Garth walked by her side. Garth carried a staff and wore a hooded cloak. The day had turned unseasonably warm, so Garth removed the cloak and folded it across the back of the horse's saddle.

In the fields and forests around them, men hauled wood in carts, while other men repaired fences and still others worked on ditches. These men were committing a sin by working on Sunday, but being in a state of grace didn't heat your house when the weather turned cold.

"Should this rebellion come to pass, will you take part?" Ediva asked Garth.

"Will you?" Garth countered.

"Yes," she replied without hesitation.

Garth's answer was more deliberate. "I suppose I'll have to, since Father's involved, though I fear there's little chance of success."

"Grugan says there will be something else going on, something that will distract the French, though I've no idea what that might be."

"It better be big, or we'll all end up dead," Garth said.

"We all end up dead, anyway. It's what we do before we die that matters."

The bells of St. Hugobert were ringing the noon hour as Badford came into view. It seemed like every time Garth came here, more new houses were going up outside the town walls. "I hate towns," he said.

"Mary be praised," Ediva said, "we have something in common."

The town's walls were slowly being converted to stone. "They're taking their time with those walls," Ediva said. "They haven't made much progress in the last few years."

Garth said, "They'd have been finished long since, but they had to rebuild the town first, after Galon burned most of it."

"Why did he do that?"

"There was a criminal named Morys Gretch. He was in league with Galon's brother Geoffrey—the one who killed the old earl. Galon didn't want Morys to escape justice, so he flushed him from hiding by setting fire to Morys's part of town. The fire spread—surprise—and took most of Badford with it."

"And this Morys? Did Galon catch him?"

"Oh, yes."

"What did he do to him?"

"You don't want to know," Garth told her.

They passed the guards on the crowded bridge and entered the town proper. They pushed down the narrow, packed street to the Saracen's Head, with its strange representation of a man's head on the sign above the door. "Who would take that for a Saracen?" Garth said.

"I suppose you know what a Saracen looks like?" Ediva said.

"No, but I'm pretty sure they don't look like that. If they did, we'd never have taken Jerusalem. Our men would all have gotten scared and run away."

They paid a boy to watch Ediva's horse and entered. The inn smelled of ale, bad food, sawdust, piss, and vomit—it smelled like the town itself, only more concentrated. Garth wrinkled his nose. "You stayed here?"

"You get used to it," Ediva lied. She pointed to a scarred man with stringy hair and a stained leather apron. "There's Milo, the owner."

Milo recognized Ediva and came over. "You back, missy? Hope you don't want your things, 'cause I sold 'em when you didn't show up to pay for your room. Find another place to ply your trade, did ye?"

Garth drew his breath.

"I was . . . taken ill," Ediva said by way of explanation.

Milo eyed the bandage wrapped around her head and snorted. " 'Ill.' Problem with a customer, was it? Services rendered not good enough? Well, that's on you."

"Watch your tongue," Garth told him.

Milo looked down his nose at Garth. "Who are you, her pimp?"

Garth's eyes widened, and Ediva knew he was going to hit Milo, so she quickly stepped between them and said, "No, he's not a pimp." She thought quickly. "In fact, he's related to Brock the Badger."

That changed Milo's attitude. "Are ye now? For real?"

"Real enough," Garth growled. "I'm his . . . his nephew."

"Whyn't ye say so sooner?" Milo said, slapping Garth's shoulder jovially. "Any friend of the Badger is a friend of the Saracen's Head. Hell, always had a soft spot for missy here— didn't I, missy? Have a bumper. On the house, as it were."

He poured Garth a wooden cup full of ale. "What brings you back?" Milo asked Ediva, his tone now convivial, almost avuncular.

"We came to speak with you," she told him.

Milo's shrewish wife, Helga, came over. "What's going on then?" She recognized Ediva. "What you doin' back here?"

"Missy's come for a talk, is all," Milo told her.

"You got a bid on our property yet?" Helga said.

Ediva feigned disappointment. "My mistress has decided to locate somewhere else."

Helga wasn't surprised. "Well, talk quick. Me and Milo got a lot o' work to do."

"We won't take up much of your time," Garth assured her. "We came to ask about Aelred of Ravenswell."

Milo made a face. "Can't say I know that name."

"Nor me," Helga said.

"He's a miller by trade," Garth said.

Milo and Helga shook their heads.

Ediva added, "Slender, curly hair, good looking. Bright blue eyes."

Recognition came over Milo's scarred face. "Oh, right. I think I know who ye mean now. 'E never said his name."

"What can you tell us about him?" Garth asked.

Milo made another face and shook his head. "Not much. Comes in every market day, right about the same time."

"Always sits with different people," Helga added. "Talking all serious, like. Not having a good time, like most."

"What kind of people?" Garth said. "Locals?"

"Come from all over, judgin' by their dress and accents," Helga said. "Kentish men, men of Wessex, Northumbrians. Scots, even."

"Hmm," said Garth. "What do they talk about?"

Helga leaned toward him, and her rancid breath punched him in the face. "Now you know, it's funny you ask, because they always lower their voices when I come by, like they don't want to be heard."

"They do the same with me," Milo said, nodding his head.

Garth looked at Ediva, who evidently had no more questions. "Well, thank you for your time," Garth told Milo and his wife.

Helga rubbed her thumb against her middle fingers. "Don't ye think that information's worth somethin'?"

"It would have been," Ediva answered with a smile. "But you sold my things, so we'll call it even."

Garth and Ediva went back outside. The reek of the city seemed almost pleasant after being indoors. "Aelred's involved in this plot for sure," Garth said.

Ediva couldn't keep the excitement from her voice. "She talked about him seeing men from all over. The plot is big, not local."

"Are you going back to Lady Blanche now?" Garth asked her.

"No. I don't want to get trapped at Brightwood Castle with all that's happening. I'll go to your father's camp instead. I can be of more use there. What about you?"

"I'm going back to Ravenswell and have a chat with Aelred. See what he really knows."

CHAPTER 49

November 2

GYTHA HANDED MILES the newly sewn banner. "What do you think?"

Miles looked it over. It was square, made from good green cloth, the kind that would hold its color, its border reinforced with rawhide lacing so that the banner would stay stiff and be visible to the men in any wind or weather. The white lion was in the center.

"Excellent work," Miles told her. "That lion looks exactly like the one on my ring."

Gytha wrinkled her brow. "Think that's what a lion really looks like?"

"I've no idea. If anyone questions it, we'll say it's a mythical beast. A unicorn, perhaps."

"Unicorns have horns," she reminded him.

"A griffin, then."

"Wings," she said.

"Well, we'll think of something. For now, it's a lion. Thank you again."

"Just tryin' to earn my keep," she said. "I'll go add oats and water to the pottage, if it's all right, and leave some in your hut for later."

"Thank you."

Of late, Gytha had taken to leaving a small pot of the pottage on Miles's fire, for nighttime, or for when he wanted to be alone. It was a nice gesture because Miles was tired all the time now. It was getting worse, too. He guessed old age was catching up with him. It wasn't strange that it had come over him all at once like this; living in the woods had that effect. Still, it couldn't have come at a worse time.

Miles attached the new banner to a makeshift staff, then carried the staff and banner to the center of the camp, men following him in growing numbers. Men had been flocking to the camp. So many, that it was hard to find room for all of them. It was hard to find room for the graves, as well, as disease and cold weather took their toll.

Bondo eyed the banner as Miles came up. "Nice flag. Always wondered what a lion looked like."

While the men looked on, Miles planted the banner in the ground by the large tree stump. There were cheers. "That's what we're fightin' for lads!" someone cried.

"No," Miles said, mounting the stump and raising a hand for quiet, "we're fighting for England. To drive out the French and restore our country to its rightful owners."

More cheering. "Kill 'em! Kill the lot of 'em!"

Miles hadn't wanted this at first, but now he was excited. He envisioned a changed country, a country whose rulers spoke the same language as its people. A country free to make its own way without worrying about problems in the lands across the Narrow Sea. He, Miles, would have a part in that change, and that feeling made his chest swell.

He went on. "There's a lot more of us now, so we're reorganizing. Frithric will be centenar; Bondo, his deputy. You'll be divided into squads of twelve, under vintenars, each with two smaller squads of six. There will be no drills. You vintenars get your men used to working together and learning each other's ways. We'll probably be fighting in small groups, at least at first. Practice archery and weapons skills. Lots of archery."

"What's our first target to be?" Frithric asked.

"St. Mary's Lodge?" guessed the shoemaker Legulf. "Easy pickin's there."

"St. Mary's Lodge has no military value," Miles said. "Our first task will be to cut off Brightwood Castle. That's the biggest prize in Trentshire. No one gets in or out. That includes by water, so we'll have to burn the docks, maybe use fishing boats for a blockade. We'll isolate Onfroi and Theobald, starve 'em out. Then we'll move on to Badford. We'll live off the land and keep to the forests as much as possible. The French knights are useless in the forest, and England is half forest—more than half around here. We've no need to meet the French in open battle."

"And after Badford?" said young Hugh Myddewinter. The boy fairly bubbled with excitement. He had no concept of war's realities.

"Depends on how events play out," Miles said. "I expect the French to raise an army and go after the Scots king, Alexander, when he comes to aid us."

"*If* he comes," Wighelm grunted.

"He'll come," Miles said with a conviction he did not necessarily feel. "When that happens, we'll harry the French as they march north, wear them down, attack their supplies and try to lure them into ambushes, the way the Welsh do to us when we attack them."

"Got it all planned out, ain't you?" said Frithric with an admiring grin.

"I've had a long time to think about it," Miles said. *My entire life.*

"Where will we link up with the Scots, d'ye think?" said Bondo.

"We'll worry about that when the time comes. If we hear that Alexander is doing well and doesn't need our help, we'll go south instead, toward Winchester, drawing men to our cause as we do."

"Winchester?" Scarlet raised his brows. "Take the treasury, d'you mean?"

"Aye, take the treasury," Miles told him. Seeing grins on many of the faces, he added, "But for the country, not for us. The French can't do much without gold, and we'll need to bring more men into our army, to buy arms and supplies."

"Can't we keep a little of it for ourselves?" Scarlet said.

"No. We're soldiers now, not outlaws."

Wighelm, who was standing with Ioco, rubbed his pugnacious jaw. "It's still hard to picture us allied with the Scots."

"True," Odda said. "Better them than the damned Frenchies, though."

Miles turned to Oswald and Oshere. "Sure you and Diote don't want to change your minds about leaving? We could use you."

Oswald shook his head. "No, the camp is getting too big for us. Like as not, we'll go tomorrow if the weather holds. We're not cut out for soldiers."

"We'll start over somewhere else," Oshere said. "Settle down."

"Dorset, maybe," said Diote. "Hear the weather's better there."

"We'll miss you," Miles told them.

"Aye, it's been fun," said Oswald.

Around the camp, the men eagerly talked and planned and bragged about what they were going to do, but Miles's enthusiasm was checked as he remembered the sheriff's hired killer.

He was certain the killer was Ioco, though he had no proof of it. He'd been certain Ioco was the camp thief, as well, but the two were not mutually exclusive. Miles had made Ioco a vintenar. It was his due; he was experienced. Miles couldn't deny him without raising suspicions.

Could Ioco have made the bow shot that killed Father Albinus? Probably. It hadn't been a difficult shot. Could he have run back to camp in time to make it look like he hadn't been involved? Miles had seen Ioco move, and he had no doubt that Ioco could run all day and never fall short of breath.

Miles could take Ioco into custody and question him, but Ioco didn't look the type to say anything, no matter how brutal the questioning. They'd probably have to kill him in the process. And what then? What if Miles was wrong, and Ioco was innocent? In that case, Miles would have tortured and killed an innocent man. That sounded like the kind of thing Galon would do.

Toward dusk, Ediva arrived in camp. The new men had not seen Ediva before, and they gawked at this pretty young woman in travel-stained clothes, with her head bandaged. "I thought you were going to Brightwood, to be with Blanche," Miles said to her.

"With rebellion in the offing?" Ediva said. "Not on your life."

She jumped from the saddle, breathless from her hard ride. "You heard that my lady's been arrested and imprisoned in the castle?"

"Aye," Miles said grimly. It was his fault. If he had let her stay in camp, none of this would have happened. What a fool he'd—

"The rumor is that her trial is to begin on Martinmas."

"What?" Miles said.

Martinmas. It was the worst possible date. Now, Miles had to gather an army and get them ready for war, and he had to rescue Blanche, as well.

"We have to save her," Ediva said.

"We will," Miles assured her. "Look, it's late, get something to eat. Then rest. I saved Father Albinus's hut for your use, in case you came back."

Ediva nodded gratefully. Scarlet took her lathered horse and led it off. "And don't eat her!" Ediva shouted after him. "I don't want to find Blossom in the pottage tomorrow."

Scarlet laughed.

It was growing dark. Ediva ate, then retired to Albinus's hut. Miles lay on his bed, thinking of Blanche and how to save her and not coming up with any good ideas.

He woke to the sounds of running feet, of yelling and things being knocked over.

CHAPTER 50

November 3 – Feast of St. Rumwold of Buckingham
8 Days Until Martinmas

MILES JUMPED FROM his bed and piled out of the hut.

Muffled yells and grunts came from Albinus's old hut, where Ediva was staying. Other men ran up in the dark, alerted by the noise.

Before Miles could get to Ediva's door, two figures crashed through the hut's flimsy wall of saplings and pine boughs. The two men were fighting. Another figure stumbled through the opening they had made and disappeared into the camp.

Miles grabbed the two men who were fighting. It was Oswald and Ioco.

Ioco.

Miles lost his self-control. Shoving Oswald away, he took Ioco by the collar and drew back his fist. "You—"

"It wasn't him!" cried Ediva. She stood in the hut's doorway, holding up her torn shift. "It was the other one. Ioco saved me."

"What?" Miles said, disbelieving. "Are you sure?"

"Yes!"

Miles lowered his fist. He should apologize to Ioco, but no words came from his mouth. He turned to Oswald, who had been grabbed by Wighelm and another man. Torches had been lit. The entire camp was there.

"Is she right?" Miles demanded of Oswald.

Oswald said nothing, the rippled skin of his burned face turned to snake-like undulations by the torchlight.

"Who was the other man?" Miles pressed. "The one who ran away?"

"I think it was his brother," Ediva said, her chest heaving.

To Oswald, Miles said, "Was it? Was it your brother?"

No answer.

Miles slapped him, hard. "Was it your brother?"

It was Ioco who answered, speaking in his deep voice. "It was Oshere, yes."

Miles turned on Ioco, accusing. "And how did you get involved?"

"I was on my way back from the latrine," Ioco said. "I saw Oswald and his brother sneak into the hut."

"Convenient," Miles said.

"It was lucky for me," Ediva snapped.

"And you didn't raise the alarm?" Miles asked Ioco, for all the world like he was blaming Ioco for what had happened.

"There wasn't time," Ioco said.

Miles swore to himself. "Find Oshere," he told Frithric.

Frithric tapped Odda and some others. They took torches and started off.

Miles turned back to Oswald. "Oswald, how could you . . .?"

Oswald shrugged, glassy eyed from drink. "She's a fine-lookin' woman. Had a bit o' wine, didn't we? Our last night in camp, thought we'd have some fun. That's what she's here for, right? You can't just keep her for your—"

Miles slapped Oswald again, so hard that he almost fell.

Frithric and his men were back with Oshere, who had been found hiding in the brush. To Miles, Oshere said, "I don't know what they been tellin' you, but I didn't do—"

"Shut up," Miles said.

"Look what we found in Oshere's hut," said Legwulf.

Legwulf held up a fat purse and jingled it. He tossed the purse to Miles, who caught it and looked inside. It was filled with coins and pieces of clipped coins.

Bondo came up. "Found a clasp in their cart belongs to me. Other things, too. Things what have gone missing."

"Told you there's a thief in camp," Wighelm said.

"Two of 'em, looks like," said Legwulf. He cast a furious eye at Diote. "Maybe three."

"Bastards been stealin' from us," shouted someone.

The talk grew louder, and soon angry shouts rang through the glade. "String 'em up!" Hang 'em!"

Oshere huddled close to his older brother, the brother who had always protected him. Miles turned to Oshere's mousey wife, Diote. "Did you know about this?"

"No," she said, "I swear it. I knew they had money, of course, but I thought it come from robbin' the . . ." She broke down crying.

"What'll we do with 'em, Miles?" Bondo said above the shouting.

Miles wished they still had Father Albinus. Albinus was able to keep a clear head while others yelled for blood. In truth, however, there was only one answer.

Ediva had thrown a cloak over her torn shift. There was a bruise on her cheek, and her lips were puffed where they'd held her mouth shut so she couldn't scream for help. She wasn't crying, though. Ediva was a tough girl who'd been in tough situations.

Miles mounted the tree stump and motioned for quiet. Gradually the glade grew silent, lit by torches. Miles raised his voice. "I told each of you when you joined what would happen if you betrayed us. I made you swear an oath that you understood. We are a brotherhood, and members of a brotherhood look after one another. They protect one another. They protect their women."

He let that sink in and went on. "But we're not just outlaws anymore. We're an army. An army that's pledged to bring freedom to our country. These two"—he indicated Oswald and Oshere—"have stolen from us. There is only one greater crime in an army, or in a brotherhood, than stealing from your comrades, and these men have committed that crime, as well. They tried to rape Ediva. I've known Ediva since she was ten, longer than I've known any of you. Ediva performed great service in the fight against Baron Aimerie. She's one of us, maybe the best of us. We can't allow this sort of thing to happen, and we won't allow it."

"So what do we do?" asked young Hugh Myddewinter, who'd become Oswald's good friend. He remembered the warning given when he joined up, but he hadn't taken it seriously. "Do we kick 'em out?"

Miles gazed at Hugh, meeting his eye, and realization grew on the boy's face as he understood what was to be done.

Ediva wanted to protest, but stopped. She knew Miles was doing what he had to.

Diote was sobbing. "What about her?" Bondo asked.

Miles hopped from the tree stump. "Diote, you say you're not part of this?"

"I'm not," she blurted.

"That's as may be," Miles said, "and only you and God know the right of it. If you were a man, you'd swing, but I don't hold with hanging women." He paused. "You can either leave camp, or stay here and make yourself useful."

Diote hung her head. In a low voice, she said, "I'll stay."

Oswald cried, "Miles, you can't do this! We been with you from the start. We didn't mean it, we were drunk. Give us another chance."

"You had your chance," Miles told him.

"But—"

"I'm sorry," Miles said.

"Please!" Oshere cried. "We haven't been shriven. Our sins won't be forgiven."

"You should have thought about that before you committed them," Miles told him. He hesitated and added, "If it helps, you can confess to me, and I'll say prayers for you."

"Thank you," Oshere said.

"Thank you, Miles," said Oswald.

To Bondo and Frithric, Miles said, "Take them away. Hold them till first light and let them pray. I'll hear their confessions then. After, we'll hang them."

The two men were dragged from the glade. The crowd followed, yelling, baying for justice from men who'd been their friends only moments before. Oswald had saved his brother's life all those years earlier, just to have it end like this.

Miles wanted to cry, he wanted to be sick. But he couldn't. It was the price of leadership, the price of command. He'd known this situation would arise at some point. It had in Wales. It always did. He just hadn't thought it would happen with Oswald and Oshere. He hugged Ediva. "Are you all right?"

"Yes," she sniffed, and suddenly she was a little girl again. "But I'd prefer not to be alone right now."

"Go to my hut. I'll sit with you till it's time to . . . till it's time."

"Must I watch?"

"No, you've been through enough."

Ediva nodded and went into Miles's hut.

Miles turned. Only one man remained in the glade.

Ioco.

He stared at Miles with those unreadable dark eyes, then he, too, turned and left.

CHAPTER 51

November 4 – Feast of St. Birstan
7 Days Until Martinmas

GARTH MADE HIS way through the forest toward his father's camp. It seemed like he spent all his time coming and going from the camp these days. It was cold, with drifting bands of rain. He had encountered only one patrol of the sheriff's men—he hid until the patrol passed—and so was able to make decent time.

When Garth had reached Aelred's house, Aelred wasn't there. Aelred's wife, Matilda, told him that Aelred had gone to see his father on some urgent matter. It had been too late in the day to set out for the camp then, so Garth had left the next morning. He had slept rough last night in the cold. He was hungry, tired, wet, and half frozen.

As he neared the camp, he heard raucous cawing and the beating of wings, and he saw a cloud of crows. Then he stopped.

Ahead, the bodies of two men dangled from a tree.

Garth recognized the men. They were brothers. What were their names? Oswald was one; Garth couldn't remember the other. They looked like they'd been there about a day. Their eyes were long gone, of course, as was most of the exposed skin. The crows were now ripping at their clothes to get to the flesh beneath.

These men must have been executed on his father's orders. But why? What the Devil was going on?

Garth entered the camp, greeting the men he knew. There were lots of new faces in the few days since he'd been here last. The men were busy, but quiet. There was a depressed air, and Garth guessed it had something to do with the hanged men.

A lot of trees had been chopped down since Garth had first been here. The once-peaceful glade had been transformed into a bustling village. His father, Aelred, and others were gathered round the central fire, warming their hands, coughing, sniffling. Garth hadn't fully realized until now how ragged these men were, how gaunt and sick and dirty.

Ediva stood behind the men at the fire, wrapped in her cloak. Dark circles framed her eyes. Her left cheek was bruised and her lips swollen, and Garth wondered if her appearance had something to do with the two hanged men, as well.

Ediva saw Garth before the others did and nodded to him. "What happened to you?" he asked her as he came up.

She looked down, her usual cheekiness absent.

"Are you all right?" he said. "Are you hurt?"

She finally met his eyes, and her voice was subdued. "Yes, I'm all right. No, I'm not—"

"Garth!" cried Miles, and it seemed like he was trying overly hard to be jovial. "Didn't expect you here. Come close, son, get warm. You look all in."

Garth edged through the men toward the fire. He held out his frozen hands to warm them. A short, stocky woman brought him a cup of wine, mulled and heavily spiced to hide its vinegary taste this late in the season. He sipped the wine, relishing its warmth. "Why were those men hanged?" he asked his father.

"They violated our rules," Miles said. He looked worn out and sick.

Garth glanced at Ediva, but she wouldn't meet his eye.

"They been up there long enough," Frithric muttered. "Best get 'em buried."

Miles nodded gloomily, and Frithric and some other men started off.

To Aelred, Garth said, "I went to your house, but you weren't there. When did you get here?"

"Yesterday evening," Aelred said. "I came to give Father details about the uprising."

"I thought you knew nothing about it," Garth said.

"I told you that because I didn't want you and Ediva involved, especially Ediva, but it's too late for that now."

Garth sipped more of the mulled wine, wrapping his hands around the warm cup. "And you know the details of the uprising because . . .?"

"Because I'm in charge of it."

CHAPTER 52

ILES JERKED HIS head up. "What!"

"What!" said Garth.

"You look surprised," Aelred said.

"We are," Garth said.

"I thought you were over that," Miles said, and all his gloominess was gone now. "Since you were almost hung and the Beardmen were disbanded, you've stopped talking about politics."

"The Beardmen never disbanded," Aelred said. "We cut our beards and went quiet. What, did you think I was going to be a good little miller and forget what happened to me? Did you think I was going to forgive? I almost died eleven years ago, for the simple reason that I was English."

"It was more than that," Miles said. "The French thought you had killed the earl of—"

"And they were only too happy to ignore any other possibility," Aelred reminded him. "Even when the truth came out, a lot of them would have preferred that I die for the crime rather than the Frenchman who actually committed it. Tell me I'm wrong."

Miles said nothing, nor did Garth, because Aelred was right.

Most of the camp had gathered around, listening intently. Ediva stood at Garth's elbow as Aelred went on. "So I brooded, and I waited. Using my contacts with the Beardmen, I established a network across the country, or most of the country, anyway. We use men like Grugan to keep in touch. What better cover than a pedlar? Pedlars can go anywhere, and they're invisible as far as the French are concerned. And I have dozens of Grugans. I meet these men at the Saracen's Head on market days. I gather news and send messages out. I've been patient, waiting till the time is ripe. And that time is now."

"Why now?" Garth asked him.

"The French have grown complacent," Aelred said. "They no longer expect us to revolt. They don't even think about it. They think they've won and there's no way they'll ever be dislodged. Well, they're in for a surprise."

Aelred was calm as he spoke, composed. But there was a disturbing gleam in his eye that Garth had never seen before. Garth said, "If you're in charge of the uprising, that means you're . . ."

Aelred nodded. "I am chief of the Beardmen, their thegn. I have been for some years, chosen by the others. And I started to plan this uprising the day I was chosen."

"Was it your idea to offer the crown to Alexander of Scotland?" Miles said.

"It was. There are no English nobles left with royal blood, and Alexander has that."

Ediva spoke up. "What about King Henry's son, William? He bears the royal blood of Wessex through his mother."

Aelred made a dismissive gesture. "He's still a creature of the French. Besides, he's descended from William the Bastard, and no kin of that man should ever be allowed to have power in this country."

Loud murmurs of approval from the men who were listening. Calls of "Aye."

"And it was your idea for Father to command the army?" Garth said.

Aelred spread his arms. "This is Father's dream, Garth, you know that. Always has been. The people love him, and he knows how to beat the French. It's not a question of giving him command. Leading the army is his right."

Miles said nothing.

"And what is your reward for all this?" Ediva asked Aelred.

"The French leaving England is my reward. It's all I've ever wanted."

Ediva looked skeptical, but she didn't say anything.

Miles said, "So what is this plan? Specifically. A general revolt to start on Martinmas?"

Aelred smiled, and there was that gleam in his eye again. "Oh, it's much better than that. Beginning on Martinmas, every person of French blood in England is to be killed."

CHAPTER 53

"WHEN YOU SAY every French person, I assume you mean the nobles?" Miles said.

"No," Aelred replied, "I mean everyone."

Miles raised his brows. "Every man of French blood?"

Aelred smiled again. "Women and children, too."

That set off a buzz around the camp. Some of the men shifted uneasily.

"My wife is French," Miles reminded Aelred. "My children by her are half French."

"They'll be protected, I've seen to that," Aelred told him.

Miles looked to Garth, then back to Aelred. "You're planning to kill a lot of people."

"We won't get them all at once, of course," Aelred said. He spoke with a preternatural calm, as though he were discussing a change in the weather, or the price of cattle at Badford market. "We'll do our best, then you and your army can hunt down the rest."

There was animated discussion among the men. Ediva spoke up. "You're talking about massacre on a scale worse than Aethelred, when he thought he could kill all the Danes in the kingdom on St. Brice's Day."

"That's actually where I got the idea," Aelred said.

"A crazy idea like that didn't work then, and it won't work now," Ediva told him. "Mary's grace, and you call yourself a Christian?"

"I call myself English," Aelred shot back. "What about you?"

"I'm as loyal to the English cause as anyone here," Ediva said. "And, unlike you, I've actually fought the French."

Aelred bristled at that.

Miles said, "I don't hold with killing women and children, Aelred."

"Women and children die all the time in war," Aelred said.

"You're not talking about war, you're talking about extermination. Evil as they are, the French didn't do that to us. Nor did the Danes."

"Only because they needed us to work 'their' lands. A man like Galon would see all of us gone at the snap of a finger if it wouldn't hurt him in the purse."

Miles shifted on his feet, because what Aelred said was true.

Aelred's comments set off a roar of talk. Some were for his plan, others against. "Do unto the Frenchies what they done unto us," Wighelm said. Beside him, Ioco nodded.

"Aye," added Odda. "If we wipe 'em out thorough like, they won't be able to come back at us later."

Bondo disagreed. "We won't be an army if we do this. We won't be soldiers. We'll just be killers, no better'n what you hire in the back alleys of Badford. Worse, even, 'cause we'll be killin' women and kids."

"There's no glory in that," Legulf added.

"Do you want glory, or do you want the French gone?" Aelred asked him.

"It's the only way to make sure we survive," Wighelm told Bondo and Legulf. "There can't be reprisals against us if the French are all dead."

"Kill the nits, and the Frenchies'll have no one to grow up and claim our lands," Odda said.

There was a lot of support for that.

Garth said, "What about the French in this country who aren't from Normandy?"

"Good question," Aelred said, and the glade quieted as the men waited for him to answer. "We'll likely have to take them on an individual basis."

"And King Henry?" Miles said.

"We can't get to Henry, unfortunately; he's in France. But by the time he learns what's happened, it will be too late. The deed will be done. I doubt Henry will be able to raise an army and mount an invasion. He can't lay hold on enough money in France, and we'll control what used to be his exchequer here. Invasion of our kingdom won't work for the French a second time."

" 'Specially with Miles leadin' us!" cried Scarlet, and there were cheers all around.

The camp was abuzz. The men could taste freedom from the French, even though they had no idea what that freedom would entail. They were excited about a future they could not envision.

"Did you think up this plan by yourself?" Miles asked Aelred.

Aelred hesitated the briefest second. "It's something the Beardmen have talked about for years," he replied. "I simply worked out the details."

"And if you're successful?" Miles said. "What comes after that? Who will run the estates? Or are the French nobles to be replaced by Scots?"

"They better not be," Wighelm cried. "We'll run the estates ourselves."

"How?" Miles said. "Who will be in charge?"

Wighelm hadn't thought about that. "Well . . ."

"That's what I mean. The entire foundation of society will have to be remade. There will be blood and suffering on a grand scale. There will be a period of anarchy, where men battle one another for wealth and power. There may not be peace in England for a generation."

Left unsaid was that Miles would be at the center of that anarchy. Because he led an army, he would become more than earl of Trent, that seemed inevitable. And because he led that army, it also seemed inevitable that he would come into conflict with Alexander of Scotland.

"A while back, you was all for this," Wighelm said. "Now you sound like you're against it."

"There's a difference," Miles said. "I can understand killing the French nobles. Most of them, anyway. They're the backbone of French power here. Without them, French rule would collapse. But what about men like Guillame of Edsworth? Good men, who look after their estates and their tenants. There are some, you know. You can't just indiscriminately slaughter everyone."

"And what about the other French?" Garth added. "What about men like Pierre Courtenay, our steward? Our friend?"

"Sacrifices must be made in war," Aelred said with that unwavering calm. "Pierre is part of the French system. I'll hate to see him go, but it's for the good of us all."

Ediva said, "And the innocent clerics and merchants? Men who've done no wrong?"

"They've taken the place of good English clerics and merchants," Aelred said. "That seems wrong enough to me."

"Who determines who's actually French?" Legulf asked. "There's been a lot of intermarriage, a lot of mixing of bloodlines in fifty years. A lot of us have some French blood."

"We'll try to be fair," Aelred said. "That's all I can tell you."

Garth was incredulous. " 'Try to be fair?' That just means grudges will be settled—you know that, Aelred. Accuse some poor bastard of being French, then kill him and take his lands, and if proof comes up otherwise, oh, well, it's too late to do anything about it now."

Ediva summed it up. "Like Miles said, it will be anarchy."

Aelred had gone insane, Miles thought. Maybe it was the beatings he'd sustained in Badford Castle's goal, maybe it was something else, but he was totally mad. Miles said, "I won't condone the killing of women and children. A free England isn't worth that."

"What are you saying, Father?" Aelred asked.

"I'm saying I can't be part of your plan. And you should have known that before you asked me to lead your army."

"I don't understand. You're pronouncing the end of your dreams, your life's ambition."

"Maybe those dreams were flawed," Miles said. "I'll never like the French, and I'll never accept them as rulers of England. But a massacre like this isn't the way to get rid of them."

"I'm sorry you feel that way, Father, but the plan is in motion, and there's nothing you or I can do to stop it."

Miles stared at him. "God save us, Aelred, I don't recognize you anymore. What's happened to you? How did you get this way?"

"Maybe I was always this way, and you never noticed," Aelred replied.

Miles was about to say more when a strangled cry came from the rear of the crowd.

Everyone turned to see young Hugh Myddewynter stumbling about, gasping and clutching his throat, his eyes bulging. Then he dropped to the ground.

CHAPTER 54

HUGH THRASHED IN the mud, his legs jerking spasmodically, eyes dilated as he clawed at his throat and gasped for breath. His chest heaved and hoarse sucking sounds came from his throat. Foam bubbled at his mouth.

With a last kick, he was still, his eyes staring.

Men backed away from him, afraid they would catch whatever he had.

Pushing through the crowd, Miles stepped forward and knelt beside Hugh. He shut the boy's eyes.

"God save us," said Diote, crossing herself.

"Is it plague?" asked Bondo, shaken.

"It's the forest spirits," Legulf said. "They done for him."

"No," said Ioco, "he was poisoned."

Miles turned. "Poisoned? What makes you say that?"

"Seen it done once, in Bristol," Ioco said. "Rival gangs in the port. Looked just like that."

Miles said, "But why Hugh? And how did whoever it was do it?"

Ioco shrugged.

Wighelm said, "Dunno if it means anything, but I seen Hugh goin' into your hut just after Aelred come."

Miles couldn't help but smile. "He likes to sneak in there and try the pottage. Thinks I don't know about it. He's convinced it's made different than the main batch . . ."

His voice tailed off. Besides Miles, only two people were allowed to tend the pottage. Ediva and . . .

"Gytha," he said, rising. "Where is she?"

Gytha was nowhere to be seen.

Realization came over Miles. "That poison was meant for me. Gytha must be the killer sent by the sheriff."

"Gytha?" said Bondo in disbelief.

"If you've got a better explanation, I'll listen to it," Miles said. "Till then, find her."

The men searched the camp and its surroundings, but Gytha was gone. The search expanded into the forest.

Ediva joined in. Garth went with her. Ediva searched west of camp, reasoning that Gytha would flee in the least likely direction. That's what Ediva would have done. The bruise under her eye, where Oshere had hit her, throbbed dully.

She weaved back and forth in a wide arc, the way Blackie had taught her. Then she stopped. "Tracks."

Garth looked over her shoulder. The tracks were barely visible in the dying light. They had been made by a woman's feet, a heavy-set woman. Short, too, judging by the spread between the tracks.

Ediva followed the footprints, Garth behind her. Other men saw them and trailed after, mindful of Ediva's reputation and sensing that she was onto something.

The tracks led over rough ground, Gytha no doubt hoping to lose her pursuers once it was dark. And she might have done, but Ediva had spent a good portion of her youth in the forest, and she was able to follow the tracks with little trouble. "She's just ahead of us," she told Garth in a low voice.

Garth motioned the men behind them to be quiet.

If Ediva had been by herself, she would have died, because as she rounded a rocky bend in the trail, she found Gytha there, dagger poised to strike.

"Stop!" shouted Garth from behind. He, too, had a dagger. It was raised above his head and ready to throw.

Gytha hesitated, and that hesitation proved her undoing as Wighelm and Ioco rushed up, bows drawn.

"Drop the dagger," Wighelm told Gytha. "Easy, like."

Gytha lowered the dagger, tossed it away.

Ioco drew his bowstring to his cheek, ready to end this.

"Hold," Garth told him. "Let's find out what she knows first."

Wighelm cried, "We've got her!"

His cry was echoed through the woods by others, and more men came up, including Miles.

"Thank you," Ediva told Garth. "You saved my life."

Garth mumbled noncommittally.

"Could you have made that throw with the knife?" she asked him.

Garth shrugged. "Don't know. Never tried it."

As the men came up, they surrounded Gytha, who showed surprisingly little fear. Odda struck her, making her stagger and drawing blood. Another man hit her, as well, dropping her to her knees. Legulf punched her in the face. More crowded round, swinging fists, kicking.

"Enough!" Miles said. He stood in front of Gytha with his arms spread protectively.

"She killed Hugh," Odda protested. "Just a lad, Hugh was."

"Many a cup I've shared with that boy," Wighelm said. "He didn't deserve this."

Miles turned to Gytha. "Were you hired by the sheriff to kill me?"

"I was," Gytha said defiantly. Blood ran down her cheek. One eye was swelling. Her hair was awry.

"Kill her!" men cried. "Hang her!"

"Wait!" Miles said, raising a hand. "Wait." To Gytha, he said, "You killed Father Albinus?"

"I didn't mean to," she said. "I kill who I'm paid to kill, no one else. I liked Albinus. But he saw me in the trees and stepped in front of you just as I let go my arrow."

Miles rubbed his jaw. "And after that, you were able to make it back to camp before we did, with no one the wiser?"

"Does it surprise you?" she said. Her short, dumpy figure seemed to preclude such speed.

"I confess, it does," Miles said.

Gytha smiled, proud of herself.

Miles said, "You put poison in my pottage?"

Some of the blood from her face ran into Gytha's mouth. She spit it out, then wiped her mouth with the back of her hand. "Aye. Dwale, I used. Been adding it gradual, so's it would look like you'd come down sick and died, then I heard you and Aelred talking about that rebellion, and I figured the sheriff would give me extra money if I got the job done quick. Didn't reckon on poor Hugh, though."

That's why Miles had been feeling run down. Poison.

"You heard her," Odda said to Miles. "She's admitted it. Now let's hang her."

A tumult of approval.

"Not yet," Miles said. To Gytha, he said, "How did you get the job to kill me? Did the sheriff come to you?"

"Not in person. He used a priest. This priest approached one of my agents, who contacted another of my agents, who contacted me." She smiled again. "I make myself hard to get hold of."

"So you've never actually met the sheriff?" Miles said.

Gytha shook her head. "He doesn't even know I'm a woman. Or where I'm based."

There was a lot of talk among the men. Garth was curious. "How did you get into this line of work?" he asked Gytha.

She shrugged. "Family died from plague. Woman alone has to make her way in the world. I wasn't going to make it on my back, not with my looks, so I learned skills. I've done well, have a nice home—won't tell you where. No one suspects me because of the way I look."

"Are you much in demand?" Garth said.

"Aye. Such is the modern world, more's the pity. Now, I'm tired of talk. Hang me, or whatever it is you got planned for me."

More tumult. "I got a rope," somebody yelled.

"Not yet," Miles said. Over the resultant outcry, he went on. "Frithric, Bondo, keep her here. Don't let her escape, but don't let her be harassed, either." He paused. "It's possible we may have need of her talents."

Frithric frowned. "What do you have in mind?"

"I'm not sure yet," Miles said. He realized something and looked around. "Where's Aelred?"

"Gone," said someone.

"He left when Hugh died," Ioco said.

Miles swore. He thought for a moment, then climbed a nearby hummock and addressed the gathering. "Any of you who wish to join my son's plot are free to leave here and do so. But I warn you, I intend to stop that plot from succeeding. If that's treason to the English cause, so be it. If this were a real revolution, I'd be in it all the way, but this is killing for the sake of killing. I'll try to stop it even if it means keeping the French as our masters for the next hundred years."

Muttering.

Miles added, "The French will be gone one day, God please, but not today, and not by these means."

The men agreed, reluctantly, as Miles himself was reluctant. "I'm sorry, lads, but that's the way it must be. I'll not spend eternity in Hell to see the French gone from England. Let the French go to Hell, instead, and join their ancestors who stole our lands."

That brought a cheer. Not a hearty cheer, but one of resignation.

Miles turned to Garth. "Go to St. Mary's Lodge. Tell Galon what's happening."

"Shouldn't I try to catch up with Aelred?" Garth said.

"There's no time. Warn Galon. Tell him I sent you. Take Ediva with you. Galon will be less inclined to kill you out of hand if she's with you."

"What about you?" Garth asked him. "What are you going to do?"

"The first thing I'm going to do is bury young Hugh. Then I'm going to rescue my wife."

CHAPTER 55

November 8 – Feast of St. Moroc of Scotland
3 Days Until Martinmas

GARTH PICKED YET another piece of straw from his beard. The damned things seemed to be breeding in there. There was straw in his shirt, as well, making him itch. "Have you ever been to St. Mary's Lodge?" he asked Ediva as they approached the walled hunting lodge.

"Never had a need," said Ediva, who didn't seem to be having as much trouble with straw in her clothing. "Lady Blanche doesn't like the place, for some reason. She won't go there."

Last night's rain had stopped, but there was a chill breeze. Ediva rode and Garth walked alongside her, carrying his staff. They'd been delayed for two days leaving camp. Ediva was suffering headaches after being assaulted by Oswald and his brother. Garth had wanted to go on alone, but Miles had been adamant that Ediva come, as well. They had spent the previous night in a tithing barn, where they had kept warm by burying themselves in straw. This morning, the kindly priest had furnished them bread and water for their onward journey.

"Ever slept in a barn before?" Garth went on.

Ediva laughed. "I've slept in lots of places. Slept under a pile of leaves once. About this time of year it was, too. Cold and wet. I was looking for your father."

Garth had never heard this story. "Did you find him?"

"Do you have to ask? Of course I did."

They joined the crowd seeking entrance to the lodge, mostly local men and women come to sell produce. As they approached the lodge gate, the two guards stationed there leveled their spears, blocking entrance. The guards were local men. "Hold on, you're Miles's son, Garth," said the first, a chunky fellow with an ill-tended beard.

The second, a fuzzy-cheeked youngster, recognized Garth, as well. "His dad's Brock the Badger," he told his companion, "with a bounty on his head."

"Is there a bounty on Garth's head, too, d'ye think?" wondered the older man.

"Not as I heard," said the youngster, obviously disappointed.

"I'm here on official business," Garth told them. Trying to make himself seem more important, he added, "As hundred pledge."

"Go on," mocked the older guard, "there ain't been a hundred court in near three years. Done with, hundred court is. Hundred pledge, too."

"Nevertheless, I'm on official business," Garth repeated. "I need to see Lord Galon."

"Well, he don't need to see you," said the older man, and both guards laughed as though this was the funniest thing they had ever heard.

"Who's the wench?" said the youngster, calming and ogling Ediva. "A right looker, she is. Might be we could—"

Ediva drew herself up, all too aware of her stained and wrinkled clothes and the unkempt hair beneath her bandage. "I am lady's maid to Blanche of Redhill, so you might want to watch how you speak to me."

The older guard snorted. "Lady Blanche? Workin' for her won't get you far. Charged with treason, she is."

Traffic at the gate had backed up, and men and women started yelling at the guards to get it moving again. "What's the hold up?" "Move it along, there!"

"Hold yer yap, Isaac!" the older guard shouted back. "You'll get in. You probably stole them hens, anyway."

More yelling.

The noise attracted the attention of Stigand, black-clad lord of Ravenswell and seneschal to Galon of Trent, who happened to be passing by. He came over to see what was the matter. Stigand's saturnine presence stopped the yelling from the people trying to get in. Most of them averted their eyes.

Stigand saw Garth. "This fellow is one of mine," he told the guards. "What are you doing here?" he demanded of Garth.

"My father sent me, my lord. With a message for Lord Galon."

"What kind of message?"

"I'm not allowed to say, my lord, not in public." Stigand knew Miles was working for Galon, Garth thought. Surely he must be able to guess what the message was about.

Stigand considered. "Very well, you may enter. But only you—not the girl."

"Oh, no, I'm coming, too," Ediva said. "I represent Lady Blanche, and she's very much a part of this."

Stigand must have intuited that it was no use arguing with Ediva. He let out his breath and motioned them both through the gate. "Thank you, my lord," Ediva said, smiling politely.

Ediva left her horse with a groom, and Stigand led them to the barn-like hall, with its central fire pit. The morning's hunt was over, and the hunters, along with the lodge's steward, Othon, and sundry guests and hangers-on, warmed themselves as best they could while eating and drinking.

Galon, as the ranking noble present, sat at the head table, drinking from a horn goblet and gnawing a pork rib, dipping it in some kind of honeyed fruit sauce. He cocked his head with interest as Stigand led Garth and Ediva forward.

Stigand bowed. "They claim to bring a message, my lord. From Miles."

Galon took a drink, washing down the pork. He raised his voice so it could be heard throughout the hall. "Everyone out."

There was a chorus of protest.

"Now!" Galon shouted, pounding the table and rising.

The hall emptied quickly.

When everyone was gone, Galon motioned Garth to begin. Garth bowed. "My lord." He told Galon what Miles had learned about the Martinmas plot, leaving out the part about his brother Aelred's involvement in it, instead referring to Aelred as "our informant."

Using his fingernail, Galon worked a bit of pork from between his teeth. "Took your father long enough to find out."

"A peasants' revolt?" Stigand scoffed. "Preposterous."

"All Normans to be killed," Galon repeated what Garth had said.

"Woman and children, too," Garth emphasized.

Galon said, "I confess, it's hardly what I expected. I had hoped for something with a bit more . . . flair. More dramatic. Dreamed up by prominent nobles whose estates I could confiscate and heads I could nail to gateways. Instead, I get peasants and the Oaf of Scotland. Still . . ."

"The peasants will never be able to make it happen," Stigand said dismissively.

"Miles seems to think it's possible," Galon told him.

"Miles is a fool. Always has been. This is either some nonsense he's made up, or it's a lie, planted by one of the king's rivals, to mask the real plot."

"Mmm." Galon turned to Garth. "Is there more?"

"Our informant wouldn't tell us," Garth replied. "It's to begin on Martinmas, that's all I know."

Galon eyed Garth narrowly. "I'm curious. Why don't you side with your countrymen in this? I should think that you and your father—especially your father—would find this sort of deviltry most appealing."

Garth returned Galon's stare forthrightly. "I don't like you people, and I wish to see you gone from our land. But, like my father, I don't hold with killing women and children. When we get rid of you, and we will, it will be through honest revolt."

"Dangerous words, Englishman," Galon said in a low voice.

"True ones, my lord," Garth replied.

Garth was aware of Ediva staring at him, as though seeing him through new eyes.

Galon said, "Mark me, but you're as impudent as your father. You know I hung him once, but he escaped. I could hang you now, and I doubt you'd be as fortunate."

"Except I'm on your side in this, my lord," Garth said, "and for the moment you need me. And my father."

Rage flared in Galon's dark eyes, like an ember that flares in a banked fire, then it subsided. "In honor of the lady's presence, I'll spare you. For the moment." He turned to Stigand. "Send messengers—gallopers, mind—to the nearby estates and to Badford Town. Tell them what's going to happen. Tell them to pass the word in turn, until the entire kingdom has been alerted."

Stigand said, "My lord, surely you don't—"

"We can't afford not to take this seriously," Galon said. "Else we might end up dead."

"But Martinmas is in only three days' time," said Stigand.

"Which is why you should already be walking out that door," Galon told him.

Stigand bowed hurriedly and left.

Galon eyed Garth, tapping a finger on the scarred table top. At last he said, "You may go. I'll decide your future later."

Garth bowed, aware how close he'd come to death. "Yes, my lord."

Garth and Ediva turned to leave.

"You," Galon told Ediva, "stay."

Garth and Ediva shared a look, then Garth departed the hall. Ediva stood before Galon.

Galon ran his eye over her, slowly, taking in her body, and there was no doubt what he was thinking. "How did you injure your head?" he asked her.

"An accident, my lord. I fell."

"You're Blanche's maid."

"Yes, my lord. Ediva." She was scared, but tried not to show it. Galon could take her right here, if he wanted, on the table top. He was strong enough, and no one would stop him.

"Tell me, Ediva," Galon said, "how would you like a place in my household? I'm a powerful man, an intimate of the king. You would spend much of your time at court."

Ediva swallowed. "No, thank you, my lord."

Galon lifted a heavy brow. "Really? You might attract the attention of some worthy young lord at court. A prosperous marriage."

And until then, I'd be your plaything, she thought.

Ediva said, "I'm happy where I am, my lord."

Galon smiled. "What if something happens to Miles, and I marry Blanche? You won't have a choice, then."

"I could leave her service and go back home."

"To a peasant's hovel? You would do that?"

If Garth could be bold, so could Ediva. "You won't marry Lady Blanche, my lord. Lord Miles will come out of this all right."

Galon stared at her, then laughed. "Is there anyone in this country who knows their place? You're a saucy wench, I'll grant you that." He went back to his food. "Let me know when you change your mind."

"I won't," she said. She bowed and left the hall.

CHAPTER 56

GARTH AND EDIVA left St. Mary's Lodge. "That was fun," Ediva said.

"Why did Galon ask you to stay?" Garth asked her.

"He wants me to be his mistress."

Garth lifted his brows. "And what did you tell him?"

"I told him his prick was too small."

Garth was shocked; he had never heard her speak that way. Then he laughed. "How's your head?" he added.

"It's still on my shoulders, so that's something. As is yours, especially after the way you talked to Galon."

"Aye," Garth said. "Father told me you might save me from Galon, and so you did. Seriously, does your head still hurt?"

Ediva shrugged and changed the subject. "So, what's next?"

Garth glanced at the sky. "I hate these short days. Makes it hard to get anything done. We'll have to spend the night at Ravenswell, then I'll go to my father in the forest."

"I'll join you," Ediva said.

Garth grinned. "I thought you were going with Lord Galon to be his mistress?"

"Ha ha," she said. "I should go to Brightwood, but I'm not. I don't want to be trapped there if rebellion breaks out. Do you think that Galon sending out a warning will be enough to stop it?"

"Possibly," Garth said, "but who knows how far the plans have advanced? We may get a rebellion whether we want one or not. We'll find out in three days."

Robert Broomall

Garth had an idea. "Do you want to give the Saracen's Head another try? Maybe Grugan will be there and we can learn something from him."

" 'We?' " said Ediva. "You mean you're not going to tell me I can't go with you?"

"I've given up on that," Garth admitted.

Ediva nodded appreciatively. "You're learning."

Upon reaching Ravenswell, they decided to visit Aelred first and took the path to the mill. More than the usual number of people were gathered at the mill in the late afternoon. Aelred was nowhere to be seen. The mill's operation had been taken over by Agmund. Agmund was the son of Grim, the former miller, executed by Galon for his part in the killing of Galon's father. Agmund loaded grain for his son Thorild on the second floor. When the grain came back as flour, Agmund took a heaping measure as his share, half again as much as Aelred had done. The manor's steward, Pierre, and the reeve, Gilbert, attempted to impose order on the waiting mob.

Agmund and Thorild gave Garth smug looks as he and Ediva approached. "Be getting' *your* grain soon, I expect, Garthie," Agmund called out. He spat, just as he would probably spit in Garth's grain. "Look forward to that."

" 'Garthie?' " Ediva said to Garth.

Garth ignored them both. "Where is Aelred?" he asked Pierre.

The steward spread his arms. "No one knows."

An old woman named Evote, waiting in line, heard them and answered. "Left in the dead of night, he did, him and all his family."

"Knew this would happen one day," said a crone named Agnes next to her.

"Irresponsible, that boy," Evote said, nodding her head vigorously. "Always was."

Garth said, "And no one knows where they went?"

"Went to the Devil, belike," said Agnes.

266

"And you've given operation of the mill to Agmund?" Garth said to Pierre.

"For the moment," the harassed Pierre replied. "Life goes on, Garth, and Agmund knows how to run the operation, even if he does take a larger share than he ought."

Gilbert the reeve added, "Mill's been shut down for days, and people need their grain milled. They have to eat."

Garth nodded acknowledgement. He went to Aelred's house and beckoned Ediva inside. "Should we be doing this?" Ediva said as she tied her horse's reins to the fence.

"I'm the closest Aelred has to kin here," Garth said. "I'm within my rights to enter."

Inside, Garth looked round the empty house, found nothing relating to the plot. The house had a deserted feeling, dead, as though it had been empty for a long time. Agmund had been too busy with the mill to loot the house yet, so everything that Aelred hadn't taken with him was still in place.

Garth rummaged in Aelred's wooden chest, looking for something relating to the plot, but, as expected, there was nothing. He found some cloth, cleaned Ediva's wound with vinegar, and put a fresh bandage on it. Then he handed her a clean chemise and kirtle. "Here."

Ediva took the proffered garments. "What I'd really like is a bath."

Garth laughed. "My God, you have been away from village life for a while, haven't you?"

He drew a pail of water from Garth's well and brought it back. "Wash up as best you can and get changed. I'll wait outside."

Ediva was used to doing things quickly. She brushed that part of her hair that wasn't covered by the bandage as best she could. Then she washed and changed and emerged from the house. She had kept her own headdress, dirty though it was.

"Feel better?" Garth said.

"Much," said Ediva. It had been years since she'd worn such coarse cloth, but the garments were clean and well scented with lavender, to keep away fleas.

The two of them made their way to Garth's house. The late autumn sun was setting, casting a thin sheen of watery light over the village, bare-branched trees pointing to the fading sky like skeletal fingers in supplication. Fragrant wood smoke drifted from hearths and smoke holes, including Garth's. He opened the door for Ediva and they stepped inside, both coughing as the smoky air filled their lungs.

Even with the windows open, the house's interior was dim in the dying light, save for a pair of tallow candles on the trestle table. "Father!" cried Alfred, Garth's oldest child, as they came in. "You're back."

"Aye," Garth said, blinking his eyes from the smoke. The dog, King, barked and slobbered over Ediva like she was his long-lost best friend. Garth said, "It's good to be home, even if it is just for the night."

"Then you're off again?"

"Aye."

Cecily said, "Hello, Ediva. You're staying with us again?"

"Yes, I hope you don't mind," Ediva said, petting the dog and getting her face licked.

"No, we're happy to have you." Cecily led Ediva to the table. "Here, have a seat."

"I'll see to your horse," Alfstan, the youngest child, told Ediva, and he left the room, a draft of chill air coming in as he opened the door.

Garth and Ediva had missed the main meal, which was at mid-morning, but Cecily brought them bread and cheese and ale, and, of course, the ever-simmering pottage. It was dark now, and the windows were shut. Garth and Ediva ate hungrily. King kept nuzzling Ediva's arm so she would give him food. Alfred pulled him back. "King, stop."

"How are things here?" Garth asked between mouthfuls.

"Good," said Alfred. "We've been sharpening the long knives, getting ready for Martinmas."

Garth thought about that. The animals that were to be slaughtered had been chosen some weeks before. "You might do better to take the animals to Rob, the butcher."

"Please?" Alfred said. "I want to butcher them myself. I know how."

"And I'm going to help," said Alfstan, who had just returned, bringing with him another draft of cold air. It had started raining.

"And me," said Cecily. "I'm going to make blood pudding."

They were old enough, Garth knew. Still . . . "You be careful," he warned the three of them. "I don't want any of you slicing off your fingers, or cutting yourselves and dying of poisoned blood."

Alfred said, "Peter told us he'd help us if we needed it, when he's done with his own animals."

As if on call, and just as they had done the last time, Peter and Garth's sister Aethelwynn showed up, King barking happily to see them. "Gilbert said you were back," Peter told Garth, taking a seat at the crowded table.

"Just for the night," Garth said.

"Something to do with Miles?" Peter guessed.

Garth shrugged noncommittally.

"That looks like Matilda's dress," Aethelwynn said to Ediva.

"It is," Ediva said. "Mine was filthy, so I borrowed this. I'll return it as soon as I'm able."

Aethelwynn waved a hand. "Don't bother, she won't be needing it."

Garth gave his sister a look. "Why?"

Wynn leaned forward in the candlelight and lowered her voice, as though someone untoward might be listening. "Don't say a word of this to anyone, do you hear?" she told the children.

"Yes, Aunt Wynn," said Cecily, eager to hear whatever Aethelwynn was going to say.

"I hear," said Alfred.

"Me, too," said Alfstan.

"Where has Aelred gone?" Garth pressed.

"They've left for the Holy Land," Aethelwynn told him. "To start over."

There was silence.

"That's the Devil of a trip," Garth said at last.

"And the Devil of a place to live when you get there," Peter added. "*If* you get there. What's going on that they've had to run so far away?"

Garth and Ediva shared a look.

Peter saw it. "Is there something we should know about?" he asked, worried.

"Something Aelred's involved in?" Wynn added.

Garth said, "There is, but I can't tell you about it, not yet."

As Peter and Wynn protested, Garth added, "You'll know in a few days. Everyone will."

"But Aelred knows already, whatever it is, and he's running from it," Peter guessed.

"More like he's running from the consequences," Garth said. "Ediva and I are involved in it, too, only on the other side."

That statement aroused the attention not only of Peter and Aethelwynn but of the children, who all started talking at once. "This is so confusing," Wynn said over the noise and the happily barking dog. "Surely you can tell us something."

"No," Garth told her. "I don't want to get you and Peter in trouble. The less you know, the better off you are, believe me."

"Thanks," Peter said. "I'll sleep much better tonight after hearing that. Whatever it is, it must be big."

"Bigger than you can imagine," Garth said. "You and Wynn take Aelred's animals. As his executor, you have my permission. Get them before Agmund steals them."

"We'll go before dawn," Peter said, with Aethelwynn nodding.

Garth said, "Now I don't want to seem inhospitable, but Ediva and I have had a long day, and we need to get some rest. We're off to Badford Town at first light."

CHAPTER 57

November 8

꒐T WAS LATE, raining outside. The fire in the charcoal brazier was low. Blanche poked Estrild, who dozed on a pallet on the floor. "It's time."

Estrild stirred, rubbing sleep from her eyes.

It was Saturday; tomorrow was a day of rest. With the longer nights, and the cold and rain, the guards were unlikely to be keeping a sharp watch. Or so Blanche hoped.

Blanche and Estrild dragged the bed sheets and clothes from under the bed, where they'd hidden them, startling some mice, who had found the folded sheets a perfect place to nest. Blanche and Estrild changed into men's clothes, including braies.

"Never wore nothing like this before," Estrild said, looking down at the braies. "How d'you hook up these hose?"

"Like this." Blanche showed her, tying points on the hose to her braies.

Both women doffed their headdresses. Blanche would miss the silk headdress; it served as a reminder of how Miles had tricked Galon. They sat on the floor and knotted the sheets together as tightly as they could, working by the light of a single candle. "Hope these knots hold," Estrild said.

"We'll find out soon enough," said Blanche.

When the two ropes were finished, Blanche and Estrild pushed the bed to the window. Blanche had picked the window opposite the keep's entrance. It was quieter on this side; they were less likely to be seen. The bed made a heavy scaping noise racket on the wooden floor as they pushed it, and they held their breaths. But no guards came.

"Probably asleep," Estrild said. "Or drunk."

"Both, with any luck," said Blanche.

The window was narrow. It would be difficult to squeeze through. "I'll go first," Blanche said.

"Are you certain I have to go with you?" Estrild said.

"I'm certain."

Estrild sighed in resignation.

Blanche knotted one end of the rope to a leg of the bed, then dropped the other out the window. She looped the second rope across her chest. "Ready?" she asked Estrild.

Estrild crossed herself. "Truth be told, my lady, I wish it was Ediva here right now, and not me. She'd probably think this was fun."

Blanche couldn't help but smile, because what Estrild said was true. "Remember, don't look down. Brace your feet against the wall."

Estrild crossed herself again. Twice.

"Here we go."

Blanche sat on the narrow window ledge, grasped the knotted sheet in both hands, twisted, and swung out into the rain.

The rope held. Blanche said a silent prayer of relief.

She started down, hand over hand, feet braced against the wall, blinking rain from her eyes. Her shoulder still hurt from the wound she'd suffered from the pitchfork, and this weather didn't make it any better. One good thing was that the knots in the linen sheets grew tighter as they got wet.

Above her, Estrild went over the side. Estrild slipped on the wet wall with a little gasp, but held on. She swung back and forth, scraping against the wall, but managed to slow her momentum, then steady herself, using her feet, and started down.

They made their way down slowly, all too aware of how they stood out against the whitewashed wall, thankful for the bad weather.

As Blanche neared the rope's end, she looked over her shoulder. The rope was not long enough. There was a drop to the ground. How far, she couldn't tell in the dark.

"Damn."

There was nothing for it. She let go.

She dropped longer than she had hoped and hit the ground hard, knocking the wind out of her. Nothing seemed to be broken, though, and she scrambled out of the way to make room for Estrild.

"There's not enough rope," Estrild whispered from above.

"I know," Blanche hissed. "Just let go."

A second's hesitation, then Estrild thumped to the ground near Blanche. "Are you all right?" Blanche asked her.

"How the Devil should I know?" Estrild said. "Never planned on jumping out of castles at my age."

Blanche beckoned the shaken Estrild, and they made their way down the hill on which the keep was built. The hill was slick from the rain and they slid part of the way. The ditch at the bottom was partially full of freezing water. Taking Estrild's hand, Blanche led her across, and they climbed up the other side. The climb was made more difficult by the wet ground. They dug hands and feet into the cold mud or grasped at protruding rocks or plant roots.

At last they reached the top and were in the castle bailey. They crouched, watching. No one moved at this late hour. At least no one they could see, for it was very dark. Fires glowed in the watch towers, but were the guards watching?

Blanche motioned Estrild forward. Bent over, they made their way to the stone wall, expecting at any second to be challenged. But nothing happened.

They crept up the wall's wooden steps to the catwalk. Stopped again at the head of the steps. Watched, listened.

Nothing. No figures appeared in the watch towers.

Blanche removed the second rope from her shoulders. She knotted one end around one of the wall's stone merlons. Then eased between the merlons, grabbed the rope, and started down. Estrild followed, more confident this time.

This rope stretched almost all the way to the bottom. The two women dropped softly down. They slid into the bailey ditch, crossed the filthy, waist-high water, and climbed out the other side. They made their way through the darkened village toward the manor house.

From the keep behind them sounded a cry of alarm.

CHAPTER 58

BLANCHE AND ESTRILD reached the manor house unseen. No one was about at this hour. The rain still fell, and it seemed to have gotten colder outside, but maybe that was because they were soaked to the skin. Behind them, on the far side of the village, lights flickered in the castle and on its walls. Distant shouts could be heard. The alarm had been raised, and Onfroi would not be slow in discovering that they had escaped and in coming after them.

The gate to the manor house wall was barred. Blanche hammered on it, the noise unnaturally loud in the pre-dawn stillness.

Nothing happened. She hammered again. "Open up!"

A sleepy voice on the other side said, "Who the Devil—?"

"It's Lady Blanche and Estrild. Open! Hurry!"

"Lady Blanche?"

"Yes, you fool. Now open!"

There was a pause. Blanche and Estrild fidgeted, looked back toward the castle, where more lights shone. More faint shouts.

A dragging noise, and the bar lifted. The door opened a fraction and an older man peered out. Blanche pushed past him, followed by Estrild.

The old man was one of the servants. Brightwood's steward, Belot, came up, clad in only a shirt and a cloak against the cold and rain. Wada and Hersent emerged from the hall behind him. Wada had thrown on his wolf-skin cloak. Belot said, "My lady, what are you—?"

"We escaped," Blanche told him. "There's no time to explain, the French will be here soon. I need a horse."

"A—?"

"A horse. Now!"

"I'll get one," Wada said, and he ran toward the stables.

Hersent said, "I'll bring food and a cloak." She hurried back inside, shouting orders for the servants.

To Blanche, Belot said, "How did you—?"

"I'll tell you later," Blanche said. "I'm going to the forest, to join Lord Miles. Estrild, you go back to Redhill. You'll be safe there. Keep to the back roads."

"If I do that, I'll need a guide," Estrild said.

"I'll take her," Hersent said, coming up with a cloak for Blanche, along with a hooded cowl, a water skin and a sack of food.

Wada led forth Blanche's black palfrey, saddled. "I'll stay here and try to hold them off. Give you a bit of time." To Hersent, he said, "I'll join you at Redhill once the French have gone."

More torches had been lit at the castle. There was more distant shouting.

Blanche latched the cloak at her throat and pulled the hood over her wet hair. She swung into the saddle and galloped off.

CHAPTER 59

November 9 – Feast of St. Benignus of Armagh
2 Days Until Martinmas

As THE FIRST hint of dawn tinted the rain-sodden sky, a party of armed men rode through the village and up to Brightwood's manor house. They were led by Onfroi of Buchy and Theobald of Jumièges. None of the men wore armor, though all had swords, and, aside from Onfroi, Theobald, and Onfroi's squire Arnot, all carried spears, as well. Dogs barked in the village and on the manor house grounds.

"Search the village, Arnot," Onfroi ordered. "Then the fields and woods. Turn the place inside out. If the bitch is here, find her."

"Yes, my lord." Arnot picked some men and they rode into the village. At the same time, another of Onfroi's men dismounted and began pounding on the manor gate with the haft of his spear. *"Ouvrez! Ouvrez!"*

No answer. The man pounded again.

"Who's there?" came a voice.

"The sheriff of Trentshire," Onfroi called. "And if you don't open this gate, I'll mount your head on top of it."

The bar was lifted and the gate squealed open. Onfroi, Theobald, and the others cantered across the bridge and into the manor yard. Dogs ran around, barking at the newcomers. Seeing the armed men, a number of people who had been in the yard slinked away. Of those who remained, Onfroi recognized the steward, Belot, with whom he'd had dealings. For some reason, the steward from Redhill, an Englishman, was there, as well, wrapped in an expensive fur cloak. Belot looked as though he'd dressed hurriedly, and the Englishman, a big man, had an iron bar in his hand.

"Where is she?" Onfroi demanded of Belot.

"Who?" said the steward innocently.

"Who do you think? Lady Blanche."

Belot spread his arms. "She's in your—"

Onfroi lashed Belot with his riding crop. "She escaped, you imbecile, as you're well aware. Now where is she?"

Belot backed away, hand to the reddening weal on his cheek. "I don't know."

"Search the house," Onfroi told his men. "Burn it to the ground if you have to."

Onfroi's bailiffs dismounted. Meanwhile, in the village, Arnot and his party kicked in doors. With Arnot gleefully taking the lead, they speared barking dogs and any man who blocked their search. Furniture was overturned, hayricks ripped apart. Outhouses and henhouses were smashed. Fires started from overturned kettles. And if a maid or two was raped, well, that was part of the search, too.

As Onfroi's bailiffs started toward the hall, the English steward--Wada, Onfroi thought his name was—attempted to block their path, brandishing the iron bar. "See here, you can't—"

"Don't tell us what we can or cannot do," Onfroi warned him.

Wada stood straight, the wolf-fur cloak conferring upon him an authority he did not merit. "This is Lord Miles's manor. Lady Blanche isn't here, and you have no right to—"

Enraged at being spoken to this way by an Englishman, Onfroi made his horse rear, the horse's hooves stamped down on Wada's head, knocking him to the ground.

Onfroi continued trampling Wada; the horse had been trained to do this. Again and again, the hooves slashed down, crushing Wada's head and upper body and leaving him a bloody mess.

Onfroi breathed heavily, curbing his horse and looking for another victim. Theobald put a hand on his arm. "Calm yourself, *mon ami*. These English aren't worth it."

While Belot and another man ran to Wada's aid, Onfroi's men searched the hall and outbuildings, not caring what they broke—or stole.

Arnot and his men rode through the manor house gate. Blood spattered Arnot's leather gambeson. "She's not in the village, my lord."

"You're certain?" Onfroi said.

"I'm certain," Arnot said. "We looked everywhere."

The rest of Onfroi's men emerged from the hall, a few carrying plunder. "Not here, my lord," said their leader.

"She's gone to Redhill," Theobald guessed.

"She knows we'll look there," Onfroi told him. "No, she's gone to the forest, to join her husband." He turned to one of his men. "Alphonse, take your dogs and look for tracks. Heading west, she'll be."

"*Oui*, my lord," said the tracker and, with his assistants, he started off.

"Mount!" Onfroi called to his men. When all were mounted, he waved a hand. "*Allons.*"

He led his men from the manor, toward the forest. Parts of the village were in flames, and Wada's body was not the only one Onfroi's party left in its wake, but none of the French seemed to care.

CHAPTER 60

November 9

"PACKED AGAIN. IS it always like this?" Garth asked Ediva as they entered the Saracen's Head. Garth visited Badford as infrequently as possible, and he'd only been to the inn a handful of times.

"Always," Ediva replied. "God knows why."

They pushed their way through the crowd and took places at one of the long tables. Their hoods were pulled way up, hiding their faces. Milo, the owner, spotted them right away, though. He came over, that smug look on his face. Garth worried that he might punch that look off Milo's face and end up in trouble with the bailiffs.

"Back again, are you, missy?" Milo said. "Can't seem to stay away, can you?" He sneered at Garth. "You and your—"

Garth pushed two silver pennies across the table; he didn't have a lot of those pennies. "Bring us each a bumper of ale, along with pottage and bread, and then leave us alone for the rest of the day. Can you manage that?"

Milo examined the pennies and shrugged. "As you wish."

They waited. People, mainly men, came and went. No sign of Grugan, though. The ale was watered, and the pottage was thin, with bits of gristle and small chunks of some kind of meat in it. "What is this?" Garth said, staring into the bowl.

"Whatever they find in the alley," Ediva said. "Cat, dog, rat—maybe an old horse, if you're lucky. They don't put honey in it, either." The bread was old and hard. Ediva rapped it smartly on the table and waited for the weevils to crawl out before sawing off a piece. She had to soak it in the pottage to make it edible.

The day passed, with no sign of Grugan. From time to time, Milo or his wife, Helga, glared at them, but they didn't come over. At last, Garth said, "It's getting late. We'd better start back to Ravenswell before darkness makes the road too—"

"Look," said Ediva.

Grugan had come in the door, conspicuous by his blue cap.

The furrow-faced pedlar took a place at one of the benches. Some of the other men at the table were pedlars like Grugan, but there were also burly peasants and a couple merchants, identifiable by their better clothes. More men joined the gathering. They huddled, talking in low voices, intense. Grugan seemed to be giving instructions. Some of the men at the table left and were replaced by newcomers. Eventually the meeting broke up and Grugan left the inn.

"Let's go," Garth told Ediva.

They waited a moment, so it wouldn't be so obvious that they were following Grugan, then they rose from their table and left. Grugan was ahead of them, headed for the center of town, the same direction he'd been going the last time Ediva had followed him.

They trailed him at a distance. It was cold, with misty drizzle. Occasional shafts of light from lamps or candles illuminated portions of the wet street. The crowd diminished rapidly with the failing light. A rat scuttled by.

Grugan weaved through the people on the narrow street, Ediva and Garth behind him at a distance. "Spry bugger," Garth muttered, and as he said that, the old man broke into a run.

"Damn," Garth swore as he and Ediva started after. "He saw us."

They chased Grugan around a corner, where they were blocked by two large men, both of whom had been with Grugan at the Saracen's Head. With a start, Ediva recognized the stocky blond who had blocked her path the last time she was here.

"You don't seriously think we didn't recognize you?" the blond said.

* * *

The blond grabbed at Ediva, but she dodged out of his grasp and kept after Grugan. She ran down the street, gaining on him, even though hindered by her cloak and dress. She spied a board leaning against a wall and picked it up as she ran past.

She wasn't going to get in a fight with Grugan. He might be old, but he was a man, and much stronger than her. She had another idea. She got closer, closer. She was right behind him now. With an underhanded toss, she sailed the board between Grugan's flailing legs, tripping him and sending him sprawling face first to the muddy street.

Before Grugan could recover from the fall, Ediva whipped the belt from her waist, pulled Grugan's hands behind his back and tied them with it. Then she took Grugan's belt and tied his feet with that.

"Don't go anywhere," she told him.

* * *

The two men attacked. Garth punched the one with the coif just below the breastbone, doubling him over. The second one, the blond, clouted Garth on the side of the head, knocking him sideways. Garth staggered, and his assailant hit him again. Garth bounced off the wall of a building and tried to grapple with the man, but Garth had been stunned by the powerful blows, and the blond man threw him to the ground, where he landed in an icy puddle. The man stood over Garth and began hitting him, throwing punches with both hands. Garth somehow got to his knees and, in desperation, lunged at the man's legs and took him down. Garth jumped forward and jammed a thumb deep into the man's eye. The man screamed and rolled around in pain.

Garth rose to his feet, unsteady. The first man had recovered and was coming at him, dagger poised to strike. Garth tried to raise an arm, but he knew he was going to be too late to ward off the blow.

Then there was a heavy thunk, and the man toppled over.

Ediva stood there, a board in her hands.

She took Garth's elbow. "Let's get out of here."

"Where's Grugan?" Garth said. His head hurt; his eyes were unfocused from the blows he'd received.

"Up the street," Ediva said.

They turned down an alley. Ahead of them, Grugan crawled away, hands and feet bound, slithering on his side in the mud. He had lost his cap.

Ediva tisked and shook her head. She walked up and tapped Grugan's skull with the wood. "Going somewhere?"

The old man swore in frustration. As he did, Garth came up. He and Ediva grabbed Grugan's arms and dragged him down the alley, even as cries for the watch sounded behind them.

They pulled Grugan down another street, into another alley. It was full dark now, hardly anyone about, because only fools and criminals were found on the streets of Badford after dark.

Garth was angry because of the beating he'd taken. He wanted to take it out on somebody, but Grugan was too old to fight, and that made Garth even angrier. He propped Grugan against the wall and took the board from Ediva. He knelt and jammed one end of the board under Grugan's jaw, knocking the old pedlar's head against the wall. "We know about the rebellion, we heard it from Aelred. We want to know the rest."

"Then you—"

He bounced Grugan's head off the wall again. "Tell us."

"You're Miles's son. Why don't you join us?"

Grugan's head hit the wall a third time. "Because we don't like killing women and kids," Garth said.

"I don't know any more," Grugan said. "I swear it."

Ediva handed Garth her dagger. "Kill him. He's no use to us, and I'm tired of standing here in the cold."

"Wait!" cried Grugan. "Wait. It's supposed to start with something big, that's all I know."

Garth and Ediva exchanged looks. "What do you mean, 'something big?'" Garth said.

"I don't know. You'll know it when it happens, that's what Aelred told me. Every Norman in England has someone assigned to kill them. When it starts, bells will toll all across the country. That'll be the signal for the general killing to begin. I'm to toll the bell here at St. Hugobert's after I do my job."

"You're supposed to kill someone? Who?"

"Ralph of Cotto." Ralph was the earl of Trent's representative in Badford.

"What about Aelred?" Garth said.

"He was to kill Pierre, Ravenswell's steward. Aelred's disappeared, though, so we had to find someone else."

"Agmund?" Garth guessed.

"How did you know?" Grugan said.

"Magic. You don't know any more about this big event?"

"I know it's going to happen at Brightwood Castle. It was supposed to start at St. Mary's Lodge, but it got switched at the last moment."

"Brightwood?" Ediva said. "Why Brightwood? Because the sheriff is there?"

"The sheriff, Theobald, all the French. They'll be there for Lady Blanche's trial on Martinmas Day."

"And if the bells don't ring?" Garth said.

"They will," Grugan told him confidently.

"If we hurry, we can reach Brightwood by Martinmas," Ediva told Garth.

"It'll mean another night of sleeping rough," Garth said.

"That's all right, I'm getting used to it. What about tonight?"

Garth lowered his voice so Grugan couldn't hear. "We can't stay in town, they'll be looking for us. We'll have to take our chances on the road."

Ediva crossed herself, and she and Garth started from the alley. Grugan was still bound hands and feet, propped against the wall. "What about me?" he cried. "Aren't you going to let me go?"

"No!" Ediva shouted back.

CHAPTER 61

November 10 – Feast of St. Leo the Great
1 Day Until Martinmas

BLANCHE LED HER black palfrey through the forest. The mare had thrown its right front shoe earlier, and so walked with a tender foot. She was slowing Blanche down. Blanche knew the sheriff's men were after her, and they could probably guess where she was headed. Her only advantage was that they didn't know which path she'd take or where, exactly, Miles's camp was. On the other hand, Onfroi and Theobald would probably have expert trackers in their employ. Blanche would leave the horse with the first person she found who wasn't likely to eat it and return for it later with a generous reward.

At least the walking kept her warm. The man's sturdy knee-length shirt and thick hose she wore were better suited for walking than a woman's dress would have been, as were the ankle-high leather shoes. She had avoided the most heavily traveled paths, skirted villages and fields. She longed to see Miles again, longed to get back to Redhill and see her children.

She worried about the children—Richard, John, Alice. With both parents accused of treason, what was to become of them? If Miles and Blanche were executed, or if they spent the rest of their lives outside the law, would Richard be permitted to inherit the family estates and take care of his siblings? Or would they all be made wards of some noble—the sheriff, perhaps, or Galon?

Or would they . . .?

The last thought was too horrible to contemplate, but contemplating it was all that she had been doing. Her children by her first husband had been killed by her husband's brother, and she would go to any lengths to prevent that sort of thing from happening again.

She hoped Estrild had made it safely back to Redhill. She had no idea what had become of Ediva. The girl seemed to have vanished into the late autumn mists. Ediva had a knack for extricating herself from difficult situations, however, or Blanche would be more worried about her.

She stopped. What had she heard?

Footsteps? A branch cracking?

She strained her ears. The horse blew and bobbed its muzzle. It had heard something, too, something it didn't like. She put a hand over the animal's muzzle, calming it.

Blanche stayed like that, but heard nothing more. It might have been an animal—a fox, maybe, or a deer. It might even have been her imagination. Her horse was still restless, though. Best to trust the animal's senses and get off the path. Hide in the trees and brush and wait for a while.

Another noise, this time in front of her. A man with a crossbow aimed stepped out of the trees, the crossbow aimed at her. She recognized him as one of the castle guards. She dropped the horse's reins and turned to run, but another crossbowman blocked her path to the rear. She tried to leave the path and escape into the trees, but a third crossbowman waited for her there.

More men appeared on the path before her—Onfroi with his shaved head, Theobald of Jumièges, Gautier of Haverham. Horsemen and men holding horses came up behind them. They must have taken another track and gotten ahead of her while she was slowed by her lame mount.

Theobald and Gautier looked smug. Theobald even raised a hand in mock greeting. "Lady Blanche! Well met!"

Onfroi said nothing. He started toward her, rage on his doughy face. He covered the distance in a few furious paces and punched Blanche in the stomach, doubling her up. He hit her on the cheek, his meaty fist like a sledgehammer, knocking her to the ground. He kicked her in the spine, making her arch her back, and when she did that, he kicked her in the stomach, doubling her up again. He kicked her in the head, but his rage was so great that it affected his aim and the kick didn't connect with full force, otherwise it might have killed her.

Theobald and Gautier rushed up and grabbed Onfroi's arms. "My lord!"

"Lord Onfroi!"

He threw them off and aimed a kick at Blanche's face. She barely avoided it and it caromed off her ear, ripping the ear open. Blanche's eyes swam, her ear rung.

Gautier grabbed Onfroi again. "Stop, my lord! You'll kill her."

"Who cares?" growled Onfroi as he struggled out of Gautier's grasp. "She's a traitor to her race, dam of a pack of mongrel dogs that need to be put down. Look at her, dressed like a man. She's nothing but a whore. Not even a whore, because she does it for free."

He kicked Blanche in the back of the head, and was grabbed by Theobald this time. Theobald said, "Who cares about her, you say? None of us. But Lord Galon has taken an interest in her, and that makes a difference."

"Galon the *Cruel*?" Onfroi mocked. "I've got plans for that pig, as well. You'll see."

He spun out of Theobald's grasp and advanced on the helpless Blanche once more, when Gautier said, "It'll look bad if you kill her like this, my lord. It's not like she's a man, who could put up a fight. Better to do it legally."

Onfroi stopped. His breathing slowed. "You're right," he said at last. "Get her up. We'll take her back to Brightwood for her trial."

Theobald and Gautier pulled Blanche roughly to her feet, making her cry out from the pain in her stomach. Blood poured from her ear over the right side of her cloak, and her head literally seemed to be spinning. Her jaw was somehow both numb and sore at the same time.

Theobald motioned one of his men to dismount. He and Onfroi's squire Arnot helped—or, rather, threw—Blanche onto the horse.

"What'll we do with her horse?" Theobald asked Onfroi.

Onfroi eyed the black palfrey.

"Put it down?" suggested Gautier.

"No, that would be cruel." Onfroi stroked the palfrey's muzzle and neck. "Wouldn't it, girl?" He indicated the man who'd given up his horse for Blanche. "You, stay with this horse. See it gets back to the castle." He picked two other men. "You two, stay with him. When the horse is shod, we'll sell it."

"Too bad we can't do that to Blanche," joked Theobald.

"You have poor taste, *mon ami*," Onfroi told him. "I would never buy anything that had been used by an Englishman. Now mount up."

CHAPTER 62

𝕿HE THREE CASTLE guards took the black palfrey back to Brightwood. Two of the guards were mounted; the third, a Burgundian named Philippe, led the lame horse.

"Why is Onfroi so worried about this damned horse?" said one of the riders, a Fleming called Ekkehard. Ekkehard was a veteran soldier but a newcomer to the castle garrison. He replaced a man whose time had expired and who had gone in search of more excitement.

The other rider, Kurt, was also Flemish. His long hair was tied behind him with a ribbon. He said, "Onfroi loves horses. He'll make a tidy profit selling this one when Blanche is gone. That's if he doesn't decide to keep it for his wife."

"Or his mistress," Ekkehard said.

"Onfroi doesn't have a mistress," Kurt said. "He's loyal to his wife."

Ekkehard snorted. "Knew there was something off about him. Where is his wife? Not in England."

"In Buchy. Tending his estates."

Philippe interrupted them. "Can't we take turns riding?" he complained. It was his horse that had been taken for Lady Blanche to ride back to Brightwood.

Kurt bit back a smile. "Lord Onfroi said nothing about taking turns."

"Besides, walking is good exercise," Ekkehard told Philippe. "It will build you up. You Burgundians are lazy."

"At least we're not thieves like you Flemings," Philippe said.

Both of the riders made surprised noises. Ekkehard placed a hand to his heart. "Who are you calling a thief? I have never stolen a thing in my life."

Kurt inclined his head modestly. "I may have robbed a few girls of their virginity, but beyond that, I'm honest as a saint."

"You stole a candlestick from the altar of the village church," Philippe told him.

"That's not stealing," Kurt said, "it's loot."

"It was our own village of Brightwood," said Phillipe.

Kurt refused to admit any wrong in what he'd done. "Serves them right for leaving it out to—"

An arrow thunked into Kurt's chest.

Kurt's eyes widened. His arms flopped around like those of a drunk seeking to regain his balance, and he toppled from the saddle.

Ekkehard and Phillipe stared, stunned. Before they could react, a large body of men emerged from the surrounding forest. How they had hidden in the leafless trees, Ekkehard and Philippe could not guess. The men were ragged, dirty, and sick; and they smelled like a latrine shaft; but they were well armed, and they looked eager to use their weapons.

"You lads should have been paying better attention," the men's leader told the guards in excellent French. He was a big man in his early fifties, heavily muscled in the back and shoulders. He gestured at the palfrey and said to Philippe, "That is my wife's horse, *monsieur*. I advise you to be honest about how you come to be in possession of it."

"Your wife?" said Philippe, and now it was his turn to go wide eyed. "Then . . . that means you must be Lord . . ."

"No, I'm King Henry, you fool," Miles said, for that was who it must be. He did not look like a lord; he was as dirty and ragged as the rest. "Now, how did you get this horse? Be quick, or you'll end up like your friend here."

Philippe stammered, "Your wife, she—"

"Address him as 'my lord,' " said one of the gang, a man with one hand.

Philippe gulped and went on. "Your wife, my lord, she escaped from Brightwood Castle. We captured her."

"Who do you mean by 'we?' " Miles snapped.

"Lord Onfroi, my lord. The sheriff. And Lord Theobald. They're taking her back to the castle for trial."

That produced a reaction among the armed men. "Trial?" said Miles, leaning in close.

"Y—yes, my lord. For treason. Her horse went lame. We were—we were ordered to bring it along after her."

"How far ahead of us are they?"

Philippe looked at the sky, tried to estimate in a way these men would understand. He was so scared that he couldn't come up with anything, and the Englishmen looked ready to kill the two guards, so Ekkehard took over. "Not far, my lord. Maybe the amount of time it'd take you to hear High Mass on Easter."

Miles stared at Ekkehard as though wondering when a man like him had ever heard High Mass. Then he spoke to his comrades, "We need to get to the castle before they do."

"Why not ambush 'em on the way?" said a nasty looking man with a much-broken nose.

Miles shook his head. "No. Too much chance of Blanche getting hurt in a fight like that."

"They have a head start, and they're mounted," the man with one hand pointed out.

"But we know the country better," said another.

"Wish Ediva was with us," one of the men said. "She'd know the fastest way."

"Be quiet, Scarlet. You act like Ediva's the only one ever been in the woods. There's others of us know the forest as well as her."

Miles said, "Odda, you and Ulf take Blanche's horse to Edsworth. Warn Guillame about the rebellion. Then meet us at Brightwood."

The one-handed men indicated the two prisoners. "What about them?"

"Kill 'em," said the man with the broken nose.

The leader shook his head. "No, take them back to camp. We'll figure out what to do with them later."

Knowing he wasn't going to be killed made Ekkehard bold. "Onfroi will have your head," he boasted to Miles.

"Maybe," Miles acknowledged. "Or maybe I'll have his."

CHAPTER 63

November 11 – Feast of St. Martin of Tours

ℳARTINMAS.

On this day began the slaughter of those animals that could not be fed through the winter—cows, pigs, goats. After the animals were killed, carcasses were drained and the blood saved for puddings and sausages. Hides were taken for leather. Meat was cut and salted—if salt was available. Hearts, brains, intestines, hooves, bones—everything was used. The first wine of the season was tasted on this date; and for at least one day of the year most everyone had a good meal of goose or beef.

Brightwood Manor was unusually quiet this early Martinmas morn. Tense. Expectant. It had been that way since Lady Blanche escaped and the sheriff and his men had set out after her, after killing the steward Wada and others. And if people knew about the large body of armed men that had gathered in the forest to the south of the castle, no one spoke of it.

* * *

"They're not letting anyone in," Diote told Miles and the others. Diote had gone to the castle as a scout, pretending to look for work, since it was unlikely anyone would suspect ill of a woman. Since Miles had spared her life, Diote had done her best to justify her place in the group, and in doing so she seemed to have blossomed, to have become more assertive and less mousey than before. She hadn't lingered at the castle—the sheriff and his men could arrive at any moment.

"Is the keep open, could you tell?" Miles asked her.

"It is," Diote replied. "The guards seem nervous. Maybe 'cause the village is so quiet."

They were gathered on the same wooded hill where, years ago, in a driving storm, Miles had prepared to attack the castle. There were nearly a hundred of them. Hersent was with them. She had returned to the manor after hearing what had happened to her husband, and Estrild had come with her. Hersent wore man's clothes and carried her bow, with a leather bracer on her arm and twin daggers at her belt. Her red hair was braided, as it had been in her outlaw days, and streaks of blue paint decorated her cheeks.

"How many men, d'ye reckon?" Miles asked Diote.

"From what I could see, a knight and maybe a dozen foot," Diote said.

Miles said, "The usual garrison's what? Theobald, two knights, and a score of mercenaries?"

"The sheriff and his men are staying there now, too," Bondo reminded him.

"Most of them are off chasing Lady Blanche," said Hersent. "Onfroi took just about every man he had for fear of you jumping them in the woods again."

There was movement in the trees. Scarlet led two people to the gathering. It was Garth and Ediva, Ediva riding and Garth on foot. The two of them—and the horse—were muddy and tired.

"Thank God," Garth said to his father. "We were hoping you'd be here. This is where the revolt is to begin."

That caused a lot of talk. "What?" Miles said as he assisted Ediva from her horse.

"We heard it from Grugan. There's to be a signal. Something big, he said. And it's to be here, at Brightwood. Today."

Ediva said, "When it happens, the church bell in the village will toll. That will be the signal for bells to ring across the country, and the killing of the French will begin."

"Every Frenchman in England has a person assigned to kill them," Garth added.

That statement drew a lot of comment.

"Is that even possible?" Hersent asked.

"Grugan says it is," Garth replied. "He says everything's in place, and they're just waiting."

Miles rubbed his jaw. "A signal to start it, you say. But you don't know what this signal will be?"

"No," Garth said. "Grugan didn't know either."

"You're sure he was telling you the truth?"

"We're sure," Ediva said, and she couldn't help but smile.

Miles turned. "Odda, take a dozen men to the church and make sure that bell doesn't get rung, no matter what."

"Aye," said Odda, and he hurried off.

Ediva embraced Estrild and Hersent. "Why are you dressed like that?" she asked Hersent. "You look like you did when you were with the Viking."

"Onfroi killed my husband," Hersent said. "Trampled him with his horse. I'm here for revenge,"

"My God," Ediva said. "I'm so sorry."

"The bastard," said Garth.

"Wada wasn't the only man killed that day," Hersent went on. "Girls were raped, as well. Onfroi's squire Arnot was behind all that."

Wighelm growled, "Still think we should be stoppin' this revolt, Miles? Me, I think we should be leadin' it."

There was loud assent to that from the men.

"A proper revolt," Scarlet added. "None o' this killin' women and young 'uns."

More assent.

"Fight 'em in the forest," Wighelm urged, "like you said."

"We have the men," Frithric said. "If there's ever to be a revolt, it has to be now."

"Aye," growled Ioco. "Aye," growled others.

Miles hesitated. Frithric was right. So was Scarlet. A proper revolt, no massacre of women and children. No help from the Scots. And Miles realized that it wouldn't just be a revolt to make England free of the French. No, Miles could fulfill his other dream, his biggest dream, to make Mercia an independent kingdom once more. With its glittering court at Tamworth, as in olden times. The Devil with Wessex and Sussex, Kent and Northumbria. The Devil with Scotland. Let them fight among themselves. Mercia would be free.

But who would rule? And now Miles freed the long-buried part of his ambition. He had Mercian royal blood. The price to pay for Mercian freedom would be him as king. With Blanche as his queen. And even as he thought that, his mind flashed to the succession, because that was how a king thought. The crown would go to Garth, of course, he was the oldest. Richard would inherit the honor of Redhill and be given other lands besides, maybe be named earl marshal. John would be bishop of Tamworth. And Alice? There was no royal blood left in the English kingdoms. She would be married to the royal house of Scotland, or Flanders or France, maybe even Burgundy or Austria. A match that would provide suitable allies against the Normans, should they try to take power again.

Miles's head was swimming with possibilities. Mercia free. Him as king. And the price for this? The cost in blood and treasure and destruction? Could he stand before God in Judgment and—

"Miles!" It was Frithric.

"What?" Miles said.

"You drifted off."

"No, I was thinking. You're right, we'll do it. We'll revolt."

A cheer rang round the assembly.

"But first we have to stop this massacre," Miles said.

"Hasn't Galon already done that?" Garth said. "He sent out a warning. Gallopers are crossing the country. The French will be on the alert for an attack."

"We can't count on his warning being successful," Miles told him.

"And we still don't know what the signal's to be."

Just then, one of the scouts, no more than a boy, came running through the woods as fast as he could. "Ten years ago, that would have been me," Ediva remarked as the boy came on.

"Or me," said Hersent, and Miles heard wistfulness in both of their voices.

The boy halted in front of Miles, breathing hard. "Five miles off, they are, my lord. No more. Lady B's with 'em, and she looks like they beat her up. Beat her bad."

Miles's eyes narrowed and his voice grew hard. "What do you mean?"

"There's blood all over her cloak, and she's not sittin' right in her saddle, like she's hurt."

Miles clenched his jaw.

"What do we do?" Frithric asked.

"Take 'em as they ride through the village," Wighelm suggested. "It's a good spot for an ambush."

"No," Miles said. He looked at the men and women around him. "Here's the plan."

CHAPTER 64

ESTRILD APPROACHED THE castle gate. Hersent was with her, the hood of her cloak pulled well up and her head down, so the guards wouldn't see the warlike blue paint on her cheeks. By ones and twos, weapons concealed beneath their cloaks, Miles and his men took places at the taverns and brothels and cook shops outside the castle walls.

Estrild and Hersent crossed the bridge to the gate. A lowered spear blocked their further advance. "What's your business here?" asked the guard with the spear. He was a Fleming with a scarred left eyebrow.

Estrild drew herself up in that fussy way she had. "I am Estrild, young man, maid to Lady Blanche. This is my lady's other maid, Ediva. We've come to tend to my lady, as is our right and duty."

The second guard, a swarthy Burgundian, eyed the two women suspiciously. "Lady Blanche isn't here, she escaped. The sheriff and Lord Theobald are out after her. If you're her maid, you should know that."

"Of course I know that," Estrild snapped, "but I'm given to understand she was captured."

The Burgundian drew himself up. "First I heard of it. The sheriff and his mean aren't back yet."

Estrild gave her companion an exasperated look. To the guards, she said, "We'll wait in the keep till they arrive, in my lady's quarters."

She started forward, but the first guard barred her entrance with the spear again. "No visitors. Sheriff's orders."

"We're not visitors, you loon, we're—"

Hersent threw back her hood and plunged a dagger into the first guard's chest. She pivoted and, with her left hand, she threw her second dagger, hitting the Burgundian in the chest, as well.

As that happened, Miles and his men rushed the gate. While Wighelm finished off the two guards, Garth tossed Hersent's bow to her, and she caught it deftly. He handed her a quiver of arrows, and they started with one group up the steps to the castle wall. Frithric led another group up the steps on the opposite side of the gate. A third group, with Miles at its head, made its way to the keep, trying to get there before somebody saw what was happening and barred the keep's entrance.

Only a handful of guards manned the bailey wall; the rest were out with Onfroi and Theobald. Two guards were the castle walk, on their way to relieve the men at the gate. Garth and Hersent shot them with arrows, and the other outlaws ran past, to overpower the rest of the guards on this side of the wall.

On the other side of the wall, it was the same. The surging group of outlaws rushed the watchtowers and neutralized the men stationed there, though one of the guards shot Ulf with a crossbow before he was killed. The remaining guards, seeing they were vastly outnumbered, surrendered. Garth's and Frithric's groups raced around the castle walls till they met on the north side, overlooking the river, and the castle wall was under control.

In the bailey, Miles's party headed for the keep. Ediva, the fastest, took a lead on the others, racing for the bridge across the keep's ditch. So far, there had not been any commotion. Then a servant raised a cry from the kitchen at the end of the yard, yelling until Wighelm ran up and knocked him senseless with his fist.

Ediva raced across the bridge and up the steps to the keep, taking the steps two at a time. A guard, alerted by the yells from the yard, made to bar the door to the keep's forebuilding. Ediva appeared, drew her bow and aimed it at him. "Don't," she ordered.

The guard raised his hands in surrender, while two more of Miles's men arrived and tied him up. Ediva and another man kept going up the steps of the forebuilding and took control of the keep's door, quickly followed by more of the outlaws, until the keep was secure.

Still hobbled by his leg wound, the knight Blaise had been left in charge of the castle while Onfroi and Theobald were gone. Hearing yells and running feet, Blaise emerged from the stables, sword drawn, and charged into the outlaws flooding the bailey. He struck down Legulf and backhanded another man, slashing open his chest. Another man jumped on him with a knife, but Blaise threw him off.

Miles started for Blaise.

"Miles! Behind you!" shouted Scarlet.

Miles turned to see cherubic Father Nicolas with an axe raised to strike. The priest was brained by Ioco with a spiked club. Miles and Ioco exchanged looks and nodded at one another.

Miles turned back. Blaise was surrounded by archers with drawn bows. Bleeding from the chest, he circled, facing the bow men, sword ready.

"Yield," Miles ordered him.

Blaise grasped the sword more firmly.

"Yield!" Miles said.

CHAPTER 65

THE SHERIFF'S PARTY approached Brightwood Castle. Shaven-headed Onfroi was in the lead, followed by Theobald of Jumièges and Gautier of Haverham. Behind them came Blanche, her hands tied in front of her, her horse's reins held by Onfroi's squire, Arnot.

For Blanche, the ride here seemed to have taken forever. Her jaw and cheek were sore. Her ribs hurt even worse. The kick to her back seemed to have damaged something inside her and made it agony to maintain a seat in the saddle. Dried blood from her ear was all over the right side of her face and down her cloak. She would have given anything to lie down and rest.

Arnot looked back at her and grinned. "Comfortable, my lady?"

"Don't address your betters unless you're asked to," Blanche told him. "Hasn't Ofroi taught you anything?"

"What makes you think you're my better?" he sneered.

"I'm breathing, aren't I?"

The insult didn't bother him. "Not for long," he said.

They had approached the castle by a roundabout path. Onfroi was leery of using the narrow village street, where peasants loyal to Blanche might make an attempt to free her. The castle gates were open, two helmeted guards stationed there. The guards stepped aside to allow Onfroi and his party to pass. Blanche noted that the guards averted their eyes from the newcomers, especially from Theobald, their commander. One of the guards looked strangely familiar, almost like Miles's man Scarlet. Blanche's heart beat faster as she glimpsed splashes of blood around the gate that had been hurriedly covered with dirt. As if he'd had the same sudden thought as Blanche, Theobald turned and looked behind him at the guards, his face wearing a puzzled frown, but Theobald had little dealings with the guards, so he shrugged and turned his eyes front once more.

The party clattered into the bailey yard. More guards manned the towers. Everything seemed normal, save there were no servants or workmen about.

Theobald frowned again. "Where is everyone? Where is Blaise? He should be here to greet us."

Onfroi glanced around suspiciously. "Something's not—"

Blanche diverted his attention, nodding her chin toward the center of the yard, where the platform that had been under construction was complete. On the platform was a wooden chopping block. Old stains discolored the area beneath the dip where the victim's neck was placed. "I see you've prepared for my trial, Lord Sheriff," Blanche said. "Why, it's as if the verdict has already been rendered."

"It has been," said Onfroi, his suspicions momentarily alleviated, "and I look forward to seeing the sentence carried out later this day."

"I've never seen a beheading before," Gautier of Haverham said.

"Really?" said Theobald, who wasn't surprised to hear this from a shire knight.

Gautier shrugged. "We've never had one around here. The only people we execute are peasants, and we hang them."

"You're in for a treat, then," Theobald told him. "Beheadings are fun. Unless the headsman makes a botch of it, of course. I saw one in the Ile de France where the fellow was so drunk it took him six swings of the axe to complete the job. Hacking away, he was, like a—"

"Look!" said Arnot. He pointed to the northeast tower of the keep.

On the tower, the sheriff's gold and black flag was coming down, and a new flag was raised in its place. This flag had a green field and on it was some kind of animal in white. Blanche's heart leaped as she recognized the lion from Miles's ring.

Onfroi said, "What the . . .?"

"Greetings, my lords!" cried a voice, and a grinning Miles stepped from between two buildings into the yard. He carried a bow; a short sword and a quiver of arrows hung from his belt.

"Arrest him!" Onfroi told his men.

"Not so fast, my lord." Still grinning, Miles waved his hand round the yard, inviting Onfroi and his party to look.

Armed men, most carrying bows, appeared from the buildings in the bailey. More men, and Hersent, appeared on the bailey wall and at the entrance to the keep, their bows ready.

Blanche thought Miles was going to give some insouciant Brock the Badger speech, but his brow darkened ominously as he took in Blanche's condition. "Who did this to my wife?"

"I did," Onfroi said. "My only regret is that I didn't let my men rape her first. All of them."

Miles threw down his bow. He drew the short sword and raced forward.

Onfroi grabbed Blanche's reins from Arnot and turned his horse. "Go!"

Some of Onfroi's men wheeled their horses and tried to escape. Others drew weapons to stay and fight. Miles ran after Onfroi but couldn't catch him. He looked to the wall, where Hersent had drawn her bow and aimed it at the fleeing Onfroi. She let loose the arrow and it tore through the rear of Onfroi's leather gambeson, ripping a wound across his back.

Arrows flew; men and horses fell. Hersent hesitated to shoot again because there was too much chance of hitting Blanche in the confusion. Onfroi guided Blanche through the melee to the gate. The guards were trying to push the heavy gate shut, but Blanche saw that Onfroi was going to beat them and squeeze through. Blanche was under no illusions what would happen to her if Onfroi escaped with her.

Ediva sprinted up and grabbed the reins of Blanche's horse. The horse pulled around violently, making Onfroi's mount stumble. Meanwhile, the gate was closing. Onfroi beat at Ediva with his fist, but she held on. One of Onfroi's men rushed at Ediva with a spear, but Ioco hit him in the head with his club. Blanche loosened her feet in the stirrups and threw herself from the saddle, landing hard. Onfroi swore and continued through the gate, which shut behind him, cutting off the retreat of his men.

Hersent ran to the wall and aimed an arrow at the fleeing Onfroi. It was as though he sensed what she was doing, because as she loosed the arrow, he weaved his horse to the right and the arrow sailed wide. Hersent swore, strung another arrow and shot it high, but it fell just behind Onfroi's galloping horse. Onfroi was out of rage.

Inside the bailey, Onfroi's squire Arnot rode at Blanche and Ediva, sword drawn. Garth picked up the downed guard's spear and thrust it into the chest of Arnot's horse. The horse reared in pain and threw its rider, and as Arnot rose, Garth rammed the spear through the front of Arnot's head.

Unable to escape, Theobald and Gautier wheeled and turned on Miles, who was running to Blanche's aid. Theobald swung his sword at Miles. Miles barely dodged the blow. He chopped at Theobald's extended sword arm with his short sword, taking the arm half off, and dragged Theobald from his horse. As Theobald cried in pain, Miles buried his sword in the Frenchman's chest.

Gautier circled the two men, trying to get in a blow with his sword. Garth jumped on him from behind, dragging him from the saddle. As Gautier rose from the dirt, Garth took Gautier's head and chin in his powerful hands and snapped his neck.

After that, the sheriff's surviving men, outnumbered, gave in quickly. Most had been killed or wounded, but Miles's men had suffered, as well. Wighelm was down, and Frithric's arm dripped blood from a jagged wound.

Blanche lay on the ground, dazed from her fall. Ediva had covered her with her body, protecting her from arrows and blades and trampling hooves. Miles ran to Blanche and helped her to her feet. She sagged against him, and he hugged her and kissed her forehead. "Are you all right?"

Blanche shook her head, trying to clear it. "I'm alive, which was more than I was expecting a short while back."

Supporting herself against Miles, Blanche turned to Ediva. "Thank you, Ediva. Like as not, you saved my life."

That's my job, my lady," Ediva said.

Garth came up. "Are you all right?" he asked Ediva.

"Few bumps and bruises," Ediva said, "An ordinary day for me, anymore."

Garth indicated the prisoners. "What are we going to do with them?" he asked Miles. "We can't stay here. The sheriff will raise every Frenchman in Trentshire and come after us."

"Reckon it's back to the forest," said Bondo, whose face was splashed with blood. "And quick."

At that moment came a cry from the wall. "Riders approaching!" It was Hersent.

"Any idea who they are?" Miles called back.

There was a moment of hesitation, then Hersent cried, "Looks like the earl of Trent. I recognize his banner."

Miles's jaw set. This was it. "Open the gate," he told his men.

The men hesitated.

"Do it," Miles said.

The men unbarred the gate and pulled it open, revealing Galon, Stigand, and a score of armed retainers.

CHAPTER 66

GALON, STIGAND, AND their men rode into the bailey yard. These were knights and men at arms, armored and ready for battle, with the white swan banner of Trent going before them.

They stopped, surveyed the carnage in the yard. They saw the armed men around them and on the walls. Saw bows nocked and drawn. Saw Hersent, wild eyed and painted for war, who couldn't wait to pull the bowstring. To their rear, Odda and his men hurried back from the church in case there was trouble.

Miles raised his hand. He looked into Galon's dark eyes. This was the moment Miles had waited for his entire life. The French gone. Mercia. Tamworth. It was all his for the taking. All he had to do was drop his hand. He took a deep beath and—

He raised his other hand. "They're friends! Lower your weapons!"

Cries of anger from his men. Hersent threw back her head in grief and rage, and for a second Miles thought she would loose her arrow anyway, but she gave in and lowered her bow, tossing it to the walkway in disgust.

Waves of self-hate and revulsion poured over Miles. The most important moment of his life, and he had backed away. He refused to be responsible for the blood and destruction and ruined lives. His conscience wouldn't permit it. The French would be driven out someday, but not by him. His time had passed.

Galon stared at him long and hard. It was like he knew what Miles had been about to do. He nodded to Miles almost imperceptibly and looked round the bailey. He saw Blanche, dressed in man's clothes, beaten and covered with blood. "What happened to you?" he said.

"Onfroi," she replied.

"No more than I would expect from him. I trust he's among the dead?"

"No," she said, "he got away."

"Pity," Galon said. To Miles, he said, "Your son informed me that this is where the English rebellion would begin, and that's why we're here. I see a lot of dead Normans and a lot of live English. Would you care to explain that?" He looked up at blue-painted Hersent, who smiled and waved to him in greeting.

French and English continued to face off. Wighelm might be down, but Miles knew that others of his men, like Ioco, were eager for a fight to start. "Onfroi was going to put my wife on trial for treason," Miles explained. He pointed to the platform in the center of the yard. "That chopping block tells you what the sentence was to be. I couldn't permit that. I had to stop it."

Galon thought that over and nodded. "I can't fault you there." His men seemed to relax a bit at that; so did Miles's.

Galon dismounted, followed by Stigand. The rest of Galon's men remained mounted, still alert for trouble. Galon passed the dead squire Arnot with the gaping wound in the front of his head, and he kicked the body. "No great loss. Couldn't stand that fellow."

He came upon the bodies of Theobald and Gautier. "Who killed these men?"

Garth started to say something, but Miles beat him to it. "I did."

Galon darted an eye at Garth, then back to Miles. "Both of them?"

"That's right, my lord," Miles said.

"Hmmm," Galon said again. He looked at the keep's tower. "Is that your green flag?"

"It is, my lord."

"How many times have you captured this castle, anyway?"

"Two," Miles said. "So far."

"Isn't it supposed to be impregnable to rabble like yours? That's the reason they build these things. We might as well just turn it over to you."

Miles said nothing.

Galon went on. "Did any of our nobles survive?"

"Blaise, my lord. He was wounded, but he'll live. He's in the chapel."

"What about the priest?"

"Killed, my lord. He came at me with an axe, and one of my men was forced to stop him."

"Hmmm."

Galon mounted the wooden platform and sat on the chopping block, overlooking the bailey yard. Black-clad Stigand stood behind him. Exhausted, bloodied, and aching all over, Blanche eased herself onto one of the steps, Ediva standing beside her.

Galon motioned to Garth. "So, about the plot, English. You and your charming, if insolent, partner," he bowed to Ediva, "told me that a signal would set it off, and that the signal would take place here."

Garth was splashed with blood. He had never killed a man before, and he was unnerved by the experience. "That's what the pedlar Grugan told us, my lord. He was one of the rebellion's organizers. He didn't know what the signal was to be, though. He said we'd know it when we saw it."

"How delightfully inscrutable," Galon remarked. "So now what? The rebellion is over? It never got underway? Your ne'er-do-well son and some grubby pedlar were its leaders? That's difficult to believe. Unless it was never real to begin with."

"It was real," said a voice.

The maid Estrild appeared and forced her way through the armed men. She knelt before Blanche and held out a dagger with both hands. "Here, my lady. I was supposed to use this to kill you."

Ediva gasped. Even Galon looked surprised.

Blanche rose from the step, a bit unsteady. "*You* were part of the plot?"

"Yes, my lady, and I'm sorry. It was Tostig gave me the order."

"Tostig!" said Blanche. Tostig, the church vicar.

"He told me it was my duty as a true Englishwoman. Told me it was what God wanted. He's been on about it for months. I never wanted to do it, but he told me I had to, told me it was a Mortal Sin if I didn't, and I would go to Hell, and . . ." She started crying.

"Aelred said that Blanche was to be spared," Miles told Estrild.

"Maybe he didn't know," Estrild sniffed. "Maybe Tostig or someone else changed the plan." She turned back to Blanche. "You can do with me as you wish, my lady."

"Return to the manor house," Blanche said sternly. "We'll speak of this later."

"How touching," Galon commented as Estrild left. To Miles he said, "Perhaps the rebellion was real, after all, and you did prevent it, for which you have my thanks." He clapped his hands derisively and rose from the block. "However. You killed the king's castellan, and the king won't be happy about that."

"Theobald tried to kill me, my lord," Miles protested. "It was self defense."

"Tell that to King Henry," Galon said. "I'm sure you'll get the chance." To Blanche he said, "Who knows, my dear, we may be married yet."

"For God's sake," Miles told Galon, "I did all this in your service."

"Really?" Galon cocked his head. "My memory may be failing me, but I don't recall telling you to kill the king's representative. I'm fairly certain that my instructions were clear. You were to stop a plot. Nothing more. Theobald wasn't part of the plot, nor was that imbecile from Haverham. No, you're on your own with these killings, Miles. We may get to see this chopping block used yet—eh, Stigand?"

"We may, my lord," Stigand said.

Blanche stepped forward, seething. "Have you no decency?" she said to Galon. "After all Miles has done for you, you're going to let him be used this way? Every time I think you've sunk as low as humanly possible, you manage to prove me wrong."

Galon cast a baleful eye on her. "You're hardly one to lecture me about decency, my lady. As I recall, you were—"

"Don't change the subject, you lard-faced . . ."

While they were arguing, Miles noticed two of Stigand's men slip away from the group and make their way out the open gate. The two men started for the village.

Where the church was.

And the bell.

Miles turned. He whipped up his bow, fitted an arrow to the string, and let fly.

The arrow whizzed past Galon's ear and struck Stigand in the chest.

CHAPTER 67

STIGAND STAGGERED FROM the arrow's impact. He took two more steps toward Galon, then faltered.

A dagger fell from his hand to the wooden platform.

Stigand took another half-step, swayed, and dropped to his knees. He toppled onto his side, the arrow protruding from his chest.

Galon unsheathed his sword. His men lowered their spears, ready to charge. Ioco and the English advanced on them. On the wall, bows were drawn once more.

Miles threw down his bow and raised his hands, placing himself between the English and French. "Stop!" he cried.

Blanche did the same. "Stop! *Arretez!*"

"Stigand was about to kill Galon," Miles shouted, "I stopped him."

The men in the yard hesitated, but their weapons remained drawn.

Miles turned to Galon. "Stigand was the leader of your plot."

For the first time since Miles had known him, Galon seemed at a loss for words. He stared at the platform, at the long dagger that had almost been plunged into his back. "Is that true?" he asked the wounded Stigand, and there was disappointment in his voice.

"Yes," Stigand breathed. "Damn you, yes."

Ediva came onto the platform, Garth behind her to protect her. Ediva knelt beside Stigand and placed his head in her lap, raising his head to make him more comfortable.

Blood pulsing from Stigand's wound reddened her already filthy cloak and dress.

"Why?" Galon asked Stigand. "I don't understand. No Englishman has profited more from his association with me—with the Normans—than you."

"You French shit," Stigand sneered. "It doesn't matter how much land and gold I've got from you. You think I don't forget what you bastards did to the North? To my family? You think I don't forget how my mother stayed alive by whoring through army camps? You think I don't forget her humiliation, the way she died? Consumed by drink to blot out the shame of what she did? I don't even know who my father was."

He coughed, paused, caught his breath. His face had taken on a greyish tinge. "My one goal in life has been to get back at you bastards. This rebellion was the culmination of that work. And it was foiled by that traitor," he lifted a weak hand, pointing, "Miles."

The courtyard buzzed.

Stigand went on. "If it wasn't for you, Miles, we'd have won. England would belong to the English again. And this one," he indicated Galon, "would be on his way to Hell, where he belongs." To Galon he said, "I planned to cut off your head and hang it above the castle gate. That was to be the signal. That's when the bell would have rung. Now . . ."

He coughed again, and blood spilled from his mouth. Ediva wiped his chin with the hem of her cloak and raised his head higher.

If Stigand had intended to make Miles feel guilty, he had succeeded. It hurt being called a traitor. It hurt a lot. Even more because it was true.

Still . . .

"You used Aelred," Miles told him.

"He was easy enough to use," Stigand said. "Him and those Beardmen, both. It was like they'd been waiting for me. Or someone like me."

Like me, Miles thought bitterly.

"You killed the original Scots plotter before he could reveal anything," Miles guessed. "Under 'questioning.' "

"That's right," Stigand said.

"And it was your idea for Galon to use me to uncover the plot."

"I suggested it, yes."

"Why me?" said Miles.

"You were the key," Stigand said. His eyes rolled up in his head, and he struggled to bring them back down and get them focused. "For some reason, people like you, Miles. They would rally to you, not to me. I knew you would never join the revolt for my sake, so I had Aelred put the idea to you. I knew you . . . couldn't say no to him."

"Yet I did say no," Miles said.

"That's right. You had to save your stinking French friends, you traitor."

"That's not the reason," Miles said. "Your plan went too far. Killing women and—"

"What do you think the French did?" Stigand said, raising his head. He coughed up more blood that went down his chin and into his beard. His voice was getting weaker, but his eyes were bright. Crazed. "They killed women and children in the North, thousands of them, starved them to death and didn't think twice about it. When you burn people's homes and destroy their crops, you're killing them as sure as if you put them to the sword."

He stopped, trying to catch his breath, as though that outburst had taken most of his remaining energy. "Fucking French . . . not a one of 'em . . . deserves . . . to live."

Blanche stepped toward Galon. "Get him help, Galon. Get that arrow out of his chest and—"

"No," Galon said heavily. "I don't want him put on trial. I don't want him tortured. He deserves better than that. Let him be."

Stigand tried to spit at Galon, but only blood came out. To Blanche he said, "You should have been English, my lady . . . Then I wouldn't have . . . had to . . ." His voice faded. "My apologies."

He laid his head back on Ediva's lap, breathing hard.

The breathing slowed.

Then stopped.

Stigand's eyes stared at nothing.

"I thought I could trust him," Galon said to himself. "But it turns out the only man I can truly trust is the man I hate the most. What a world we live in."

And at that moment, Galon looked very old, and very sad.

CHAPTER 68

𝕿HEY WERE IN the hall of Brightwood Castle. Miles and his companions had trailed along after Galon, uninvited, as though they had every right to be here. The warmth from the blazing hearth felt good, especially to Miles, after weeks of living in the forest.

Galon sat at the head table, gloomily drinking from an engraved pewter cup. Miles stood before him, with Garth and Ediva behind. Blanche, bruised and covered with blood, sat at a trestle table that hadn't been removed after the midday meal, resting her head on her arms. Miles's flag had been lowered from the staff and replaced with the white swan of Trent. Miles's men had gone to the manor house, while most of Galon's men warmed themselves in the barracks, though two stood guard in the lower hall and two more on the gallery. Dogs wandered back and forth or dozed by the fire, resting after a hectic day.

Miles fetched cups from a sideboard and poured wine for Blanche, himself, and the others.

"Did I say you could do that?" Galon snapped.

"No," Miles said.

He kept pouring. Blanche hoped the wine would dull the pain from her beating. Ediva, filthy, her dress and cloak covered with Stigand's blood, drank gratefully, as did Garth.

"That was a damned good shot you made with the bow," Galon growled to Miles. "You might have hit me, you know."

"Who do you think taught Aelred to shoot?" Miles said. "I was once the champion poacher of Trentshire."

"Why am I not surprised?" Galon said. He banged his cup on the table. "Damn you, Miles! Every time I see you, I end up more in your debt. This time, I literally owe you my life."

"The king owes Miles, as well," Blanche added.

"He knows that," Galon said irritably. "Or he will. I keep my promises. I'm sure he'll reward you handsomely." He gulped more wine. "You've done well, Miles, I congratulate you. You've complicated things for me, though. My seneschal is gone, thanks to you. And much as it pains me to say it—and it pains me a lot—you're the obvious man to replace him."

Miles bowed his head in appreciation. "I'm grateful for the offer, my lord, but I must refuse."

"Why?" Galon sat straighter, surprised. "Stigand has a number of fine estates in Normandy and France, plus a few in England. They'd all be yours. That's a lot of wealth you're passing up. Not to mention prestige and power."

"I don't want lands in France," Miles said. "I don't want prestige or power. I don't want anything that keeps me from my family. Besides . . ."

"Yes?" Galon said.

"I wouldn't be your seneschal a week before you and I were trying to kill each other."

"That's the part I was looking forward to," Galon admitted. "Still, I don't know where else to look."

Miles thought. "Perhaps old Etienne's son would take the position. Etienne did a good job for your father."

"Hmmm," Galon said. "Very well, I'll take him under advisement. So you'll take no reward for what you've done?"

Blanche lifted her head from her place at the table. "We'll take Haverham."

Both men stared at her.

Blanche went on. "Gautier is dead, and it's a rich manor. I want something for what you've put us through."

"Haverham is not in my gift," Galon said, "but I dare say I can arrange it with the king. Ravenswell will need a new lord, as well, and that *is* in my gift. Do you want . . .?"

"How about Garth, my lord?" Miles said.

Garth was startled—he hadn't expected this. Nor had Galon.

"He's earned it," Miles told Galon. "If you don't want to knight him, give it to him as a lay person. Plenty of bankers and churchmen have manors, and they're not knights."

Galon thought again, drinking more wine. "Oh, very well. We lost one English landowner when you killed Stigand, I guess the country won't fall apart if we have another." He stabbed a thick finger at Garth. "You'll owe me knight's service, though. On time, and in silver."

"Yes, my lord," said Garth, still wide eyed with surprise at this sudden turn of events.

"With Theobald dead, this trash heap of a castle will need a new castellan, as well," Galon mused, looking around.

Miles said, "If I may make a suggestion, my lord? How about Blaise? He's a good man, honest and clever. Becoming castellan would be a big opportunity for him."

Galon stared at Miles.

"Yes, my lord?" Miles said.

"I'm just wondering," Galon said. "Are there any more of the king's decisions you'd like to make? Replace the archbishop of Canterbury, perhaps?"

"No, my lord," Miles said evenly, "I'm fine with the current archbishop. But there are some things I'd like for myself."

"Yes?" Galon sighed.

"I want the charges against me and my wife dropped."

"That's the sheriff's remit, but the king will make him do it. I'll see to that."

Miles went on. "And my men are to be pardoned and permitted to return to their homes."

Galon actually grinned at that request. "Pardon all those outlaws? Onfroi will have apoplexy. I'll gladly get the king to agree to that."

Miles knew that a lot, if not most, of his men would return to the greenwood and resume their lives of outlawry—Frithric and Bondo, Ioco and the rest. They had nowhere else to go. Maybe one of them would become the new Brock the Badger.

"Anything else?" Galon said.

"No, my lord," Miles said. "That's all."

Galon leaned back in the chair, steepling his fingers over his chest. "You do realize that the sheriff will remain a threat to you? You've humiliated him and he'll want revenge."

"I know," Miles said.

"He's a threat to me, as well," Galon said. "He wants my place at the king's council and he desires my lands in France. So it seems we have a common enemy."

Miles gave Galon a cold smile. "I may have the answer to your—to *our*—problem, my lord."

Galon leaned forward. "I'm listening."

"Onfroi hired someone to kill me." Miles was careful not to reveal that the killer was a woman. "That person is now in custody at my camp. I believe he would be amenable to working for you, should you be interested. He is reputed to be among the most skilled at his profession."

"He failed to kill you," Galon pointed out.

"Bad luck," Miles said. "On the first attempt, one of my men stepped in front of me and took an arrow meant for me. On the second attempt, he tried to poison me, but someone else took the poison by mistake."

"And you think this fellow would work for me?"

"I'm certain of it. He owes me his life."

Galon rolled his eyes. "Is there anyone around here who doesn't? I must say, I'm surprised Saint Miles would recommend a solution like this."

Blanche was surprised, too. "You would do that?" she asked Miles.

"I came here planning to kill Onfroi," Miles said. "Onfroi knows that, and he won't rest until he's found some kind of drummed-up charge to have me executed. Plus, he tried to kill you once, and he'll try again. And there's what he did to Wada. Onfroi's not an honorable man, he doesn't deserve an honorable death."

Galon mulled the idea, smiling to himself.

Miles said, "Shall I to send you word on how to contact the fellow?"

"Yes, yes, very well," Galon said. "Now get out of here, before I do what I should have done years ago and hang the lot of you."

CHAPTER 69

MILES AND HIS companions left the keep and started across the bailey yard to the gate. Miles and Blanche walked side by side. Garth and Ediva were behind them, both of them deep in thought. The bodies had been removed from the yard, though blood was splashed here and there over the sere grass and dirt.

Miles had been given the green flag. It was folded, difficult because of the rawhide stiffening, and tucked under his arm. It would hang in the hall at Redhill.

Blanche ached all over. She yearned to get to the manor house, get cleaned up, and rest. She turned to Miles. "Are you comfortable with what you've done? With the sheriff?"

"I'm not proud of it," Miles told her, "but I'm comfortable with it. There's no way for me to get at Onfroi, but there's lot of ways for him to get at us. Let Galon deal with him."

"And the revolt?" she said. "What about that?"

"I don't know," Miles admitted. His dream had been there for the taking, so close that he could have touched it had it been a tangible object. He could have led his revolt, he could have become king of Mercia, but in the end he'd been unwilling to let his pride and ambition plunge the country into bloodshed. The dream was ended now, never to be revived.

Had he done the right thing? He'd spend the rest of his life wondering about that, and if he was fortunate enough to get into Heaven when he died, he'd wonder about it there, too. "It was my decision," he said. "I'll have to live with it."

"That means you'll have to live with the French, as well," Blanche pointed out.

Miles would have put an arm round her bruised waist, but he knew that would hurt her, so he smiled. "As I've said before, some of the French are easier to live with than others."

From behind, Ediva said, "What about Estrild, my lady? What will you do with her?"

"I don't know," Blanche said. "Estrild's always been loyal. She stuck by me through this and helped me escape from the castle. I might not have made it without her."

"Please, give her another chance," Ediva said. "She's a good person."

"I'll have to think on it," Blanche said. To Miles she said, "There's Tostig to consider, as well. 'Twas he who put Estrild up to killing me. Telling her it was the will of God, of all things."

"Him I'll dismiss," Miles said. "He's supposed to be a holy man, and he suborns the killing of his mistress? We'll find another vicar. If need be, we'll do without."

Ediva said, "So you'll . . . what? Just turn him loose on the highway?"

"If he didn't have benefit of clergy, I might hang him," Miles said. He remembered something. "Redhill will need a new steward."

"And provision must be made for Hersent and her children," Blanche said.

Miles thought of Wada, thought of Onfroi killing him, trampling him with his horse. No, he had made the right decision about Onfroi. He had no regrets about recommending the killer Diote to Galon. His only regret was that he wouldn't be able to do the job himself.

Blanche went on. "A lot of people will be in trouble because of this plot—all across the country, if Aelred and Stigand are to be believed. Likely some on our estates, as well. I imagine someone was assigned to kill Belot."

Miles lifted his brows. "Probably best not to dig too deep. Bury it and forget about it. The ringleaders have been dealt with. The bells never rang. Nothing good can come from a witch hunt."

Blanche nodded. "I was thinking the same thing. I hope the other barons have enough sense not to pursue this."

"The other barons will follow Galon's lead, and I think he's prepared to let it lie. He has other things on his mind."

They passed through the castle gate, crossed the bridge, and emerged into the open, facing the village and the fields and wide forests beyond, golden in the end-of-autumn sun. Miles turned to Garth. "You've been awfully quiet. Aren't you excited? You're to be lord of Ravenswell."

"Trying to get used to the idea, I guess," Garth said. "I've been thinking about what needs to be done on the estate. The first order of business will be to find a new miller. And it won't be Agmund. Maybe we could give Wat a try. He's young, but he was Aelred's apprentice."

"Whatever you do, you'll have Pierre helping you. You couldn't ask for a better steward."

"You think he'll have a problem working for me? After all these years of him giving me orders?"

"Knowing Pierre, I think he'll be proud to do it." Miles said.

Miles removed the niello-inlaid ring from his finger. "This belongs to you now. Wear it well."

Garth stared at the ring. "I . . . I . . ."

Miles put the ring on Garth's finger.

"Thank you, Father," Garth said.

Miles clapped him on the back. "All that remains now is to find you a new wife."

"He's already found one," Ediva said with a smile. "He just doesn't know it yet."

"Oh?" Garth said. Then he realized what she meant. "Oh," he said. Then he realized that he quite liked that idea. "Oh," he said.

The other three grinned at him.

"Tell me," said Garth, "is the man always the last to know these things?"

Miles and Blanche looked at each other, and they answered with one voice. "Yes."

BOOKS BY ROBERT BROOMALL

A Case of Murdrum (Miles Edwulfson 1)
The Castle (Miles Edwulfson 2)
California Kingdoms
Texas Kingdoms
The Lawmen
The Bank Robber
Dead Man's Crossing (Jake Moran 1)
Dead Man's Town (Jake Moran 2)
Dead Man's Canyon (Jake Moran 3)
Death's Head (Roger of Huntley 1)
The Red King (Roger of Huntley 2)
Death and Glory (Roger of Huntley 3)
K Company (K Company 1)
Conroy's First Command (K Company 2)
The Dispatch Rider (K Company 3)
Murder in the Seventh Cavalry
Scalp Hunters (Cole Taggart 1)
Paradise Mountain (Cole Taggart 2)
Wild Bill and the Dinosaur Hunters

ABOUT THE AUTHOR

Robert Broomall is the author of a number of published novels, including the popular *Death's Head* (Roger of Huntley) trilogy. Besides writing, his chief interests are travel and history, especially military history, the Old West, and the Middle Ages. He also likes to cook, but don't eat with him unless you like brown sugar and Worcestershire sauce.

Amazon author page: https://www.amazon.com/author/robertbroomall

Facebook:
https://www.facebook.com/RobertBroomall.author

Printed in Great Britain
by Amazon

26743890R00189